The Commodity Of Love

For Bob(?)

Glad we met. Thanks for trying to help (I was born to write novels) but the world doesn't pay me to) so now (I make Top 20 instead of working on #8... either way) I hope you enjoy this story(?) my favorite!

3/22/18

Other Titles by I. Alexander Olchowski

The Karma Of Butterflies (unpublished)
Strings Of Attachment (unpublished)
The Relevance Of Men
The Farmer
Buskondre

The Commodity Of Love

A NOVEL BY

I. Alexander Olchowski

The Commodity Of Love is a work of fiction.
Names, characters, places and incidents are the products of the author's
imagination or are used fictitiously. Any resemblance to actual events,
locales, or persons, living or dead, is entirely coincidental.

Cover painting (The Hump) by Dr. Steven Olchowski
Cover and book design by Melissa Mykal Batalin
Author photo by Anonymous

Printed in the United States of America

The Troy Book Makers • Troy, New York
www.thetroybookmakers.com

To order additional copies of this title, contact your favorite local
bookstore, visit tbmbooks.com or visit slowbookmovement.com

ISBN: 978-1-935534-914

This novel is dedicated first to my father, Dr. Steven Olchowski, who was a great surgeon for more than thirty years. Now he has blossomed into a fine painter. There is awesome power in art. By including my dad in this project, both as one of my sources of inspiration and as the painter of the cover, we have grown closer even while our physical distance remains.

I would also like to dedicate these words to everyone suffering from heart disease, a pervasive killer the world around, and to those doctors and researchers working on combating it.

Finally, this book honors the world's great rivers. Our freshwater resources are now more threatened than ever. If a reader has extra time and resources, please consider donating them to help a river in need.

Thanks to my readers, especially to Charles Banker. Also Dan Weiss, Sky Smeed, and Michelle Lydon.

Thank you all for reading my novel. Without readers a writer has no purpose. I cherish feedback of any kind, so feel free to get in touch through my website.

I. Alexander Olchowski
slowbookmovement.com

Once there was a tree . . .
and she loved a little boy.
And the tree was happy.
    - THE GIVING TREE

"Lovers come and go,
the river roll roll roll."
            - JERRY GARCIA

DR. KATHRYN STONE HAD BEEN WAITING for this day, her protégé driving them northwest on I-89 into the undulated heart of the Green Mountain State. It was a sunny Saturday afternoon in September. The northern New England air was predictably crisp and cool. Markus' upbeat mood mirrored the weather as he guided his red Prius along the highway's smooth pavement, this his regular commute for years now, traveling back and forth from Dartmouth General Hospital to his old Vermont farmhouse. Markus seemed to be wearing a permanent half-grin of excitement during the entire hour-long drive, while Kathryn endured mostly heavy emotions, her apprehension and dread building to a crescendo as the two heart transplant surgeons drew closer to the farmhouse. The man in the driver's seat had been her student, best friend, chief resident, and, now, her colleague. The one relationship left for them to explore lurked within the gaps of silence in every one of their conversations, constantly stalking the empty air space between them. She looked forward to exploring this penultimate avenue of connection with Markus Green. But before their relationship could embark upon these yet-to-be-charted romantic waters, and the sea storms they were bound to encounter on this adventure, Kathryn first needed to lay eyes on whatever it was he'd constructed inside his old farmhouse. Markus had been hinting at the bold scale and borderline risky nature of his clandestine home renovation project for some time, but he'd yet to provide her with any real specifics about it, repeatedly promising a personal tour as soon as he finished.

Her hands, damp from the clammy side effects of agitation, clenched into involuntary fists when she noticed the mountain resembling a whale's tail rising tall in the sky off to their west. Markus often talked about Camel's Hump, how the distinctive domed peak was a beacon guiding him towards the country comforts of home. They were getting close.

"I think it looks more like the tail fin of some giant ocean creature than the hump of a camel. Don't you think?" Kathryn asked him.

"From this direction, yeah, but when you see it from the west the summit looks very much like a single-humped dromedary. So whoever named it must have been looking from over by Lake Champlain. I actually like this perspective better."

"Yeah. Wales are definitely cooler than camels."

"Definitely."

Kathryn was halfheartedly trying to lighten her mood, but her sense of foreboding was only getting heavier the closer they got to his house, and the mysterious project he would soon reveal.

"So I never asked - why Vermont?"

"Part of me just figured that if I get busted someday, Vermont might take it a little easier on me! No but seriously, I just like the way it feels over here a lot more than New Hampshire. There's more light. And more farm - "

"What do you mean busted Markus? Are you doing something illegal out here?"

"Not exactly," he answered too quickly. "It's kind of a gray area. You'll see."

They were off the highway now, on a narrow country road that hug the bank of a swiftly flowing river. Soon Markus was pulling the nearly silent hybrid into his long gravel driveway.

"It's absolutely gorgeous here, don't you think?"

Once out of the car Markus flung his arms up into the air and spun in a circle, opening his palms to the cerulean sky, to the sloping lime green fields surrounding his house, and, finally, to the peak with its conical summit of large boulders completing the pastoral scene.

"It is very beautiful, Markus. Even to a city girl."

"Well I'm a suburban boy. But if I'd grown up here instead, I might have turned out sort of normal."

"You're normal enough." Kathryn nodded at the low white house with chipping paint. Red wooden shutters were closed tight over every first floor window. "Are you going to show me around or not?" she asked.

"Let's go!"

The side door of his house led into a dark, musty mud room, the kind of entryway often found in old New England farmhouses. A space for the kids to kick off boots, hang coats, drop mittens.

"Seems normal so far," Kathryn joked.

Markus had his hand on the steel handle of a thick wooden door. Beside the handle was a built-in combination lock. With his free hand he typed in an elaborate code. The deadbolt released with the sound of metal sliding through metal. Markus pushed the heavy door open. A suction sound enveloped them as they stepped into darkness. Markus reached down and found Kathryn's hand.

"This is a very special moment for me," he said. "Thank you for being here."

She squeezed his hand back. Markus flipped on the lights, illuminating the vast space, what was the entire first floor of the sprawling farmhouse. Every interior wall had been removed. The four remaining walls were blanketed in stainless steel. Powerful lights were embedded in the plastic ceiling. The floor was polished white marble. An operating table occupied the middle of the space, flanked by all the requisite accompaniments: IV stands, moveable spotlights, racks of stainless steel tools, sterilization sinks, an EKG machine, waste disposal buckets, cabinets filled with syringes and rubber gloves and anesthetic drugs, racks of slippers and scrubs, an open-air shower, and a bank of screens and keyboards. A heart/lung machine on wheels lurked off to the side, loaded with dials and switches. Hoses and wires hung off it in loops. A circular saw with a diamond studded blade, specially designed for cutting through a person's chest plate, rested on a shelf at the base of the machine.

"This is amazing, Markus," Kathryn said warmly.

"You like it?"

"I do. You did a great job with the design. Any surgeon would be happy to operate in here."

"Thanks, Kathryn. That means a lot to hear."

The scene was another version of one Dr. Stone knew well. She spent most of her waking hours in operating rooms not unlike the one she was now standing in, except the structure housing this OR was a two-hundred fifty year old farmhouse instead of a modern-day hospital. What then caught her attention was a row of mini-fridges lining the far wall. A cylindrical black tank was suspended up high above them on a platform. Clear plastic tubes filled with greenish liquid spread out from the tank, across the back wall, and down behind each mini-fridge. She could see this green sludge pumping through the tubes.

"Of course I have some questions," Kathryn said, heading across the room. "First of all, what's in all these little refrigerators back here?" she asked him over a shoulder.

"My hearts."

Kathryn froze. "Excuse me?"

"My hearts," Markus answered. "Go and take a look if you want."

"Oh God, Markus. What have you done."

1

MARKUS GREENE

Grosse Pointe

IT WOULD HAVE BEEN a normal fifth grade day at the Shores elementary school, if it weren't for the fact that Markus had to recite the alphabet while standing up at his desk, the focal point of the entire class. This was his worst kind of nightmare-come-true. Markus Greene was shy. He possessed a particularly acute form of reticence, with two primary side effects. First, when in the company of more than one other person, Markus basically didn't talk. And when life forced him into being the center of attention, as life can often do, his pores would close up as his temperature rose, forcing hot blood to flush his skin bright red from collarbone to temple. Most everyone couldn't help noticing this physical reaction, teachers and parents and other students alike. Some of the less-sensitive kids in the class would comment about his face burning so bright with embarrassment, not bothering to whisper, even in his presence.

"See how red he is?"

"Look at his face!"

Of course overhearing these comments only intensified the shade of red blanketing his face and neck, ears and scalp, the heat not receding until he was able to extricate himself from the situation, hiding in a bathroom or some forgotten hallway, any place where no eyes were boring into him. Today, while reciting the alphabet in front of the entire class, the future heart surgeon, shy, borderline speechless Markus Greene, the only one in the class who still believed in Santa Claus, stumbled on his first attempt, drawing a blank after the letter F. His next try fizzled at K. And this performance was coming from one of the smartest students in the class, one of a handful selected for the honors sections of math and science. His head throbbed with heat. Comments were being exchanged across the rows of desks. Markus finally made it through the whole alphabet on his third attempt, his voice shaking. He excused himself to go to the bathroom, returning almost half an hour later, when the red, deep red shade of embarrassment had finally retreated from his cheeks. The only way he was able to endure the rest of the day, while the other kids left him entirely alone because they didn't know what to say, even his only true friend Andrew Pelham, was the certainty that his mother would be picking him up at the bus stop in her station wagon. In four hours his mother would rescue him.

The rest of the school day was a blur of solitude. His face still felt hot on the bus ride home, sitting alone, listening to Guns & Roses on his Walkman. At the bus stop he climbed into his mother's idling Suburu. Smiling, she hugged him, then clicked off the audio tape of *A Tale Of Two Cities*, turning her attention fully upon her son. She was dressed in tennis whites, all the way down to the short socks and shiny white Reebok's. Markus could smell her sweat, salty and fresh, no hint of the classic B.O. None of that stinking sweat men could so readily produce. Other days Bethany would be in her gardening clothes, an old t-shirt and worn blue jeans. Sandals. Smelling like dirt. Fresh from a couple hours pulling weeds in the garden space she rented on the outskirts of town.

"How was school, honey?"

"Okay."

Markus never told her about the embarrassing times. Not to spare her. He just didn't want to relive the experience. But his mother knew about the alphabet assignment. She'd helped him practice it for a few nights in a row.

"Did you get through the alphabet all right?"

"I did, Mom. I got a B+, because it took me three times," Markus admitted heavily.

"Well, that's a very good grade."

"Ya, I know."

He wasn't going to say anything more about it. She reached over a hand, rubbed him on the head. "I think we should celebrate."

"Sundaes?" His voice lifted with the word.

"Yes. Great big hot fudge sundaes."

And so then the rest of his afternoon, like every school day afternoon, stretched out in front of him, time becoming a dog on its back revealing its belly for a long scratch, the drawn out afternoon Markus would share with his mother, that gentle slide into evening. There would be the celebratory sundaes, a board game on the living room floor, and his daily half-hour allotment of cartoons. And then came dinner.

With dinner came his father. Rupert hardly paused between his commute and the dining room table, stopping just long enough to shed his suit jacket, peck Bethany on the cheek, and pour himself a scotch. Rupert Greene was the founding owner of Scoreboard Franks, makers of very popular, all-beef hot dogs. Rupert, a self-made man, worked long hours, and the company thrived under his leadership. Scoreboard owned slaughterhouses up and down the Midwest. Its office headquarters were in downtown Detroit. In those days Markus' reaction to his father's presence was the same one he employed when thrust into a group of peers. He hid behind silence. Which was really the best thing for the whole family. Rupert had little interest in hearing about after-school sundaes and trips to art museums. There was nothing for him to talk to his son about because, at least up to that point of development, his only son had shown no interest whatsoever in sports. So on this evening, like most evenings, Markus ate in silence. His father's overwhelming masculinity, a personality made physical by his abundant, thick black body hair and baritone voice that occasionally belted out opera solos, easily overwhelmed any urge Markus might have had to express himself at the table. His dad dominated the dinner conversations with adult subjects meant solely for his wife's ears. Rupert's two favorite subjects were the endless fluctuation of the beef markets and the endless corruption of the Chicago political world. Bethany listened attentively to his every word, feigning interest in two subjects she despised, holding strong to her theory that a healthy marriage was more realistic if one partner had some degree of acting ability. She'd been a drama major in college, and her old skills on the stage, unnecessary during their early years of courting, now had these dinner table opportunities to reawaken and shine.

After dinner each family member retreated to a specific comfort spot to digest. Rupert sunk into the leather couch in his den to watch whatever game of whatever sport he could locate with the great black metal satellite dish occupying an entire corner of the backyard. Bethany secluded herself in her office upstairs, putting in time organizing aspects of Markus' life, researching summer camps, mapping out his next round of doctor's visits on the Sierra Club calendar she devoted to keeping track of what had to be done to ensure her son's health and well-being. Then, if there was any time left before the bedtime phase of the day, she would write a letter to some state politician protesting the latest environmental travesty taking place in the wilds of northern Michigan. Her dabbling in conservation had developed only after moving to the Shores, born out of her guilt over living a comfortable life in a wealthy suburb. But having grown up in Montana, with Yellowstone right around the corner, Bethany knew firsthand the benefits of wilderness, even if these were being revealed mostly in hindsight now that she no longer had access to them. Markus spent the post-dinner hours in his bedroom off the kitchen, leaving his door open to let in the lingering smells of his mother's cooking while he dutifully made his way through whatever homework he'd been assigned. Then came the dual rewards of his bed and his mother's soft voice reading him a story, ushering him slowly into sweet sleep.

Bethany Greene could have succeeded at whatever she'd chosen to do with her life. She chose motherhood the day Markus was born, and put all her effort into perfecting this timeless art, staying light on her feet, flexible, always available for her son's every need without smothering him. She learned how to hone her intense motherly concern into forms Markus could easily access no matter his age. She adapted the specific nature of her care over time. It evolved and grew on pace with her son's stages of development until Bethany mastered the skill of motherhood, a career that didn't require any degree, with no set path to follow. If becoming a mother was a professional field, then she would have been granted a Ph.D. with the highest of honors. In the early years she memorized all the classic lullabies, and her soft singing voice could soothe Markus to sleep at any hour, in any situation. She made her own organic baby food from scratch, knitted his Halloween costumes, threw themed birthday parties for her silent son, inviting magicians and clowns and all his classmates. Bethany assisted with every field trip, and helped out at all the class bake sales.

She cherished the after-school dates with Markus, as she referred to them when chatting with her friends. They explored city parks and visited museums, grocery shopped and, on certain special occasions, went out for late afternoon hot fudge sundaes, hand-in-hand the whole time. Bethany made them breakfast while Rupert made his commute, packed Markus a lunch, and prepared him his favorite snacks in between their after school activities and dinner time, before her husband got home from work. But the best part of her day came at the end of every night, when she read to her son while seated on the edge of his bed. Markus often requested *The Giving Tree*, a sad story about a tree that gives all of itself to a boy, until the boy becomes a man and realizes how much he's taken from the poor tree still willing to give him its stump, all it has left. The story made him tear up no matter how many times his mother read it to him. But it was a warm, gentle sadness. Markus loved that tree, and he told her so. Sleep always came so easily after his mother read to him, sometimes before Bethany had even shut the door to his bedroom, trying hard not to make a sound.

All through childhood Markus looked for the tree that kept giving in his dreams, vowing to himself that if he found it there, he wouldn't take a single thing. A couple years before Markus hit puberty the bedtime reading sessions with his mother ended, and *The Giving Tree* stayed on the shelf. He grew slightly restless, no longer content to spend all his time out of school engaged in the diverse activities Bethany put together for him. He began turning down her offers to do things after school, heading outside on his own instead. Soon he was slipping out beyond the borders of the backyard grass to explore the extension of the half-acre lot that was the same as all the other half-acre lots on all the other streets in the neighborhood - a large, square lawn halted by a patch of scruffy woods. Few people, adults or children, ever ventured into these fragments of forest. But Markus heard their pull, and yielded to it. Bethany, suddenly left alone in the house for hours at a time, grew anxious. Well before dinner time she would call her son home from the back porch. It became an after school ritual that went on for a few years, even in the deepest darkest months of winter, when Markus would put on enough layers to stay warm for hours out back.

Markus listened to her voice penetrate the woods, always a soft calling at first. He loved the woods, because there were things to find among the trees. His favorites were the large rocks scattered about. On this day, like most days, he was sitting on top of the biggest boulder pretending it was a horse, some great black stallion galloping across the wild western prairie, both of them characters in one of the Louie L'Amour books he was currently hooked on. Other times he would imagine the rock to be a sea vessel, anything that could carry him away to a more interesting place than the suburban neighborhoods repeating themselves for miles and miles around him. The only way to escape it was in a car. And Markus was still years away from driving.

"Markus Greene, come home now!" Bethany shouted, her tone shifting away from the siren-like call she'd employed a moment before, her angelic mother voice promising the unique gifts only a mom could bestow upon a son. Now she was shouting his name with authority, resorting to the clenched fist of parental control, a dominance supported by the simple reality that she was calling her son back home to the shelter she and Rupert provided, the roof, the kitchen full of food. And if that wasn't enough, his mother also had the keys to the car. And if all of these things weren't enough, as Markus compared them to his relative state of freedom there in the patch of woods, riding his boulder, there was the warmth beckoning him. Even though there was a hot summer sun still shining strong in September, another kind of heat source awaited him within the sheet rock walls of the behemoth house. Markus looked around. There was nothing like the warmth contained in his mother's voice out here in this patch of forgotten forest. It was this promise, contained in Bethany's calling, which never failed to draw him out from the trees. The Ritz crackers with peanut butter that he knew awaited him on the kitchen counter would be a nice bonus. There were no Ritz crackers in the woods. It was time to go home.

After dinner and his father, after the sunset and homework, his boulder stayed in the patch of forest while Markus waited in bed for his mother's visit. He was reading to himself now, cowboy stories mostly, but her soothing goodnight wishes still blanketed him with the snugness of a sleeping bag woven with the threads of comfort and care, the same thing *The Giving Tree* read aloud had once provided. In bed Markus forgot about his woods, and the trap of endless neighborhoods, and the unexpected mysteries of testosterone. The mystery of his father, who so often seemed like a stranger, a man to whom he wasn't even related. Markus would forget all these concerns in exchange for the feeling his mother would leave behind in his room, the cocoon of warmth, a bath he could float in while waiting for sleep, and with it the sweet dreams he'd just been promised.

"What's for breakfast?" he asked her, like he did each night while she lingered in his doorway for as long as he needed her to be there.

"Cinnamon French Toast," she answered definitively, knowing he liked that answer, one she had the ingredients to follow through on.

"Okay. Goodnight, Mom."

"Goodnight, Markus."

Mother and son maintained this circle of affection for many years, sealed tight every night by their dreams. The ceiling and floor between them were not nearly enough of a barrier to prevent their waking connection from living on in the subconscious realms, an around the clock bond that fed them both. They often shared the same dreams, recreating an after school activity of some kind, time at the playground with the shiny corkscrew slide, fast food treats, the glowing rocks inside a dark room in the science museum. They each dreamed up the scenes from their opposite perspectives, vantage points that were happy and fulfilled. Their relationship was the driving force behind their daily lives. It became an entity in itself, self-sustaining, the warmth and energy it created every day propelling them forward into the future, giving them each a specific identity to hold onto. Bethany was the fully devoted mom who still made time to be a dutiful wife and a good citizen. Markus was the nice shy boy always trying to please his mother with good grades and books finished, indulging in fleeting fantasies of escape while riding his boulder. And Rupert, although he wasn't consciously aware of it, found sustenance from the leftovers of this pure love being exchanged within the cavernous mansion he came home to every night, largely content in his role as the provider for his nuclear family, forcing himself to put aside his fears about Markus' lack of development into some kind of manhood a father could celebrate. In this way the family circle held strong.

At school Markus became known as the boy who didn't talk. Some of those less sensitive classmates, the ones who gossiped out loud about his red face episodes, would ask him the same blunt question over and over.

"Why don't you talk?"

Markus never had an answer to this question, so he always shrugged his shoulders in response to it. He wanted to talk like all the other kids. He just never knew what to say. His thoughts didn't easily coalesce into words he could use to share them, at least not before the situation had shifted, the way situations do for kids, in one eye blink. Markus' shyness grew and solidified over the years into an acute form. He absolutely dreaded being called on in class. The terror preceding any kind of oral presentation kept him up through entire nights. Surprisingly, when spending time with one of his select few friends he would talk and laugh, opening up fully within the safe bounds of these one-on-one friendships. But among groups of his peers, at the lunch table or during recess, Markus never spoke a word. He hated it when more than one pair of eyes was focused on him, and did everything he could to deflect attention from himself within group situations. But certain facts ensured he couldn't always avoid being the focus of a conversation. For one thing, he was always taller than anyone else in his class by a measurable amount. And his father's hot dog company was famous. As the years went along this almost debilitating shyness failed to recede at all. So Markus simply endured it, living for the afternoons in his backyard forest riding his boulder, the home-cooked dinners, the stories about cowboys and wolves he read while awaiting sleep in his cozy bed with Star Wars sheets. And his last thought of every day was the breakfast his mother had just promised him while standing in his doorway, wishing him sweet dreams. His dreams were always sweet.

Markus made very few friends while growing up, but the ones he did choose to befriend received the full focus of his loyalty. The select boys he chose to hang out with one-on-one came to see that Markus was much more than just a shy kid who got the best grades in the class. He liked boys that would come visit his boulder, kids who agreed to explore the backyard scraps of woods with him. His best friend for years was Andrew Pelham. They turned the boulder into a spacecraft, drew up a keyboard by hand on note cards Bethany laminated for them, and flew the rocket ship boulder up into space, where they encountered all kinds of things, whatever Markus' brain came up with. After Andrew came Roger, who loved nature, and helped Markus conduct a variety of field experiments in his miniature forest. They counted frogs and beetles, observed birds, peered into ground hog dens with a flashlight. Then came the unlikely bond with Jake Boletti.

Jake was the class clown, a renegade of sorts who was drawn to Markus perhaps due to their contrast in personalities. Jake didn't come visit Markus' boulder after school like Andrew and Roger had. Their friendship took place during school, where they came to rely on each other in an unspoken way. Markus supported Jake's antics by secretly facilitating some of his pranks, then laughing louder than anyone else, creating an immediate audience Jake began to feed off. And in turn the boisterous boy with much to say gradually started drawing Markus out of his silent shell, making an effort to encourage his shy friend to offer his viewpoint within a group, en- couraging Markus to speak up, using his finely-tuned bullying skills to force the other kids to listen. And then, in the midst of puberty's onslaught, Jake would be the catalyst for a great change in Markus, a shift from his drawn out childhood into the dark wilderness of adolescence.

That year was sixth grade, and Markus still believed in Santa Claus, holding out a full two years beyond any other member of the class. He was certain that the white-bearded, big-bellied man from the North Pole really did exist, and, thanks to Bethany's expertise, nothing had happened to prove otherwise. But one day as the holiday break was approaching, Jake took his friend aside during a recess Whiffleball game.

"Santa Claus isn't real, Markus. Your mother is Santa," Jake told him firmly.

"What?"

"You're the last one in our class who still believes the fairy tale, Markus. I can't be your friend anymore if you're still going to think Santa is real."

Markus needed Jake's friendship more than he needed to believe in Santa Claus.

"How do you know?" he asked, wanting some kind of proof.

"Next time you're alone in the house, search all the closets. You'll find the presents Santa is going to bring you for Christmas. Sorry Markus. But somebody had to tell you, and the class picked me to do it. You have to start growing up now. It's sixth grade!"

For all his life Markus would never forget how sad he was that Christmas, struggling to accept the shattering of the magic of childhood, to forget all those hours he'd spent staring at the sky out his window, wide-awake all night, trying to catch a glimpse of reindeer. Although he'd never seen a shooting star except in movies, he figured that was what Santa's sleigh would look like. Markus pretended to believe even after finding all the hidden presents just like Jake had predicted. He faked that he still believed for his mother's sake, because it seemed she delighted even more in the fairy tale of Santa Claus than he did, and relished her job of keeping the myth alive for a few years after the mothers of all his classmates had given up on pulling off the ritual. By the time next Christmas came around Bethany finally dropped the act, knowing without having to ask that her son's years of pure innocence had officially come to an end. She endured a similar hollow withdrawal during that holiday season as Markus had suffered through the year before. The myths of childhood crumbled one by one as the Easter Bunny and tooth fairy were erased from their shared world, ushering them forward into the next phases of their lives.

The Shores, as locals called it, held the distinction of being the wealthiest suburb in the country, while the city lurking just a few miles away, Detroit, was being annually crowned as the murder capital of America. In Grosse Pointe vast front lawns glimmered, garnished by perfectly manicured landscaping, the yards like picture frames, each one framing a palatial mansion. These houses were more luxurious the closer they were to the lake, a lake so large one couldn't see the opposite shore, yet it still wasn't big enough qualify as a Great Lake. Markus began emerging from his oasis of trees to roam the winding, pristine sidewalks, entranced by the palaces enclosed behind automatic black steel gates. His favorite had eight rooftops, all sloping in different angles, capped by orange, terra-cotta shingles, with an interior courtyard of fountains and flower gardens that could be glimpsed through brick archways. They could have been the homes of drug barons and rappers, mafia kingpins, political royalty. But most were owned by law-abiding CEO's, men who'd sacrificed decades of their lives to climb the cubicle rungs of corporate ladders. Men like Rupert Greene. The houses were their rewards to themselves, victory prizes waiting for them every night, each one gated off from the grit and grime of the nearby city. Detroit's dirt never blew into Grosse Pointe. Highways transported the bosses from suburban oases to their sparkling office buildings rising high above the blood-soaked concrete that carpeted the Motor City in a thirty square mile sprawl. On the outskirts of it all the car giants' factories pumped out bigger vehicles every year, their cash flows increasing in direct correlation to the size of the SUV's.

The tall cylindrical towers of the Renaissance Building captivated Markus on those rare occasions he wound up downtown with his mother. It rose above the skyline in a dramatic fashion, making him think of the City Of Oz. *There's no place like home.* Dorothy's words would always ring in his ears while downtown. When Markus would look down at his feet, and think of clicking his heels like Dorothy did, the home he imagined being transported to wasn't his family's house, but the boulder in his backyard woods. Bethany didn't like being downtown either, so they always retreated back to their neighborhood as soon as their business had been taken care of, which was fine with Markus. Detroit was a looming beast, an urban wilderness more frightening to him than any wild landscape he could imagine. He'd rather be face-to-face with a grizzly bear than with the average resident of downtown Detroit.

On those rare occasions when Rupert decided to interject himself between Bethany and Markus, attempting the role of an engaged father, he mostly stumbled and flailed, then retreated before his masculine pride could be damaged, at least in his own eyes. His most common attempt at forming some kind of parental connection with his only child was to invite Markus into the den to watch a sports event of some kind. By this point Markus liked watching sports, especially baseball, because it relaxed him. So father and son would share a few summer Saturday afternoons watching the Cubs lose to whoever they were playing. Markus loved the brick walls and ivy of Wrigley Field. Rupert even took him there to see a game once, a magical experience for the boy. One day Markus asked his father why he didn't root for the White Sox, because they won a lot more games, and were also from Rupert's home city. His father abruptly clicked off the big-screen TV, one of the earliest kind, with the colored projector lights shining from behind. He spoke in a deep, serious voice.

"My father, your grandfather, was a Cub fan. So I am too. And so are you. That's just how it works, son."

"Okay," Markus said.

This was another one of his father's rules that men must use to guide them through life, rules Markus never really understood. Yet this familial edict was able to undermine the quality of these baseball-watching sessions, at least for Markus, because he was becoming more of a Tigers fan every year, a secret he would keep from his father well into adulthood. By the time he admitted this break from Greene patriarchal tradition, at least when it came to sports team allegiance, too much had taken place in between for it to matter at all.

Markus graduated from his intimate Montessori school after eighth grade, and began as a freshman at the public high school while his handful of friends went off to boarding schools, an option Markus had never considered, unable to fathom the thought of being far away from his mother. Those first two years of high school were horrific. Just after he'd gotten somewhat confident enough to speak up in a group thanks to Jake, without his friend there to encourage him, Markus regressed dramatically. He had no idea how to be accepted by one of the tight cliques of friends that had formed their circles in the public middle school years before, and had come to the high school intact. Lunchtime was a daily nightmare. Every group had its own table in the cafeteria. Markus was quickly labeled a loner, and had to locate empty ends of tables, scraps of space to occupy while he inhaled some food, feeling the stares of so many eyes on the back of his neck like thousands of pins pricking his skin, the flush of red heat rising relentlessly up his neck. His solution was to take his lunch into the boy's bathroom. He would pick the biggest stall, close the lid of the toilet, and sit there eating his food alone, bothered only by the occasional flush of a urinal. The pain of eating the lunch his mother still packed for him all by himself, while breathing the smells of liquid soap and stale urine, paled in comparison to the torture of the cafeteria scene. He maintained this ritual for the rest of freshman year, and all of his sophomore one, never sharing this sad aspect of his life with anyone. He lived for the hours after school spent in his patch of woods, where he invented stories about Native Americans and explorers while sitting on his boulder, kept company by squirrels and songbirds and trees.

Those first two years of high school felt like five or six to Markus. He didn't make a single new friend. He became numb, stuck within the bubble of his still-forming self, utterly alone. The things that comforted him before became things he now hid behind. He went through the motions with his family, baseball games with Rupert, Sunday morning talks with Bethany. The boulder no longer inspired his imagination the way it had for years, failed to instill the optimistic sense of adventure it once did. His patch of forest suddenly seemed very small. The trees were not dense enough to do a good job at hiding him. So he spent a lot of time in his room, reading and studying. Markus got good grades. But his position on the bottom tier of the social spectrum kept him from having the confidence to join the baseball team, even though he yearned to play. He didn't go to a single dance, or partake in any extra-curricular activities. He became aware of a tightening sensation in his chest, like an essential part of him was closing up on itself. Markus knew, even while having to look through the clouded haze of adolescence, that this was no way to live, that his suffering could somehow be alleviated.

He enlisted the help of his mother, informing her of his need to make a big change. After weeks of diligent research Bethany found out about a new charter school downtown. They visited during a school day. When Markus discovered the junior class had a total of thirty-nine students, compared to his class of over three-hundred, he was sold. He quickly became a big fish in this smaller pond, finally shedding some of the shyness that had haunted him for so many years. He made some new friends, giving Bethany some much needed relief that her over-mothering, as her friends referred to her style of raising Markus, hadn't turned him into a socially inept teenager. And he pitched for the baseball team, leading to an unprecedented level of attention from his father, even if Rupert's interest in having a concrete relationship with him faded once the season ended, as his son never joined the basketball or soccer teams.

All of a sudden Markus started getting dates. With his mother's warm feminine presence so readily available over the years, combined with his shyness that bordered on being a disability, he hadn't put a lot of time and energy into thinking about the opposite sex, even into his teenage years. But around the age of seventeen, the cup Bethany had been so religiously filling with love began to overflow, so to speak. Thanks largely to his mother's influence, and what his father would call "good genes", Markus was smart and handsome, sensitive and caring. And he was suddenly eager to share himself with others. The recipients of this sharing tended to be young, mostly brown-skinned females from Detroit. Blessed with natural charm and a quick wit, Markus had little trouble getting dates with a variety of girls, and the Latinas quickly became his favorites. He largely avoided the parties, which worked to his advantage somehow, making him mysterious in a way that girls wanted to further investigate. And even though he got mostly A's while taking all the honors classes he could, Markus didn't have to devote much time to studying. This left plenty of windows for romantic pursuit wide open. So he went over the top in doling out his seemingly endless supply of warm affection. And the girls couldn't get enough of it.

How did Markus transform himself from a shy nerd, a borderline loser, into a stud in the span of roughly one summer? He simply started talking. Not just to one friend at a time, but out loud in groups of peers like he'd been starting to do in eighth grade. These groups were made up of relatively equal proportions of guys and girls. He made a few jokes. He shared some of his more complex thoughts, philosophical musings on the potentially deeper nature of things, the kinds of thoughts he'd always had. Finding himself surrounded by peers seeking more than public school had to offer, their brains expanding together, most of them were hungry for the kinds of ideas Markus regularly pondered. He went to the dances, where he quickly discovered that simply by not getting drunk in the parking lot, by dancing as best he could, and talking to the girls he danced with about whatever they wanted to talk about, the end results of these simple behaviors would be extremely positive. In other words, Markus began hooking up.

Within the various circles of self-respecting females in his school, a girl was never called a slut for hooking up with Markus on a first date. Instead such an accomplishment was always considered worthy of respect and admiration. When courting these girls, and courting was what he did, Markus employed techniques expected of a man well beyond his age. He could turn a class president into a ravenous sexpot, could transform a science nerd into a wannabe porn star. But it was never sexual conquest he was angling for. Physical contact was usually just an end result of what he felt possessed to share, to the point of being ravaged by his pent up urge to care for someone if more than a couple weeks went by without having a new girl to shower with his bountiful affection. Markus never expected the end results of his amorous endeavors, the kisses and caresses, cuddles and squeezes, no matter how many times the pattern repeated itself. He quickly decided the best thing he could do was relish these situations, soak up each moment, cherishing the leftover saliva of an overeager overachiever before it had a chance to dry on the skin of his upper lip.

He enjoyed kissing girls, moving into territory still largely a wilderness for them both, into the unmapped terrain of lust, new frontiers demanding exploration and promising rewards, succulent fruits to be savored from within the bright sunbeam of youth. But these romantic escapades rarely resulted in Markus having sex. It seemed to him that his dick wasn't the commodity these girls were looking for anyway. They wanted the other things he offered, sweet and tender things, the romantic stuff handsome men did for women in movies, not the grunting, thrusting kinds of things most every other guy in school wanted to do. After spending a string of intimate hours with a girlfriend, after whispering compliments about the degree of her beauty into the crease where her neck met her jaw, after softly kissing the back of her hand, holding hands until palms grew slippery with sweat, after a string of hours spent indulging in this kind of delicate intimacy, Markus couldn't help taking note of a certain lightness inside, as if his internal organs had gone on a diet and lost some pounds of weight. He hardly felt the ground he walked on. Gravity seemed to have less of an effect over him. He didn't mind this floating sensation. It felt good, like being young should, an intoxicating kind of freedom. So Markus simply took note of it, got used to being lighter on his feet after romancing one of his dates. He started a journal, and wrote poetry about the girls, the poems helping him leave each of these whirlwind experiences behind.

Each poem came out in a burst, a flurry of words that formed their own rhythm, sometimes rhyming, sometimes not. The only other experience he knew of that resembled writing a good poem was a wet dream. After giving a new poem release, birthing it onto the blank pages of a journal, Markus would feel similar to the morning after coming in his sleep. Empty in a good way. Calm and relaxed. The need to write a poem about his girlfriends overrode any need to have sex with them, allowing him to move on from one girl to the next without much guilt, avoiding the dangers of emotional attachment. Of course his take-it-or-leave-it attitude to sex only made the girls want him even more. Whenever they compared him to the other popular guys in school, all with a kind of tunnel vision focused only on vaginal conquest, Markus stood out in their eyes as a different kind of boy, an irresistible combination of intelligence, good looks and sharp wit. And he treated every date like she was the center of his universe. At least for one night his girl would feel like the sun around which his planet revolved, leading many of the girls he courted to spend the rest of their single lives seeking out a similar kind of man, searches that often wound up futile. Because there was no such thing. Markus wasn't a man. He was still just a boy, and would be the first to admit this fact.

A few days after being on a date with a girl, as the school week swept him back into the daily concerns of tests and homework, Markus would feel himself slowly return in full, and would again walk firmly on the ground. He didn't really like this floating sensation his dates induced, and welcomed a gradual return into his feet. But he didn't stop his indulgence in giving, because it felt so good in the moment. After testing the waters with a few different girls during the first months of his junior year he wound up settling on one. Her name was Marisol. She was a Puerto Rican drama major, a senior, and a virgin. His friends teased him relentlessly for taking on such a project, as a girl like Marisol was called, an endeavor more than one of them had embarked upon unsuccessfully. But Markus loved the challenge of getting close to her, how it made the rewards she slowly offered back so much more rewarding, like not slapping his hand away when he cupped her perfect butt in her perfectly snug jeans. And, over the course of the months he devoted to securing her as his girlfriend, she inspired him to write more than a few poems.

I WISH

I wish, for one moment
that the world would fade away

one thing at a time
in liquid retreat
dissolving into a sea of
muted color

leaving you and me
standing on an island
the size of our feet
and nothing more.

Me and you.

And nothing more.

He finally had sex with her six months into their relationship,
following a three-course picnic he prepared and served on a white
tablecloth atop his boulder, an illicit bottle of Dom Perignon smug-
gled from his father's extensive collection capping the scene, all of it
illuminated by an orange Midwestern sunset. The setting sun gave
them the veil they needed to lay the tablecloth atop a bed of leaves
on the ground. The white cloth became their island. Marisol wanted
to save it afterward, telling him it was a family tradition. Markus
had heard some wild stories about Puerto Ricans, especially when it
came to sex, but this topped them all. After dropping her off back
home that night, the blood-stained tablecloth tucked proudly under
her shirt as she bounded up to the front door, Markus watched her
tight ass bounce from side to side, barely contained by her blue jeans.
His ass. At least for that moment. And for the last three hours that
had preceded it, while feeding her, while complimenting the degree
of her beauty before ravishing her naked brown body sprawled out
on the forest floor. He felt lighter than ever, high on a kind of drug,
and figured it might be a week before he came back down this time.
Markus compared the airiness in his bones, this inner emptiness, to
the way he felt after writing a poem. Crafting poetry left him empty
in a different way. They were two different kinds of giving. One kind
took much more from him than the other. Making love to Marisol
had been a waterfall of giving, an eight-hour span of time from

when he started cooking for her to now, having just dropped her off at home. A sustained outpouring of love that left him feeling all emptied out inside. Writing a poem about her happened in a timeless burst, and what got emptied was fully replaced when he handed her the poem, watched her face light up in response. Of course her face had been glowing all evening long, Markus reminded himself. But he couldn't help dwelling on the fuel it had taken from him in order to maintain her state of shining, a condition he felt responsible to induce, and then perpetuate. Because he could induce it, simply by employing his gentle touch, by sharing his quiet spark for life through whispered words. It all felt so good. But writing a poem felt even better. Writing poetry set him free. And freedom was his ultimate goal. He was seventeen years old, with an entire life spread out in front of him, a blank canvas waiting for him to paint in the details with whatever colors he chose. There were many more colors in the world than red and white.

During the days after Markus had sex with Marisol he would notice pains in his chest, shock waves radiating from his heart. At one point they became so intense he asked Bethany to bring him to see a cardiologist, who did a few tests and told him he had a completely normal heart. These chest pains, whatever they were, would always recede in about a week, along with the accompanying lightness inside. One evening, during the summer before Marisol went off to college, they were in the back of a movie theater waiting for the credits to roll and the lights to go down so they could start making out. Markus talked about the empty feeling she inspired, but left out the chest pains.

"That's funny," she said after listening to his description of what loving her did to him. "I usually feel the opposite after a date with you. Full, like I just ate one of my grandma's great big meals. I'm all full and warm inside. And it lasts for days! Then I have to see you again, to get that full feeling back."

"I see."

It was the first time Markus had heard his effect on his girlfriends articulated for him. He decided it made perfect sense. After Marisol went off to Columbia on a full scholarship that fall, following a few weekends commuting to see each other they both realized that holding on to their relationship was holding them both in the past, and mutually agreed to set each other free. Markus went back to the style of dating he'd done early on in his junior year, dabbling in romance, moving fairly swiftly from one girl to the next. After being let go not a single one held any ill feelings towards Markus. Each came to view her time as the sole recipient of his overzealous ardor as a gift to be treasured. So he got hooked on giving, on doling out his care. He listened to all the deepest thoughts of his girls, growing accustomed to a peculiar tingling behind his eyes, coming to accept this as a side-effect of his insatiable desire to love. He showered them all with his bountiful affection. When he felt even the hint of pain in his chest after a date he took it as a sign to call things off immediately. Instead of having sex with them, Markus wrote poems about every girl. And he always made a copy for himself.

The Poet

AS HIS SENIOR YEAR wound to a close, after all the application deadlines for colleges had passed by without Markus having submitted a single one, his parents tried to accept the reality that their only child had no plans to further his education. Neither were happy about this, and each employed various methods of protesting. Bethany tried to withdraw the remaining forms of her motherly attention during that last summer of Markus living at home. She stopped cooking dinner, forcing Rupert to bring home takeout and Markus to find his own sustenance, because he refused to eat the greasy food in Styrofoam boxes. He became a vegetarian, and started making his own meals in the kitchen while his parents ate dinner without him. Bethany halted the long conversations with her son on Sunday mornings, something both of them still looked forward to, the side of their relationship that fit into the category of friendship, a ritual that had outlasted most every other one they'd shared over the years.

While Rupert read his Wall Street Journal, Bethany and Markus would discuss deep subjects over cups of coffee, topics like global warming and human evolution, things their other friends had little interest dissecting through conversation. Markus missed his mother's cooking more than he expected. But he missed those Sunday morning conversations even more. So instead he would take a cup of strong coffee and his journal out to his boulder, where he'd plumb the depths of his mental musings alone, using his pen and a caffeine buzz to pursue strains of ideas that captivated him, the kinds of ideas he used to discuss with his mother. The poems he cranked out on these occasions gave him some form of satisfaction, allowing him to move forward through the summer without these things he'd come to take for granted, home-cooked meals and long talks with the one person who understood him the best.

As a proud graduate of Northwestern, which he'd attended on a full scholarship, Rupert Greene had more trouble accepting his son's rejection of both a traditional academic path into adulthood, and the classic, competitive sport-fueled rise into manhood. Lacking the skills to communicate these feelings to his son, Rupert resorted to strange, immature behaviors instead. He took the keys to the car he'd bought for Markus the year before and buried them in the backyard one morning before dawn. Markus tripped over the mound of fresh dirt that same afternoon, on his way out to his miniature forest. After digging up the keys Markus promptly reburied them, allowing his father the small victory, deciding it would be more of a test to leave home without a vehicle to fall back on. Rupert's next strategy was to cite examples of the kind of work Markus would wind up doing to make a living. He never spoke directly to his son, but rather out loud to Bethany at the dinner table in between bites of Kentucky Fried Chicken, while Markus sautéed strips of marinated tofu in the kitchen.

"Well, he'd better get used to hearing one question - can I get fries with that?" This was Rupert's most common prediction, always talking loud enough to be certain Markus overheard him above the sounds of olive oil spitting in a pan.

"He might want to look into being a garbage man," was another favorite line, condemning his son to a lifetime of menial labor. "At least garbage men have unions. And health insurance. Can't say that about waiting tables."

"Never seen the kid pounding a nail. He might want to start practicing."

Bethany sometimes fired back. "That's enough, Rupy. There's nothing wrong with being a carpenter. It's an honorable profession."

Occasionally Markus defended himself from the kitchen. "I'm

going to live off selling my poems. How many times do I have to tell you guys that?"

He repeated this statement to his parents many times that summer, until he noticed the detrimental effects it was having on both of them, and began keeping silent in response to his father's predictions of his future livelihood. Making money never crossed his mind, even after leaving the safe haven of the suburban home in exchange for surviving on the streets of random towns and cities. Markus had grown up witnessing his father devote the majority of his waking hours towards earning money without reaping any visible happiness from this narrow pursuit. Rupert lived for the fleeting contentment of Sunday afternoons, after the lawn was mowed and all the bills were paid, when the sports came on TV. Markus vowed he would live for every day. Every hour, second, and minute. Because life was too short to do anything else.

Markus Greene left home the day he turned eighteen. Not to go to college, like every other graduating senior in his class of forty. The idea of college bored him. He left to become a poet. On foot, with an army duffel bag slung over one shoulder, a blank journal in his back pocket, a new pen in his front. Inside the olive green bag were his favorite clothes, a tent, sleeping bag, cook-stove, three more blank journals, and copies of all the poems he'd written. Markus took pride in the fact that his own two feet were carrying him away from the only home he'd ever known. He intentionally chose a route that took him past his favorite house, the one with the eight terracotta shingled rooftops. Staring at the exotic estate, Markus felt his usual twinge of a wish to one day own such a palace himself. But now, taking this thought a step further, he clearly saw that the only way to obtain such a house would be to bow down before the god of money, to willingly enlist as a slave to capitalism, to sacrifice his best years, his youth, in exchange for a salary. Like his father had done a long time ago, never looking back.

Markus smiled. It was a smile for himself, for his future. He knew he was setting out to begin a much different kind of life, one all his own, with no guarantee of a secure end destination. Concepts like the pursuit of money and a career had no foothold whatsoever in his psyche, and wouldn't for many years. Markus left home with one focused purpose - to give away the boundless currency of love bursting at the seams of his skin. He would give it away one poem at a time, asking for only a dollar a piece, just enough to survive. Viewed behind the veil of these thoughts the palace in front of him lost most of the glowing allure it had always held for Markus. And then something happened that he'd never seen before. The black metal gate began sliding open, parting to either side. A silver car emerged from the interior of the vast house, and made its way along the winding, sapling-lined driveway. Markus stood still. The car, a sparkling Mercedes with tinted windows, stopped beside him. The driver's window lowered. Markus bent down to peer into the car. The driver was a bald man of an age he couldn't determine, forty, or sixty, or something in between. He wore sunglasses and a white linen shirt, half-unbuttoned.

"You're the kid who likes to stare at my house, aren't ya?"

Markus glanced over his shoulder, eying the two video cameras perched atop either side of the gate. He turned back to face the man.

"Yup. Your house has always fascinated me, ever since I was a little kid."

"You want it?"

"What?"

"Just kidding." The bald man didn't laugh. "Designed it myself. It's my baby. Those clay shingles were handmade in Italy."

"Wow."

"Exactly. So, where you heading, kid? Off to war or something?" He nodded at the duffel bag lying on the sidewalk.

"You could say that. I'm leaving home to become a poet."

"No shit."

The man nodded his approval. Then he spun to reach into the dark leather depths of the backseat. Markus stood up. The man reached out a hand. His hand was holding a worn, tattered book. Markus cocked his head to read the title as he took hold of it.

"Siddhartha?"

"The Buddha's story. My all-time favorite book. I carry it everywhere I go. It's my bible. Now it's yours."

"But I can't ta -"

"Wanna' know the ending?"

"Not really."

"It ends at a river. And it begins right now."

Markus was about to say thank you when the window zoomed up. The car pulled out into the road, and sped away. The metal gate clanged closed. Markus looked up into one of the cameras perched atop the brick pillars. He mouthed the two words slowly, without emitting any sound. *Thank you.*

He spent that night in his tent on the grassy shore of Lake St. Clair, beside a busy four-lane road, less than a mile from the house he'd lived in for eighteen years. The next morning, after hardly finding any sleep during the night due to a combination of nerves and traffic noise, he stood gazing across the huge lake that wasn't a Great Lake, even with its liquid horizon that could have been the ocean. Listening to the endless roar of the traffic speeding past behind him, Markus considered a water-based departure from home, weighing the option of boarding some kind of vessel at the port, a craft bound for Lake Erie. This hypothetical boat would continue on through the famous canal and into the Hudson before spitting him out into the Atlantic beside New York City. It was a bold vision for the first phase of his journey, the oyster shell of his new world being split wide open in his mind. Markus considered the idea for a couple minutes, until the memory of the one and only time his father had taken him out on the lake resurfaced. Rupert had chartered a fishing boat in an attempt at bonding over something besides watching professional sports. After landing a six pound walleye on his second cast, Markus spent the rest of the afternoon clutching his stomach and vomiting repeatedly over the railing. So he let this particular version of his departure from home go, packed up his tent, and stood awkwardly beside the road with his duffel bag slung over a shoulder. He thrust his virginal hitchhiking thumb into the traffic with as much confidence as he could muster, trying hard to keep it from shaking. Three hours later he was sitting on a five-gallon bucket in the back of a windowless panel van, heading to Milwaukee with two unemployed painters hoping to find work in a beer brewery.

"For all the free beer," they kept telling him, even though he never asked for the rationale behind their random career shift. Markus was busy composing a poem in his head, a heightened, romantic version of the last twenty-four hours, successfully distracting himself from natural fears about the immediate future made more potent by hunger and a lack of sleep.

Markus did become a poet after leaving home, in the sense that he wrote a lot of poems. And a lot of people read them. After reading one of his poems most people handed Markus a dollar. They did this because he always asked for one, and because he often had the appearance of a young man dying of starvation. He did endure his fair share of hunger pains and sleepless nights during his first year after leaving home, experiences he considered to be extremely valuable aspects of this period of aestheticism. Markus wasn't above bartering by any means, often trading an original napkin poem for a banana, or a doggie bag of leftovers from a fancy restaurant. He relished these old-fashioned customers, poetry patrons that enabled him to bypass the exchange of money for food, a trade of commodities he never enjoyed. The only book Markus Greene kept in his possession during these years was *Siddhartha*. He read the Buddha's story many times over, finding the tale of self-discovery to be exciting and comforting at the same time.

What began as a year of adventure, initially a blind attempt to forge some separation from his mother, became two years, and then three. Most of Markus' early poetry, bursts of inspiration scribbled on napkins in bus station bathrooms, were, in essence, love songs. The memories of his high school sweethearts at first provided plenty of fodder for these spontaneous works of art, many of which were second and third drafts of poems he'd saved during high school. He began gaining confidence from the volume of his sales, his daily revenues easily surpassing the saxophone players in subway stations and the fiddlers on sidewalk corners, other artists he competed with for customers. His poetry evolved from youthful expressions of romantic interest into distillations of certain moments he happened to notice, children sharing some prized discovery, a tired dog heading for home, the sun setting on a minor league baseball game in a small Midwestern town. Markus wasn't sure if his poems were getting any better, but he didn't really care. There was no such thing as a perfect poem.

He had the clichéd look of another young person going to desperate lengths in an attempt to find himself. But Markus wasn't trying to find himself. He was doing the exact opposite, trying to give his self to the masses, to share the love he carried inside him with the world. He reached great pinnacles during these three years, and also deep depths. He dove in dumpsters for dinner, did live web cam shows for frustrated gay men to earn a few bucks, all the while avoiding college, and any other trappings of what his father called a Normal Life, the kind of life young Markus shunned with passion. And he avoided getting involved in any kind of romantic relationship. He'd decided shortly after leaving home that giving himself to just one individual would have been unfair. There were too many needy ones out there, too many people desperate for a little dose of what he had to share. That was how he viewed his poetry, like medicinal shot glasses of love doled out to those who needed them. He could have kept doing it forever, bonding with bums, crashing on the futons of strangers, always moving, discovering cities and towns and cornfields alike, channeling Kerouac and Dylan while building an intimate connection with America.

During this first year of wandering his often-empty stomach and dilapidated appearance scared him, driving him down into miniature depressions, until Markus learned to feed off new things. Instead of relying on his weekend dates to lift him up off the ground, like he had during high school, he cultivated the ability to elevate himself through the heightened moments he stumbled into, daily jewels of experience sparkling outside the bounds of regular reality. Markus fed off being a witness to these things, ingesting the special scenes he observed, digesting them in his mind before regurgitating them in a new poem scrawled onto a napkin and sold on the street for a dollar. Laughter overheard lifted him. So did old men playing chess in a park. Lovers hand-in-hand at a cafe. Kids splashing in puddles. He felt connected to all of humanity through his focused observations that led to so many poems. Of course Markus had to fend off relatively constant feelings of separateness, the nagging notion that he should be laughing too. Maybe he should be holding his lover's hand at a cafe. He was able to make it through these instances of doubt by telling himself that being separate was a necessary state in order to find material for the next poem. His poetry was his religion. His survival. He needed the process of writing poetry more than he needed people. And all along he maintained a constant awareness of his youth, since being young would allow these years to be a phase, experiences he could later lump together and catalog as one chapter of his younger days.

Markus came to view his poetry customers as one big extended family. He could picture most of their faces, and liked to think of individual customers, and the specific poem the person had purchased, while trying to fall asleep in some less than comfortable situation. Markus thrived on giving his poems away. He was certain that each one decreased the burden of his love, took a little more of the weight off his shoulders, helped with his quest to one day be

free of it, so he could move on and do other things. Many customers asked him personal questions. He tried to answer them honestly.

"Isn't this a precarious way to make a living?" they often asked.

"Yes."

"Where do you sleep?"

"Tonight I'll be under the stars in center field of the baseball park
down by the river."

Answers like that often resulted in the offer of a bed to sleep in,
especially down south, gestures of hospitality Markus usually turned
down politely, favoring the adventure of finding a place to sleep.
There was one question he hated above all others. It was the most
common one of all, except during July and August.

"Shouldn't you be in college or something?"

The question made Markus clench up with anger, a reaction he
fought hard to subdue with grace. Sometimes, on a hot humid day,
on a crowded street corner, he snapped a reply.

"Shouldn't you be at the office?" was one. Another was "Why, so
I can have a safe, comfortable life? Screw safe and comfortable." But
most times he was able to summon a calm reply. "I'll probably go to
college someday," he'd say.

Overall Markus loved his interactions with everyday people.
When he stopped moving long enough to look at the overall picture
he would see how his creative, work, and social lives were all intertwined as one. This worked out great for over a year, until he began
needing something more. He needed a friend.

Markus never stayed in one place long enough for it to feel like
home, never longer than a few months. A nomadic lifestyle. He
wasn't looking for a home, so he kept moving. Markus moved on
once he began to run out of customers eager to buy his poems. Although certain locations had steady flows of tourists, Markus found
that locals were his most reliable customers. People warmed up to
him over time. They came to see him as more than just a lost drifter,
and eventually wound up purchasing a poem not due to a love of

poetry, necessarily, but rather the simple desire for a window into what they'd decided was a rather complex, intriguing young man who also happened to be a nice guy, with a quick and easy smile.

Trying to maintain a clean slate when it came to relationships, remaining open to a wide-range of poetry-inducing experiences, Markus didn't pursue any girls during these years. His fully-developed romantic side learned how to thrive off the exchange of a furtive glance, a coy half-smile thrown over a shoulder. He could survive for days off the glimpse of a pair of young eyes, eyes momentarily drawn to what he might have to offer. He engaged in brief flirting sessions before showing, with subtle body language, that he was already taken. Poetry had taken him. And his poems were literally just enough to provide shelter from the storms. They had the full focus of his commitment. When he went out to clubs he danced with girls without getting names or numbers, subsisting off the fleeting intimacy of his pelvis moving in rhythm with another, briefly bound to a beautiful young stranger, their bodies joined by shared youth and the pounding beats of music. He was happy to let these threads of connection with various girls slip by without grasping onto them, exchanging the pleasure of intimacy for a poem about the possibilities contained in a fleeting connection not pursued. His reward for not pursuing would be a new poem.

After more than a year of existing solely on evanescent interactions with people who never became much more than strangers, places where he never became much more than a visitor, Markus had ziz-zagged across the western half of the country, and found himself north of San Francisco. He was satisfied at having reached California while subsisting solely off poetry sales, resisting his mother's repeated offers to send him cash. Once there, however, after the manifest destiny rush over laying eyes on the Pacific Ocean had faded, Markus was accosted by a sudden, intense form of loneliness.

Making his way up into Humboldt County, his poetry thriving from the inspiration of Redwoods and Pacific Coast cliffs, he began to consciously seek out a friend. Markus wanted a guy friend similar to his elementary school buddies, a peer of some kind, the type of friend he could learn some things from. The problem was he wasn't sure any potential peers existed.

After a flurry of poems spilled out of him in response to the pine needle-infused, sea salt-tinged beauty of Northern California, his mind set free by the depth of the dramatic landscape combined with the bright green, crystallized pot most everyone seemed to smoke, and offer up in a way that made turning down a few puffs an insult to the region's culture, Markus became mired in a state of writer's block, lost within the map he'd been drawing for himself to follow. In an attempt to get his brain back to a blank slate of creativity he enrolled in a week-long meditation retreat at a Buddhist monastery perched on a grassy slope above the Pacific. He reveled in the stark wood and stone simplicity of the silent chambers, the deep repeating chants, the hours spent emptying his mind of all thought, learning how to drop each one as quickly as it arose. He enjoyed the vegetarian food, discovered a deep kind of contentment while performing his daily weeding duties in the monastery's garden. And he didn't speak a single word for seven days. After this week of silence, imbued with the kind of peace the ancient religion was created to inspire, his mind a smooth glassy pond empty of thought, Markus emerged feeling reborn. The first person he spoke to was a fellow participant, a twenty-something guy who struck Markus as someone in the midst of an abstract journey perhaps similar to the one he was on. They stood together under the great, arching stone doorway of the monastery, looking down the winding road that would lead them both back into the daily realities they'd abandoned a week before. The sharp sunlight struck the guy's shaved head.

"I'm Markus." His own voice sounded strange to him, like it belonged to someone else.

"Cool."

"What's your name?"

"I lost my name a while back. Left it in Yosemite, on top of El Capitan, with the ghost of John Muir."

They started walking down the long driveway. Markus took note of the nameless guy's wiry calf muscles, his strong and sturdy gait.

"Are you looking for a new name?" he asked eventually.

"I am. Maybe you can help me find one."

"Okay. And maybe you can help me lose mine."

"Deal."

And so began their friendship. A few days later they drank mushroom tea on a deserted Oregon beach, their minds expanding out into the cosmos, touching stars with thoughts, returning to focus in on individual grains of sand, the mushrooms teaching them how a sand grain and a star could be the same. The mushrooms allowed Markus to thrust his hand into DaVinci's river of time, stopping the relentless current so he could feel an extended moment, the past striking the back of his hand while the future spilled away from his palm. He looked into this gap he'd created, and was able to see himself as an old man and an infant, simultaneously. He saw where he was in the present, standing on the brink of manhood, most of his life still to be lived. By the time it was all over the mushrooms had shown him that there was much more to things than what he saw on a daily basis, layers of reality beyond the scope of regular human perception. When the sun rose behind them, striking the saltwater horizon in front of them, they'd constructed a city in the sand. A city of sandy skyscrapers with seashells for windows and driftwood foundations. To celebrate the dawn, and the dangers of attachment, a lesson taught by Buddhism and the mushrooms both, the two friends crushed the sandcastle city with their bare feet. They stomped it down in a tribal kind of dance, hooting and hollering with uninhibited joy, a rapture as pure and clear as the dawn light filtering through the sea mist.

"I lost my name last night!" Markus shouted.

"Congratulations," screamed his new friend. "I found my name last night. Call me Ishmael!"

"That's the first line of Moby Dick," Markus said, suddenly serious.

"Never read it. The name chose me."

"Fair enough. Ishmael."

The two friends went on to explore other realms beyond altered states of consciousness. They backpacked into wilderness areas and fished rivers, attended all-night raves on secret beaches and kayaked ocean bays. They became like little kids together, treating the northern half of California as their personal playground. They made camp fires and drank whiskey, sharing long stories of past lovers, dreaming up images of future ones. They talked philosophy and economics, helping each other with their shared pursuit of constructing an identity for the kind of world they wanted to live in, even if neither was certain that this world existed. It did exist, was taking shape during all their shared moments, glued together by the raw power of will combined with imagination. Ishmael showed Markus how to feel the energy of a tree, how the trunk became a magnet between his palms held a few inches from the bark, a force drawing his hands together when he tried to pull them apart. Markus taught Ishmael his techniques for coming up with a poem, encouraging him to let the pen move across the paper freely, following thoughts until a rhythm arose. Once their friendship had become a universe all its own they both knew it was time to part ways, forever bound by an unspoken promise to stay true to what they'd found together, a shared foundation that could only be added to as individuals moving forward again on two separate paths. After separating, Markus became aware that this friendship with Ishmael, lubricated by their chosen activities, had permanently shaped a part of his personality, just like Andrew Pelham and Jake Boletti had, parts of a whole still predominantly defined by his mother's pervading influence.

As Markus moved into his third year away from home the main focus of his attention began shifting away from people and more to nature. He took note of landscapes, lost himself in the textures of clouds, drank in the angles of sunlight, tasted the rain with his bare skin. And he wrote poems about it all. These poems honored individual trees, like an old oak on the edge of an Iowa cornfield he spent the night sleeping under. They celebrated single mountains looming over valleys, honed in on the personalities of ponds. Markus wrote poems that gave life to rocks, although even the glowing red rocks of Arizona couldn't hold up to the memory of his backyard boulder, so he wrote one about what he remembered of that rock too, from his new perspective far away from it. He penned verses describing encounters with birds and deer, fields and forests, valleys and mountains. These nature poems sold well, and he was able to save up to buy a tent, which allowed him to find comfortable, peaceful places to sleep, spots that offered even greater immersion into the natural world, which was steadily becoming his primary inspiration. Markus began avoiding all cities, choosing to linger on the outskirts of towns just large enough to provide him with a market of potential customers. Without knowing it he was following in the footprints of poets like Emerson and Whitman, wandering from one natural bliss to the next, chasing butterflies without a net, only the hope that the fluttering creature would stop long enough for him to bend down close, to take in a view of the bright patterns of color splashed across a pair of wings, to spend the time getting to know the insect well enough to write a poem about it.

THE MOUNTAIN

The mountain holds the earth back
and speaks in a deep voice
that bellows from its core.

It rumbles "halt" to the ground
pushing from behind.

The city?

The mountain holds the earth
while the sky moves by in clouds.
They whisper a tease,
urging the mountain
to lose its weight,
to move with the wind.
The mountain breathes
slow and heavy,
holding the earth back.

It used to be jealous of the clouds
and their freedom.

Now it holds the earth
and waits,
knowing that every passing cloud
will return again and again,
each time a different shape,
each time the same water.

The mountain holds,
breathing slow.

On the extremely rare occasion that he was able to sell enough poems to afford it, Markus would get himself a nice hotel room, at a Marriot, or Holiday Inn Suites. He'd indulge in the soft, comfortable bed, watch TV, brew some complimentary coffee. He would take three or four showers over the course of his twenty-four hour stay, relishing the rare experience of shampoo lather in his hair. Usually unable to afford room service, he would order some food sent to a room down the hall, to be left outside the door without a knock, and billed to that room number. After the food was dropped off he'd sneak down and snatch it for himself. These were his first experiences testing the limitations of his morality. He didn't like the feeling of engaging in an activity that was so close to stealing, and halted this practice after indulging in it a couple of times. His favorite thing about these rare hotel experiences was when he'd sit down at the desk in his room shortly before checking out to pen an original poem on the hotel's pad of paper. He'd leave this poem there on the first page of the pad for either the housekeeper or the next guest to find. During the days following a hotel stay Markus enjoyed thinking about the unknown stranger that got to have this complimentary poem, while he tried to distract himself from memories of the clean-smelling fluffy pillows of the hotel bed, struggling to find a scrap of comfort from some hard piece of ground.

After more than three years of scribbling had passed, after thousands of napkins sold for a dollar each, Markus finally came to the undeniable conclusion that the emotion of love was either too simple, or too complicated, for words. Even his best poems failed to fully articulate what he felt coursing through his bloodstream in seemingly endless supply. He began to view the writing of poems as an act of observing a tiny fragment of life as it passed, and then recording it. Markus knew he needed to learn how to do something greater than that. He needed to become a man. And men were not poets. In these three years spent being a professional poet he hadn't gone on one date. The high school girls had wanted him because of his performances on the baseball mound and his AP grades, for his quick wit and subtle charm. The poems he'd given them were only bonuses, small prizes of teenage romance to be hung on a wall for a time before being forgotten in a box or drawer. Markus had kept the poems alive, resurrecting them over these years, fine-tuning the little pieces of his love they represented into gifts for strangers. After coming to these realizations the first thing he did was call up his father, knowing it was a shift in direction that Rupert would want to hear about.

"So what are you going to do now, son?" Rupert asked, his voice lifting with renewed expectations for his son's eventual outcome in life.

"Good question, Dad. I only know two things at this point."

"And what are those?"

"I'm moving to Vermont, and I'm quitting writing poems."

"Oh," Rupert said, deflating with the word, obviously hoping for a more detailed, practical plan of action.

"Don't worry, Dad. I'll be okay. And I have no regrets. I've learned so much these last three years, more than college could have ever taught me."

"I won't worry, Markus. Worrying is your mother's job."

"What's your job then?"

Rupert took in a deep breath. "To push you forward into the next thing. Something I haven't ever done."

"What would you push me into now, Dad?"

"Money, Markus. You need to make money, and lots of it, or you'll never become the man you need to be."

A long silence followed the strongest words Rupert had ever spoken to his son. This gap in the conversation was punctuated by the squawking of a tropical bird on Rupert's end of the line.

"Dad?"

"Yes son?"

"What's that sound?"

"My new pet. It's a macaw. Beautiful bird. I can't wait for you to meet him."

"I can't wait either," Markus said, trying hard to mean the words.

By the end of it all, having pushed the envelopes of decadence and nothingness, Markus decided that a person's happiness basically came down to whether or not he had someone to have dinner with.

This had been a rare event for him since leaving home. According to this theory, conversation was a necessary component of digestion, leading to a relaxing conclusion of the day, enabling the evening to culminate in a few hours of contentment before bed. Whatever one did during the day itself was done in absolute solitude, no matter how many people happened to be participating. The sum total of these daily actions was called a person's path. And although the few people that knew him spoke of Markus as if he was an unfocused hippie headed for a life of destitution, the reality was that he always made sure he was walking forward in a specific direction, one that he'd chosen. When his road as a poet turned out to be a spur, a side trail with the potential dead-endings of poverty, suicide, and alcoholism, Markus turned down a new trail, a path that would prove his doubters, namely his long-suffering parents, wrong.

He was living in White River Junction, a post-industrial ghost town in central Vermont. He hadn't written a poem in six weeks, a self-imposed fast from composing new strings of verse. Restless but broke, he found himself drawn across the river, to the campus of Dartmouth College. Markus spent whole days in the school's science library, consuming biology and chemistry and physics textbooks, filling his journals with the intricacies of photosynthesis, the orbits of electrons, wavelengths of sound and light. He got hooked on using his brain in entirely new ways, exploring the backwaters of his neural circuitry. Although he'd stopped writing original poems he still relied on poetry sales to support himself, and quickly discovered the well-funded students at Dartmouth to be willing customers. So he spent his nights in a dilapidated studio apartment in the forgotten town across the river, reprinting some of his best nature poetry over the past three years, still using his trademark diner napkins for stationary. He'd break up his marathon study sessions in the library with an hour or two selling poems on a card table he set up in the middle of the grassy quad. Some of his customers were frustrated frat boys eager to impress freshman girls. Markus was able to boost his income substantially by charging them to compose poems for specific girls. To accomplish this, while also sticking to his vow not to write anymore new poetry, he recycled some of his early high school work and changed a detail or two, rhyming romantic mush these manly football players would then pass off as their own, often returning on Monday to share success stories, thanking Markus profusely, offering cash bonuses as tokens of appreciation for helping them get laid on Saturday night.

Markus' favorite customer on campus was a man with curly white hair and weathered, tan skin. He assumed the well-dressed man was a professor of some kind. But Markus never prodded him while accepting the exorbitant prices the gentleman insisted on paying for one napkin poem a week. Other professors bought his poetry, although none so regularly, but this one stood out from the rest of the faculty members for a different reason. This teacher didn't look like the others, who struck Markus as college students with twenty extra years added on to their appearance, twenty-somethings in forty-something bodies, adults who'd never left the safe bubble of academia. This teacher was different. He seemed to have lived many lives, had experienced multiple incarnations, and was still far from living out his last. These things Markus knew before even learning the man's name.

After a few months had passed, with winter break approaching, Markus was consumed with organic chemistry. He would study the complex formulas even during his midday breaks selling poems in the quad. When his favorite professor stopped by one Friday afternoon in late November, Markus was so consumed by the chapter on hydrogen, a gas that fascinated him, he didn't notice his regular customer standing at the table, eager to make his weekly purchase of a hand-written napkin poem for which he would pay fifty dollars cash. The professor bent down to eye the title of the thick book Markus was so engrossed in.

"What does a poet need to know about organic chemistry?" he asked, a delighted smile spreading across his face.

Markus snapped his head up. "Oh, sorry, I didn't see you there." He closed the textbook and placed it on the ground. He nervously organized that day's display of napkin poems on the table. "To be honest, sir, I'm not a poet anymore. These are all reprints of poems I wrote in the past. That sounds ironic, I'm sure, but my poetry is just how I'm supporting myself while I follow a new path."

The professor nodded while he browsed the selections of poems laid out on the table.

"And what path is that?"

"Science," Markus said firmly. "I can't get enough of science ever since I wandered into the library here at Dartmouth."

The professor stood up straight. He extended a hand. Markus rose to shake it. He was surprised by the strength of the older man's grip.

"It's time I properly introduced myself. I'm Dr. Karl Fredericks, president of Dartmouth's School Of Medicine."

"Oh," Markus said softly. "I'm Markus Greene. Retired poet."

Dr. Fredericks nodded. "Nice to meet you, Markus. Well, it's a shame you're giving up writing poems, because I think you're a genius. And you're alive! The only other poets I've ever liked, guys like Whitman and Frost, are all dead. Kind of a bummer, you know?"

"Yeah, that's part of the problem. Poetry doesn't usually pay off in this lifetime."

"Well, given your newfound love of science, have you considered going to medical school? That's a great way to get your fill of science."

"Medical school? But I don't even have a college degree. Sir. Doctor, sir."

The president shrugged his shoulders. "Did you take the SAT's?"

"I did. Scored a 1420."

"Okay. Then I can probably make an exception for you. Here at Dartmouth there's such a thing called honorary admission. Robert Frost got an honorary degree from Dartmouth, you know." He pointed to a poem titled *SING A SMILE*. "I'll take this one," he said, bending down to write out a check for one thousand dollars. He handed the check to Markus, holding up a palm to cut off his immediate protests. "Use this to buy some new clothes. Some kind of a suit. You'll need to look decent when I present you to our board. But there's no need to be nervous. If I tell them to let you in, they will."

So the next week, at the age of twenty-one, Markus Greene was accepted to medical school without ever having attended college. All he had to do to win the board's unanimous approval was promise to go into primary care when it came time to choose a specialty. There was a shortage of these kinds of doctors, and the school would receive additional federal funding for every student they graduated in this specialty.

SING A SMILE

SomeSing
SomeSing their blues away
until the blues can only stay

SomeSing
SomeSing with only one lung
one smoke for every tune they've sung

SomeSing for the next meal
strumming scrawny bones
across strings stretched tight

SomeSing so they can heal
eyes to the sky aching to see
a sign that all will be right

Sing your life away
Sometime
Some lonely day

Sing
SomeSing
until a smile gets stuck on your face.

The Baker

ONCE MARKUS TRANSFERRED to the charter school and became like a pitcher tipped at a permanent angle, his abundant affection pouring out for lucky female recipients, Bethany fractured into a broken prism. Her mother love, which had been flourishing and evolving for sixteen years, seventeen if Markus' time in her womb could be counted, suddenly fragmented, scattering in many directions now that she was left with no immediately available outlet. It refused to diminish, however, even as she grasped at all the fleeting moments alone with her son in their cavernous house, her affection following avenues that could only become dead-ends. She knew the days of Markus being the main recipient of her care were over. It was just the suddenness of this transition that shocked her. It wound up taking most of those two years for Bethany to gather up the shards of her still-potent urge to love someone in the same way she had Markus. She grew frantic over her failure to find a new recipient for what she'd doled out solely to her only son over all the years, a wellspring of warmth her husband had never possessed an ability to fully tap.

Rupert had long ago gotten accustomed to leaving and returning in the darkness, pursuing his waning sexual desires a few times a year, under the sheets and in the dark, right before bed. They were very different people. Bethany read books. Rupert watched late night television. Bethany woke up early to write letters to friends. Rupert woke up early to put on the day's suit. She hardly spent any time in their vast bathroom. He spent more time in there preening himself than he did awake in the adjacent bedroom. Rupert had a peacock position in the outside world. He was a male who had to show his tail feathers often, and therefore needed them to be glistening at all times. Bethany understood this, and gave him that first hour of the day to himself, the hour that balanced against the one they spent alone together right before bed, with her novels and his Jay Leno.

The problem with this scenario was that Bethany was an early-morning lover. She was rarely horny at night, while Rupert was the opposite. Early on in the marriage they'd been able to oblige these preferences for each other, shifting their inherent body rhythms, bending themselves to accommodate love's physical needs. Over the years they'd settled back into individual patterns. Bethany often masturbated in the early mornings, getting herself off quietly to a steamy scene in some work of historical fiction while her husband prepared himself for that day's battle in the bathroom. Rupert didn't need to masturbate. His libido had plummeted long ago, rising up out of the shadows of his middle age a few times per year. When it did, perhaps after a night out to dinner in celebration of his birthday, Bethany would make sure she rose to meet the occasion. They were able to get enough of what they needed from each other that the marriage had survived over the years, sometimes getting by on fumes of intimacy, other times thriving on visceral closeness. After Markus left home Bethany quickly resumed cooking dinner every night. And Rupert worked as hard and long as ever, bringing home surplus amounts of bacon, a portion of which she invested in the stock market every year. As their money swelled she was able to feel comfortable siphoning some off to fund two long-held dreams - to start her own business, and to pay the tuition bill for her son to attend an institute of higher education. Now that Markus had been accepted to medical school, Bethany could cross one of these goals off the list. It was time to focus on herself for a change. Because if she didn't, no one else was going to.

She began to consciously store up her love inside, where it slowly fused into a new form of the emotion, one that would demand a much different outlet than her only son. It was a drawn-out, painful metamorphosis. She spent long hours staring out the back sliding glass window, sometimes calling Markus' name even though she knew he wasn't out there in the woods. She occasionally constructed Ritz cracker and peanut butter sandwiches for him, leaving them on the counter for a phantom son, eventually eating them herself the same way she used to eat the cookies and drink the glass of milk she once placed by the chimney every Christmas Eve, so the plate would have realistic crumbs, so the glass would be clouded on one side with the evaporated traces of milk. After flailing around in cyberspace in search of outlets for natural resource conservation activism, finding little satisfaction in this endeavor, she began making overnight forays to the Upper Peninsula, suddenly eager to commune with some of the wild places she'd helped preserve from her suburban outpost over the years of raising Markus, leaving Rupert behind to bond with his new pet. But when she noticed how her husband had so swiftly and completely replaced their son with the macaw, Bethany figured she must be trying the wrong things. She finally found the missing outlet for her bottled up love about six months after Markus left the house to be a wandering poet. She started baking bread, treating each loaf that emerged from her ovens with the kind of attentive care worthy of a newborn baby.

Bethany spent the next three years becoming fully absorbed in the baking world, exploring the nuances of the craft. She made a pilgrimage to a well-known artisan bakery in the Catskills, where she worked side-by-side with their master baker for ten days. Pierre Lufont, an eighth generation traditional French baker, took her under his flour-coated wing. Bethany let herself be swept away by the sweat-soaked passion of Mr. Lufont. She became enthralled by the little pieces of dough stuck to his glistening forearms, how his whole strong, wiry body was involved in sliding the loaves across the great stone surface of the domed brick oven. She regularly found herself entranced by reflections of the yellow flames in the master baker's black eyes. By the end of her time there the two could work together for hours in silence, moving as one person. Bethany was shocked that a man could exist for so long without talking. Rupert needed to maintain a steady outpouring of words in all social situations, including every waking second he shared with her, as if talking was as necessary to his waking existence as breathing. Unless there was a sports game on. Football was the best at keeping her husband quiet for hours on end, making fall Sundays some of Bethany's most relaxing days of the year.

By the time Markus was about to enter Medical School his mother was completely obsessed with the building blocks of bread. She'd studied the chemistry of yeast, learning all the details of this diligent microorganism. After yeast Bethany's focus had turned to flour, and then to the wheat her flour was milled from. She went on a solo tour of the organic wheat fields of Northern Vermont, the same sort of trip one might take to the vineyards of Napa Valley, a pilgrimage that had the side benefit of a visit with her son before he began classes. It was the first time they'd been together for more than a few hours in a setting other than the Grosse Pointe castle. After forty-eight hours in the quaint Ivy-league town, after sharing lattes and pizzas, after apple-picking and art gallery browsing, their visit culminated with Markus cooking his mother breakfast in his tiny apartment just off main street in town.

"Remember how I always asked you what was for breakfast every night when you tucked me in bed?" Markus asked over the crackling sound of frying eggs.

"Of course I do. I always loved making you breakfast, Markus."

He looked down at the eggs he was frying, and seemed to be doubting his ability to imbue the food with that one crucial ingredient his mother always imparted into her own cooking. He glanced at the loaf of bread sitting on his cutting board. Bethany had baked it the night before, teaching her son the nuances of the process, humming soft songs under her breath while she kneaded it. He flipped the eggs to finish them off over-easy, got out a knife, and sliced into the bread.

"I'm glad you came for a visit, Mom."

"I'm glad I came too, honey. I love you so much, Markus."

"I love you too, Mom."

Bethany left later that morning to head for the wheat fields up north. Her last image of Markus was him sitting on his futon, clutching the half-loaf of bread, wanting to cry but unable to produce any tears. She knew his sadness was coming from a weak and selfish place, and therefore made no effort to assuage it. Bethany sensed the source of his sadness was some realization, during the course of her fleeting visit, that he hadn't taken every last drop of what she'd tried to give him during his childhood. Some he'd missed because of teenage blindness. Some he'd rejected, choosing the escape of his boulder or a book. Her son was sad because there was no time left to replenish what he'd let slip past him without gathering it all up and storing it inside. Now it was his turn to cook the breakfasts of his life. The torch had to be passed, so to speak, but he seemed to be resisting. So Bethany would just have to hope that he'd stocked up enough of the precious resource she'd offered to him so freely, so abundantly over the years, some quantity large enough to allow him to become a great man, strong enough to build the bridge from his mother to another woman, the mother of his own children. She knew he would need more than good intentions and half a loaf of bread to accomplish this task. He would need to finish medical school. And he hadn't even been to his first class.

Bethany fully indulged in her tour across the Northeast Kingdom, stopping in at farmhouses attached to rolling fields of grain, leaving with zip-lock baggies filled with wheat berries she brought home to grind by hand in her kitchen. If it could still be called a kitchen. Upon arriving back in Grosse Pointe buzzing with inspiration, Bethany immediately knew it was time to convert the entire first floor of the couple's suburban mansion into her personal bakery. After announcing this intention to her husband and deflecting his weak, half-hearted protest, the construction crew was called in. She had them put in a bank of sparkling professional ovens where the dining room used to be. The original kitchen became a walk-in proofing room filled with racks on wheels stacked with cornmeal-coated trays. The former living room, where the couple had once held well attended, glamorous cocktail parties, was emptied of all furniture, the plush carpet floor replaced with shiny ceramic tiles. Bins of flour, a giant Hobart mixer, a hand-operated wheat grinder, and a long wooden kneading table filled up most of the vast space beneath the cathedral ceiling.

Once there was no more room on the main floor of the house to accommodate further expansion of her rapidly expanding business, Bethany built an adobe, wood-fired oven in the backyard. The adobe came from sacred Hopi land in the New Mexico desert, and was hand-delivered by an old Native American driving a battered Chevy pickup. She had cords of sustainably harvested wood trucked down from northern Michigan. After being shut down by the town fire marshal three times, Bethany finally got the traditional oven rolling. She would fire it up five evenings a week, spending the entire night baking round crusty loaves, sweating, stripping layers, her mind consumed with thoughts of Pierre Lufont, while her heart gave itself away over and over with every loaf of bread she pulled from the domed oven beneath the starless suburban sky.

Head Tutor

DESPITE HIS NEW PASSION for science Markus struggled with the med school regimen, and quickly succeeded in making the president nervous. He flunked his first exam. The following week he was called into Dr. Frederick's office. The powerful, respected man had gone out on a limb by accepting a wandering poet, one who'd never graduated college, into the Dartmouth program. Markus wasn't nervous during their meeting. But neither was he aware of the seriousness of failing even one test. Being given the opportunity to attend medical school was an unexpected gift that had fallen in his lap, one that his parents had practically begged him to accept. Pleasing them by enrolling was a bonus. He was doing this for himself. Otherwise he knew he'd never make it through.

None of this changed the fact that Markus hated every aspect of medical school. He wasn't a quitter, but failure was an option he was strongly considering, even as he sat across from the man responsible for dramatically altering the entire course of his life. Markus respected the president, saw him for the renaissance man he was: a lover of poetry and medicine, marathon runner, skilled pianist, and devoted family man. All of these aspects of the president's multifaceted life were on display in the lush office: framed photos of children and grandchildren scattered about deep shelves filled with leather bound medical journals, shining gold trophies from collegiate cross-country races in a glass display, a baby grand piano beneath the only window. But what struck Markus the most, of course, were a few of his original napkin poems, framed and occupying more prominent positions on the wall than the doctor's four diplomas, including one of his all-time favorites, a poem he'd written in his patch of suburban woods during the spring of his senior year of high school.

SPRING

Spring happens like that!
Like love,
in a burst.

Infinite shades of green
are bursting by roadsides.

The sun grows bolder by the day,
and how the moon is to the sea
is how the sun sometimes is
to my heart,
a gravitational force
warming the tides of my blood,
turning them towards You.

Spring spins my internal compass
affording new angles,
new views.

Every day has the same possibility.

I wake up not knowing the details.

Sitting there across from the president, the guilt over failing the first exam settled into Markus' gut. He squirmed and fidgeted, waiting for the man to speak his mind.

"As you know, Markus, I took a great risk in granting you admission to our medical college. It won't be the end of my world if you drop out. I'll still be here. You'll be . . .wherever. Back on the streets writing poems. But I think you want to finish. Am I right?"

Markus nodded. He wanted to please this man the way a son wanted to please a father. He fidgeted and squirmed, avoiding the president's heavy gaze.

"I'm not a quitter, sir," he said firmly. "But I haven't taken a test like that one in over three years. And it was a lot harder than anything I did in high school."

The president nodded slowly. "I understand. But Markus, you scored a 1420 on your SAT's, and got straight A's all through high school. To stay and pass our program, all you'll need to do is hone your short term memory skills, something most any person can achieve. Takes more discipline and persistence than intelligence, by far. Trust me. Do you think you possess these two qualities, Mr. Greene?"

"Honestly, sir, I don't know."

The president clapped his hands. "Well, if anything, going through the training to become a doctor will force you to find out. Fast. But I didn't invite you here to lecture you. I want to help. You need a tutor, an expert studier, because that's what you need to learn how to do. Study. Which, when it comes down to it, is just another word for memorization. This sounds boring, I know. Most students expect far greater challenges in medical school, but there aren't. Those come in residency, when you're a slave working ninety hour weeks. Not to say it's easy by any means. But the strategies for success are simple ones. Skills that can be taught like any other. Now, I'm sure studying for a test won't give you the same rush that writing a poem does." The president glanced at the shining black piano under the window. "But that's okay. I think that if you can make it through this whole thing, and all that means is getting 66's instead of 29's, you'll like the end result."

"The money?" Markus asked bluntly.

"That's part of it, yes. But I'd say the least rewarding part. Really just makes for excellent vacations. Assuming you have the energy to take them." The president stood up slowly, his slender hands pushing into his thighs. "I want you to meet our tutor. Nice guy. Ken Gabriel is his name. Smart as a whip. Ken will set you straight."

By the time Markus was due to meet Ken Gabriel a week later he knew the man was a professional studier, a graduate of the medical college who never went on to residency, staying put instead to accept the president's offer of a full-time, salaried position as Head Tutor. After five years on the job Ken had helped raise the rank of the students' test scores from fifty-third in the country to second. By then he was rumored to be earning a hundred grand a year. And the students knew that he loved his job. Their initial meeting was in the college's medical library, a cave-like expanse of rooms, each one divided by towering walls of thick books, walls that caught any excess light beyond what illuminated the polished wooden study table occupying the center of each room. Making his way towards the designated location for their meeting, Markus guided himself through the tall looming stacks with the help of a map printout. He felt like he was penetrating the chambers of a prison. Each successive room was a holding cell designed for long stretches of solitary confinement with only medical books for company. He kept trying to remind himself it was only a library. Just like he kept telling himself many times each day that medical school wasn't going to kill him. This was his biggest fear at that stage. But it wasn't a physical death he worried about. What Markus feared most was that the extremity of these next four years would do irreversible damage to his most important possession, something he'd never thought could possibly be lost even while trying to shed it in bits and pieces ever since leaving home.

When he reached the designated room, the one starred in blue ink on his little map, Markus was brooding heavily. His mood had been darkening the further he progressed into the progressively darker chambers of the library. Sitting there at the round, glossy table in the middle of the square room was Ken Gabriel. The only tutor in the world earning six figures stood up and extended a large hand. There was a brisk efficiency to his movements, a sleek professionalism to his outfit, the silk purple shirt, emerald tie, black suit pants.

"Ken Gabriel. Head Tutor."

"Pleased to meet you, Ken. Markus Greene."

Ken motioned to the empty chair at the table. Markus sat down, placing his notebook and pen in front of him. Ken settled into his chair. He had no materials. The tutor leaned his elbows on the shiny table. He crossed his hands.

"So. The president tells me you're a poet."

"I was a poet," Markus said. "I don't write poems anymore."

"I see." Ken smiled. "And why is that?"

Markus shrugged. "The day I got into this school I wrote my last poem. Drew a line in the sand, so that old life wouldn't be able to sneak back and distract me from the studying I'd be doing here. Maybe being a poet is like going insane - kinda fun at first, but doesn't really pay off in the long run."

"Did you study for that first exam, the one you scored a 29 on?" Ken asked, leaning forward, visibly hanging on his new pupil's answer.

"I did, actually."

Ken nodded slowly. "Well good. I need to hear that you're at least willing to try. If you aren't, then I can't possibly succeed at my job."

Markus scanned the square room. His eyes took in the repeating shelves of books, trying to feel comfortable sequestered within them. He forced himself not to feel like they were preventing him from getting enough oxygen. The moment took on a charged, heightened feeling. Ken Gabriel was giving him a black-and-white choice, right then and there. Markus guessed this was the first stage of Ken's regular training program, an assumption he'd later confirm to be accurate.

"Yes, Ken. I'm ready to try. Actually, I'll do more than try." Ken lifted his eyebrows. "Exactly what do you mean by that?"

"I'm prepared to make myself into a blank canvas, a blob of clay, raw material for you to work with. That's what I mean."

"Well, I'm not a painter. Or a sculptor."

"I know. You're a tutor."

"Yes, I am. And you, Markus Greene, are my only student."

Ken Gabriel usually took on many students at once, often juggling ten or fifteen first year students along with a handful still struggling in their second. But the president had asked Ken to devote himself to Markus full-time, taking on no others until the former poet without a college diploma started passing exams on a regular basis. Markus had to report for daily meetings with Ken deep inside the stacks. They met six days a week, only taking Sundays off, a day Markus was still expected to study during most of his waking hours. The initial sessions were forty-five minutes of Basic Skills Training, as Ken called these early lessons focused on specific methods of studying, from note cards to highlighting to acronyms. These evolved into three-hour marathon meetings by a month into the semester, grueling affairs that left Markus entirely drained of energy, eyeballs throbbing, brain dazed by the onslaught of so many formulas and diagrams. Ken became more like a drill sergeant as the semester went on, purposefully avoiding a friendship with his prized student, never engaging him outside the library, never chit-chatting about the weather. Markus was allowed to bring food and drinks, but had to eat while studying. He was allowed one trip to the bathroom during the course of the three hours. There were daily review quizzes, flash card drills, even a yogic breathing technique Ken promised would increase the oxygen flow to Markus' brain during an exam.

After a couple months of this rigorous training his grades began to plateau in the upper eighties, placing him at the top of the class.

Markus had been begging his tutor to meet outside from the beginning, swearing he needed the fresh air in order to focus clearly. Ken finally relented to this request in late October, and they began having their Friday meetings out in the quad, weather permitting. Markus liked to study while leaning against the base of a campus tree, one of the regal oaks or confident maples lining the paved pathways, their trunks adorned with the nooks and crannies of centuries' old bark. The trees gave him clarity of mind, allowing him to hone in on the essence of formulas. And he gave the trees a fleeting connection to the human world, a realm they were normally forced to observe from a distance. To Markus even the trees at Dartmouth seemed wiser than the average trees found in a forest, or along a neighborhood street. Like the students, most of whom were smarter than the average young person, the trees didn't go out of their way to broadcast their elevated status. He felt that both Dartmouth's trees and its students refrained from bragging, happy to exist within the charmed bubble of the school, a place where intellect collected to form a miniature atmosphere, one that often swelled to encompass the pine-cloaked mountains and the classic New England town tucked beneath them.

To Markus the Dartmouth community was close to being an entirely balanced local ecosystem, equal parts natural, intellectual, and cultural. The community was far from perfect. And this was fine with Markus. He knew perfection was not only impossible, it was also boring. He enjoyed the overall vibe of the place while also looking forward to those times when the bubble got popped, whether by the antics of an undergrad frat pledge, or by the clique of local bums that haunted the coffee shops and dumpsters in town. Most of his fellow students, immersed so intensely in their studies, had no conception of the greater community outside the medical school. So Markus did his best to explore whenever he was able to escape his duty to Ken and the lecture classes and all the huge books. Once off campus he envisioned himself as a hunter out gathering stories from another world, tales he would bring back to share with the rest of his tribe. He brought back stories of his experiences in town like carcasses slung over a shoulder, visceral tales that enthralled his classmates, affording them brief distractions from their everyday lives spent entombed in the stale, sterile atmospheres of labs and libraries.

Markus never felt like he belonged in this overly serious clan he found himself a member of, and ventured out into the community in search of people with whom he could more easily connect. Musicians and drunks. Carpenters and bakers. Guys with bellies and tattoos, who liked to play poker and watch football on Sunday afternoons. He loved escaping the enclosed world of med school to vicariously taste their proletariat lives, the kind of life that would never be his. They called him M-dog. He shared their cheap beer, traded stories about women, laughed at their jokes. They were the sort of regular guys not so prone to over-thinking that they were able to appreciate what Markus had to share, the flow of his warmth, that source of pure feeling he used to pour into his poems, but now reserved for friends.

His style of friendship was entirely foreign to these men. At first they thought he was gay, until he told enough stories about his first-hand experiences with a Puerto Rican virgin to convince them otherwise. They'd never known a man who listened like Markus did, who seemed so genuinely interested in learning the details of their specific makeup as men. He was the kind of friend who would say what he liked about those he befriended, and would then make the concerted effort to encourage his friends to express these particular traits he liked in them, forging strong friendships in the process. Two of his best friends in the group were Jim Bellvone and Rick Midland. Jim was a carpenter, and always wanted to practice his card tricks, so Markus became like a little kid in awe of every one, pretending to be greatly impressed even by tricks he'd seen before, or ones he could figure out before Jim finished them. Rick, a state trooper, had a passion for making barbeque spare ribs, so Markus would bring him special cuts of pork he bought from a local farm and recipes for new techniques, then lend himself to be Rick's assistant during the slow roasting process, while the rest of the guys occupied themselves with the usual distractions of beer and football and long discussions about the benefits and pitfalls of marriage.

"When are you gonna settle down, M-dog," the guys often teased. "You're gonna be a surgeon. You'll have the pic of any litter!"

Markus did his best to fend off these comments in a casual way. "I'm not a surgeon yet," he pointed out. "Still got years to go. I'm barely halfway through training."

"Well, you ain't gonna make it if you keep hangin' out with us on the weekends!"

Of course not one of his friends in town wanted Markus to stop hanging out. They all had a kind of unspoken appreciation for the fact that this future doctor found their company desirable. His presence at their cavemen gatherings of red meat and football lent just the right hint of sophistication to the scene. Markus also provided the guys with a readily available justification for these events, which usually consumed entire weekend days, when defending themselves against the protests of wives and girlfriends.

"If a doctor is going to be there, it can't be that bad, right baby?" became a classic excuse.

But the most important thing was that they all just liked Markus as a friend, because he made them feel better about being themselves. And while bathing in the glow he poured over them so naturally, as he slowly and steadily opened himself up to share his light with these men he began to cherish, none of them would have guessed Markus was utterly paranoid that the commodity of his love was suddenly beginning to run dangerously low. Because it seemed to all of them that he had an unlimited amount of it to give. Only Markus himself knew the toll his studies were taking on him, the lack of sleep, meals inhaled on the go, whole strings of days blending into the same blur of textbooks and lecture halls, flash cards and cups of coffee. The problem was that in order to simply survive the intense rigors of med school, Markus was being forced to consume what he held inside for himself. He began to view this necessary shift as a kind of spiritual masturbation, feeding his love to himself in the name of survival, because there was no other choice. He had to go forward. He had to survive. But at the same time Markus couldn't help entertaining the tempting notion of going back, as long as he did so in moderation. Maybe he could go back to his mother from time to time, and replace some of what he was losing a little more of every day. A voice in his head told him repeatedly that this wasn't an option. But he didn't listen, and tried it anyway.

The Only Game

MARKUS BOUND HIMSELF to the slavery of medical school. There was no other way to make it through. At first he figured the fact that his commitment to the training left hardly any time to share himself with others could be a good thing. Until he began to consider the fear that his love might actually be a limited resource, an internal bank account he'd been drawing from too often over the past decade. Soon he was panicking with the real worry that if he didn't give his care and attention to his friends whenever he could, the once endless springs of his love would dry up even faster than they already seemed to be. The obligation to his studies, a duty occupying most of his waking hours, left him with little free time to be with others. With an erratic schedule that often required studying all weekend, his relationships with his buddies in town began to slide. Driven by a kind of panic he chose to try resurrecting his dormant dating skills, to pour whatever emotion was leftover inside of him onto any receptive females he could find, making sure not to regress into writing poetry about them in the process. His phase as a poet had also been a celibate period, although this was not something he'd consciously intended at the time. Markus had been so obsessed with fine-tuning his poems for sale on street corners and inside subway tunnels that there just wasn't any time to pursue women. He'd been single-minded in his devotion to saving his love for the poems, for sharing a piece of his heart with whoever was in need, whether man, woman, or child. So it had been over three years since he'd even kissed a girl. Or gone on a date.

Markus endured a series of romantic setbacks right away, the kind of rejections he'd never experienced before, causing him to suspect the worst, that there really was nothing left inside. After his string of defeats on the playing fields of the local dating scene, shot down by Filipina nurses, coffee shop baristas, and fellow med students alike, out of desperation he began making one weekend pilgrimage a month back to his mother's house. Although he hated admitting it to himself, Markus knew he came home looking to refill his reservoir of love, to soak up her warm affection, hoping to replenish his own tank for the next round of living. What he didn't account for was the fact that Bethany was no longer the same woman. She was still a source of abundant love, but her motherly care was now being channeled in an entirely new direction.

Bethany Greene gave herself fully to her bread, day after day. Her life was a daily devotion to the loaves, a walking meditation through flour and water and yeast. When Markus came for a weekend, always the busiest time of her week, she was unable to provide him with what he'd come there to receive. She needed to save it all for her bread. Markus quickly recognized the futility of these visits yet kept them up anyway, going through the motions of a mature adult returning to visit his proud parents, when in reality he came home as a kind of beggar, desperate to retrieve what was slipping away. His parents were very proud of him, but neither one of them knew about the inner terror he was going through, because he didn't tell them.

During these weekend visits back home Markus struggled to accept the reality that his mother could no longer be a warm source of refueling. Following this blatantly clear realization he hit rock bottom, and regressed into infantile behavior. He made the grueling drive home every other weekend, skipping Monday classes to extend his stay. Over the course of three days he would eat five or six entire loaves of his mother's bread. And when he left to go back to school on Monday afternoons, he would ask for as many loaves as she could spare.

THE COMMODITY OF LOVE ❧ 65

"I like to give them to friends," Markus would say, hoping to justify loading ten round, crusty loaves into the trunk of his hatchback.

He would give one to Ken Gabriel, another to the president, and then keep eight for himself, eating two slices three times a day, hoping the one ingredient he couldn't taste would temporarily bolster his seemingly dwindling internal storehouse of love. Markus soon developed an intolerance to glucose from eating so much bread, and was beset by fevers. Dramatic red rashes broke out all over his body. Bethany adapted to this crisis by learning how to bake with spelt flour, and made him special gluten-free loaves. But when Markus discovered he'd gained fifteen pounds due to all these extra calories he went cold turkey, halting his weekend trips home, then declining his mother's subsequent offers to ship boxes of her artisan loaves to him in New Hampshire.

A few months into the semester he came to the undeniable conclusion that medical school was having an extremely adverse effect on the essential makeup of his self. He began to doubt the wisdom of his decision to become a doctor. What started simply as an infatuation with protons and electrons had led him into a life that no longer felt like his own. He was horrified by the notion that the unconditional love he'd always felt just beneath the surface of his skin, coursing through his blood in a constant, steady supply, was retreating, cowering deep down into his core. With every Ken Gabriel study session, with every grueling lecture class and every exam, Markus was becoming a little less human. Or at least that was how it felt to him. Toward the end of what would be his last weekend home, following his acknowledgment of the limitations underlying these retreats, he decided to request one-on-one conversations with both of his parents. They each received a day's notice to think of what advice they wanted to share in regards to what he described simply as a failure to find anything that resembled happiness. This was the reasonable way he came up with to express the phenomenon he was undergoing, one he tended to think about in more abstract terms they wouldn't be able to grasp.

Expelled from the first floor of his own house now that it had been converted into a commercial bakery, Rupert responded by having the basement reconstructed into a private retreat. He was spending most of his free time down there, trying out various hobbies while holding long, mostly one-way conversations with his pet macaw, during which he often questioned the sanity of his wife. He referred to her as the Mad Baker, but only when talking to his macaw. Markus chose the time for their talk intentionally, midway through the one o'clock football game, leaving plenty of time before Rupert's beloved Chicago Bears would take the field at four. This was a window when his father would likely be both relaxed, because he hadn't been to work in a day and a half, and excited, because his favorite team was heavily favored in their game against the Dolphins. But Markus had no choice when it came to the location of this father-son exchange. He would have to venture down into Rupert's lair.

Markus had only seen the space once before, when it was newly completed and he'd felt obligated to join one of the tours his father gave of the basement theater to interested neighbors on weekend afternoons. He remembered how Rupert had conveniently ignored the fact that almost every tour guest lingered longer, and seemed more enthralled by, his wife's industrial baking kitchen upstairs. This time, descending the carpeted stairs slowly, Markus was struck by a sharp aroma that stung his nostrils, a smell he guessed to be macaw shit mixed with cedar shavings. He'd yet to lay eyes on his father's cherished bird. When the last stair gave way to a sprawling basement, Markus found himself standing before a great golden cage hanging by four steel cables bolted to the ceiling. The pastel blue and yellow macaw was bathed in the soft shine from spotlights embedded in the polished bamboo floor.

Enthralled by the sight of the exotic bird Markus walked towards it, ignoring the vibrating boom coming from the far end of the space, where Rupert's ten-foot tall speakers shook with football stadium noise. The macaw, perched on a white plastic bar in the middle of his radiant cage, bobbed its head up and down, holding one eye fixed on Markus with a piercing stare. The bird stopped its incessant bobbing. Markus halted. He was five feet from the cage.

"The Only Game," the bird squawked.

Markus cocked his head.

"The Only Game," the macaw repeated, bobbing up and down with the words.

Markus assumed the bird was talking about football. He looked over at the bank of leather couches forming a half-circle in front of the giant projector screen on the far wall. His father's white head was lost in the holographic swirl of a football game. Rupert was the only person Markus knew to have a 3D television projector, a device that had just become available, and retailed for over five thousand dollars.

"Gotta win," spouted the macaw.

Markus turned back to face the bird. "Who's playing?"

"Gotta win the Only Game!"

"You're one crazy parrot," Markus said.

He turned to walk towards the thundering rumble of sound coming from the opposite side of the basement.

"The Mad Baker!" the macaw screamed. "Crazy Mad Baker!"

Markus saw his dad's head turn. Rupert's face scrunched up with embarrassment. The bird's voice had overpowered the exuberant announcers. As Markus was approaching the back of the couch a virtual football screamed towards his head. He ducked. A life-sized, leather-gloved receiver leaped through the air, passing through the couch like a ghost before catching the ball and sprinting off towards the wall. Rupert let out a deep laugh as Markus stood up warily.

"Almost got clocked by that nice tight spiral, eh son?"

Markus climbed over the back of the couch, glancing nervously from side to side, half expecting the avatar of a middle linebacker to tackle him before he could sit down.

"Christ pops," he said, settling nervously into the soft black leather. "You don't even need glasses for this?"

"Nope," Rupert said proudly, letting a thick hand blanket his son's kneecap. "Brand new technology. I'm the first in the neighborhood. There'll be a special tour next Saturday. You should bring some friends from school."

Markus leaned his head back into the couch, surprised to see a bank of speakers on the ceiling. He thought about how his father was always the first to get the newest home entertainment systems to come out. Markus would never forget the giant satellite dish that still occupied a far corner of their backyard. It had been one of the first in the country for home use. Rupert had ordered it direct from NASA. Neighbors of all ages showed up for a series of weekend tours, events that went on for over a year, until someone else in the neighborhood bought one, and dishes in backyards were suddenly no longer a novelty. Markus remembered his father bragging to anyone who'd listen about being able to watch Canadian feeds of the Olympics broadcast hours and hours of the events without commercial interruption, without the mushy stories on U.S. athletes Rupert always hated. But what he'd always been most ecstatic about was his ability to angle the dish in order to receive any football game being played on a given Sunday afternoon.

"Remember when you used to send me out to wipe the snow off the dish with a broom if the game wouldn't come in?" Markus asked.

Rupert smiled. "Of course I do. You loved that job!"

"Actually I hated it."

"Oh."

Although Markus had welcomed any excuse to wander the outskirts of the yard, and usually lingered there well after the dish-clearing task had been completed. He liked to find the base of a certain hemlock, where the snow had been blocked from reaching the ground by the web of needled branches. He would sit on a bed of soft dead leaves, feeling protected by the tree, enjoying the silence punctuated by a chickadee singing its simple song. He always appreciated the company of chickadees in the backyard woods during winter, when most other birds had ventured south at the first hint of fall. Even as a young child he'd delighted in their unique blend of innocence and confidence, chirping optimistically straight through the dead of winter. Snapping back into the present moment, Markus asked his father to turn off the game.

"But the Bears," Rupert muttered, squirming, glancing at the series of remote controls lined up on the glass coffee table in front of them.

"The Bears don't play until four, Dad. I checked the schedule. It's only two th -"

Markus was interrupted by a running back coming straight at the couch. He dove to down to one side in an attempt to avoid the path of the charging player.

Rupert laughed again, louder than before. "All right, I'll turn it off. I don't think you're ready for 3D football."

"I'm not," Markus admitted, sitting back upright.

Rupert stood up and walked over to a vast wall of mahogany shelves surrounding a bar stocked with fine liquors. Beside the bar was a glass humidor filled with racks of cigars. Rupert opened the glass door, reached in, and pulled out two long silver tubes. He unscrewed them, unveiling two large cigars. With a scissor-like tool he snipped off the ends, grabbed a jade ashtray, and returned to the couch. He placed the ashtray on the coffee table, then handed Markus a cigar.

"Cohiba," Markus said, reading the yellow and brown paper label.

"The real deal, son," Rupert said, winking. "Straight from Havana. Rolled on the inner thighs of beautiful Cuban women," he continued, closing his eyes briefly, reveling in some fantasy that Markus had no interest in imagining. But perhaps sharing a cigar with his father, engaging in the manly ritual for the first time in his life, would make their upcoming talk go more smoothly.

"Dad?"

Rupert opened his eyes. "Yes son?"

"Let's light these suckers up and get down to business."

Fifteen minutes later the two men were enshrouded in gray, heavy smoke. Neither had yet uttered another word. Markus was busy trying to negotiate the intense buzz now overtaking him, the kind of high akin to the effects of strong coffee, but with certain key differences. For one thing his entire mouth was numb. His scalp tingled. And the urge to vomit came and went repeatedly. The best part of the cigar's effect was its ability to transport him, lifting his mind up and out of his father's excessive basement. His imagination wandered to tropical destinations, places where the ancestors of his Latina high school lovers had come from. Then he remembered the brightly-colored bird in the golden cage at the other end of the room.

"The Mad Baker, huh?"

Rupert grimaced. "That nickname stays in this basement. Okay son? Between you and me. And my bird."

"Sure thing, Dad. But what did your parrot mean about winning the only game? Was it talking about the Bears?"

"He's not a parrot. He's a macaw."

"Sorry."

"No problem. Now, the Only Game, well, that's a term I came up with while rehearsing for this little talk you wanted to have."

"You rehearsed for this?"

Rupert took a long series of productive puffs on his Cohiba. By this point the two men could barely see each other through all the smoke.

"I did. I'm no good at this kind of stuff, son. You know that. I imagine most fathers aren't. So not only did I rehearse what I wanted to tell you, but I also had my macaw memorize my entire monologue. And I'd like to ask if it would be okay for him to deliver it. What do you think?"

Markus leaned forward to rest his half-finished cigar on the lip of the green ashtray. He shook his head. "You're serious, aren't you?"

Rupert nodded, placing his own cigar beside his son's. He stood up and beckoned Markus towards the cage. The bird watched them approach. The macaw seemed to know it was about to perform. Rupert veered towards the wall to brighten the spotlights illuminating the golden cage. Rejoining his son, draping one arm around Markus' shoulders, he gave the bird a signal with his free hand.

"The Only Game," he prompted, as if the upcoming monologue was one of many the bird had stored up in its tiny brain.

The macaw bobbed its head a few times, shook its feathers, stretched one claw, and then the other. "Buuwaah. The Only Game. Only one game to play. Gotta win. Simple rules. Find a mate. Bwuaah. Have sex. Bwuaah. Find a career. Make money. Buaahh. Support offspring. Get through time. Buwaah. Many hours to get through. The Grind. Buwaah. A desert. Be a camel. Wait for next meal. Wait for next sex. Bwuok. Killing time. One day only next meal. No more sex. Try Viagra. Bu. Wahh. The Only Game. Gotta play. Son. Buuwaaaah."

The macaw entered a prolonged period of head-bobbing, visibly proud of himself, expecting a reward. Rupert clapped in praise of his pet's performance. He reached into his pocket to pull out a piece of dried mango, and held it between the bars of the cage. The bird snatched it from him, then flew up to his swing at the very top of the cage to savor his prize.

"There," Rupert said, rubbing his hands together. "Any questions?"

"Your macaw called me son."

"He did. Was that awkward?"

Markus checked his watch. "The Bears will be on soon. I have to go up and talk to mom."

"Okay son."

Markus found his mother brushing an egg wash across a row of twisted, shiny challah loaves. He watched her dance around the long wooden table, dipping her brush in the bowl of melted butter, coating the loaves with the passionate strokes of a painter.

"I have to tell you something tragic, Mom," Markus announced.

Bethany took in a quick breath of concern. She rested her brush in the butter bowl.

"What's wrong honey?"

"I'm pretty sure I gave away all my love. And I'm only 29. That's what."

His mother chuckled. "Oh don't be silly."

"I'm not being silly, Mom. I'm serious."

"What did your father have to say down there?"

Markus took in a deep breath. "He had the bird do the talking."

"You're kidding."

"Nope."

His mother huffed with disdain. "I did overhear him practicing some kind of speech in his basement last week, but I never thought he'd have the parrot deliver it."

"It's a macaw."

"Whatever. So, tell me, what's your proof of this crazy notion?"

"The proof is that I can feel it."

"Oh really? And what does it feel like?"

Markus began to attempt an explanation, then stopped himself. Any possible description of his state could only sound cliché when spoken out loud, some combination of the words cold, hollow, and empty. And he saw what his mother's reaction would be too, that half-smile of wisdom he used to take strength from but would now only be defeated by, knowing how far he was from being a wise person himself. So he told her the absolute truth, using most direct language possible.

"Mom - what you gave me - is gone."

"That's not possible, Markus," Bethany said, flashing the sagacious smile he'd predicted as she resumed painting her loaves with melted butter. "All I gave you was my love, honey. And love can't be lost."

"I think maybe it can." Markus kicked at the floor in frustration. "Why did you have to give me so much of it? That's the problem."

"What do you mean?"

"I mean, I was like your little pet project for eighteen years. I still believed in Santa in sixth grade for Christ's sake! That's just not normal. In school I didn't talk. I ate lunch on the toilet. Alone. I wasn't a normal kid, Mom. And now I'm some kind of man-boy that you created. You filled me up with so much of your love that I've been unable to find my own - I've spent years trying to give what you put inside me away, to get back to square one, some blank slate of manhood so I'll have a chance at falling in love with a woman someday. But now there's no more time. I'm a slave to medicine, heading down into the dark tunnel of my career, which will demand my complete devotion. There's nothing to lose, though, because I've got nothing left to give. So screw it!"

Markus was breathing heavily following this outburst. He paced in agitated circles around his mother's sparkling bakery. Bethany stood above the shining loaves of challah. A brush suspended in one hand dripped butter onto the wooden counter. Her face held a combination of sorrow and care. But her words of response came out strong. It was the only way she knew how to speak to her son. With the strength of one generation addressing the next.

"I don't regret anything I gave you, Markus. You were a special boy. And you ARE becoming a man. I can see it in your eyes. All you have to do is make the leap."

"But I don't know what I'm leaping into," Markus lamented, standing across from her, fifty loaves of bread between them.

"The specifics don't matter, honey. You only have to jump, and trust that you'll land on firm ground."

Maybe it was hearing the word jump that made him do it. Or maybe he just wanted to prove his level of desperation to the person who still knew him the best. So he gave in to blind impulse and jumped right then, onto the wooden table, belly-flopping on top of the shiny twisted loaves. He tore at the bread, ripping off chunks, biting into as many pieces of the egg-laden dough as he could while Bethany called down the stairs to her husband with mild degree of urgency. Markus flung himself off the table, bread flying in all directions, bits of challah stuck to his face.

"He can't see me like this," he said, nodding grimly towards the basement stairs before shouldering his already-packed duffel bag and stepping out the door. After climbing into his car Markus looked up to see his mother and father standing side-by-side on the front step. They were both trying hard to smile while waving tentative goodbyes.

"Some of the loaves didn't hit the floor," Bethany called out to him in her softest, most motherly voice. "Wouldn't you like to take them with you?"

"I'm off bread!" Markus shouted while pulling out of the driveway, spinning stones with his tires. "How many times do I have to tell you that?"

He let the grueling, nine-hour drive back to Dartmouth be the beginning of this leap his mother had spoken about. Markus didn't like the feeling at all, but decided that might be a good sign. Maybe sometimes the right thing to do was the hardest thing, and being hard was the proof it was the only thing he should be doing.

The Gondola Club

WHAT FOLLOWED FOR MARKUS WAS a year of purgatory, a numb wasteland largely void of emotion. He was growing increasingly paranoid that he'd greatly depleted the core of his essence during all his years spent indulging in romance and poetry, spreading his affection out among thousands, behaving like some kind of Johnny Appleseed of the heart. Except Johnny's trees had always provided the tree-planter with fruits, and therefore new seeds. But where were the fruits of Markus' many labors of love? He had nothing concrete to show for all that energy expended. None of the girls he'd wooed were by his side. His poems were in the hands of strangers, most of them likely forgotten by then, lost in dusty stacks of books and papers. Thrown out. Recycled. Decomposing in ditches. Except for the framed napkins hanging on the president's wall, and a few laminated ones his mother had hanging on the door of her walk-in cooler. But what were those scribbled words, entombed behind glass, sealed within plastic, able to give him back? Nothing. His perspective shifting with age, Markus began to wonder if there was any point in sharing love without the hope that it would one day come back around? If not in the form of a wife lying beside him at night, and children to cuddle with in the morning, than at least something warm enough to assuage the acute pain of loneliness now assaulting him on a regular basis.

His grades began to slip. He didn't care. As far as he could tell there was no point to anything. It was a mid-life crisis, and he wasn't yet thirty years old. He started skipping classes, spending long hours leaning against his favorite trees in the quad, daydreaming about his childhood boulder in the backyard woods. All he wanted to do was go back in time, start over again, choose different paths with destinations opposite from this life he'd stumbled into, the bubble of academia, a career track largely set in stone. Markus failed another exam during this time. He kept waiting to be summoned into the president's office. But he never got a call. Instead he got a gift. It was there outside his apartment door one morning, a polished wooden stick about four feet tall. There was a note attached with twine, a tiny card with handwritten words inside.

This is my old walking stick, from my days in med school. Juniper. I found it on a walk in a Utah canyon. It's a gift. One you should use. Start walking, Markus. Walk until your feet burn. That might just cure what ails you.

Karl F.

Markus decided to accept the president's gift, and with it his advice. He walked the way Forrest Gump ran. Because he had to. He walked like it was the only thing he had to do, but for no specific reason. He walked every day, for miles and miles. Markus liked the feeling of it right away, and didn't try to figure out why this incessant bipedalism felt so good. The walking helped calm down his mind. He became addicted to it. He sold his car, content to walk back and forth between town, the large apartment his parents helped him afford, and the Dartmouth campus. On weekends he walked up into the mountains, often covering distances of thirty miles or more on a given Saturday. He explored any trails he stumbled upon, heading into forests and up mountains. When he got tired of the trails he could reach on foot, Markus got rides from his classmates out of town so he could discover new territory to explore.

By the end of the third year his manic walking habit was well known throughout the Dartmouth community. His body had become rippled with muscle, his face smooth and tan from the elements. When Markus wasn't walking he was studying. He poured himself into his school work, and rose back up to the top of the class in his third year. His primary goal each day was to distract his mind from the nagging emptiness in his chest. When he wasn't studying or sleeping, Markus was walking. This compulsive locomotion did bring him some of the deep, inner satisfaction he craved. And it was a great way to kill free time, to distract himself from the hollowness in his chest, becoming even more empty in the process. He didn't go home for Christmas that year. He came to accept the void inside, forcing himself to get accustomed to it, to prepare for a lifetime spent living with it the same way one came to accept cancer, or some other life-threatening disease. Markus told himself that maybe every adult lived this way. But the example of his mother haunted him. She was living proof that a rich life full of love was possible. His mind cast about for some theory to latch onto that might be able to explain what had gone wrong. Maybe what had filled him up before was bound to dwindle and fade by the time he reached the age of thirty. But he couldn't help thinking that it might have been different, that he'd had the chance to hold onto his love, to preserve and grow it, but had instead chosen to give it all away in the intoxicating blur of youth. He'd given it to the dozen high school sweethearts during the process of sweeping them off their twenty-four feet. And he'd handed a piece of his love away to each of the thousands of strangers who'd bought his poems, thinking it would all eventually come back around, not really caring if it didn't, because he'd had plenty to spare. So now Markus had nothing left to lose. Or so he thought. What he still had was his freedom. Without freedom, love wasn't even an issue. But being an American from a privileged upbringing, he took this most basic of liberties for granted.

By the beginning of his fourth year the spell of walking began wearing thin. His walks had become more about visiting his trees. He'd discovered some very special trees while ambling through the forests surrounding Hanover. Most were old-growth, having aged over the centuries into a variety of sizes due to variations in sun and wind and altitude. Many had witnessed the Green Mountain Boys fight the Revolutionary War from their fixed viewpoints on the land. Markus had a mental list of his favorites, cataloged into a kind of GPS system built into his mind. He didn't need a digital accessory to find these trees. He just walked to where they were in the forest. He tried to visit each of them once a month. When he arrived at one of his old trees Markus would admire it from a distance at first, able to feel their warm, tractor-beam embrace from fifty feet away sometimes, as if the tree had a gravity of its own. Once he decided that the tree had accepted him as a guest into its world he would move in close to sit at the base, resting his back against the ancient trunk like he used to do in Dartmouth's quad. While gazing up into the canopy Markus would feel protected, not only from the elements, but from all the concerns of the outside world. He would take long, slow breaths, listening to the subtle sounds around him, like a woodpecker's rata-tat tapping, or a breeze rustling the leaves high above. He liked to reach around to finger the contours of bark. The deep crevices of an oak. A beech's hard smoothness. The peeling paper of a birch. These heightened moments outside the bounds of his everyday existence always brought back warm memories of his backyard woods, the protective hemlocks, the friendly chickadees, and his boulder.

Markus fed off these intimate moments with his favorite trees, filling up on something new and old, feeding a primal, child-like type of hunger, sustenance others found in churches or temples or baseball stadiums. What he used to find riding his boulder. Maybe, even, the same kind of fullness Marisol had described feeling after a movie date with him all those years ago, as if she'd just eaten one of her grandma's home-cooked meals. The same satiation Markus always felt after the thousands of meals his mother had crafted for him with such care. If he'd been forced to choose a favorite tree, it would not have been an easy choice at all, but he likely would have picked an old twisted birch that clung to one of the high rocky ridge lines so prevalent in the White Mountains. He almost considered it another species entirely, so different this tree was from birches found at lower altitudes, in flat forests, along the edges of hay fields. Those younger white birches had a warmth to them, a soothing, feminine kind of aura. This old one had grown neither tall nor thick over the centuries, like most of Markus' other trees. But the white paper had long ago peeled off entirely, replaced by dark gray, rough bark that would have caused the average observer to assume it wasn't a birch at all. Markus felt this tree was not feminine and not masculine either, that it had transcended such narrow definitions to become defined simply by the raw strength and perseverance it had needed to survive for so long being lashed by the brunt of violent storms, buried under snow, coated with ice for months on end. The old birch had survived long enough to evolve beyond its original birchness, becoming a tree unique to itself, worthy of the same amount of reverence that a redwood received. Markus knew he was the only human being to honor its remarkable presence by spending time leaning against its gnarled trunk, a trunk with a strength rivaling steel.

After a few hours spent basking in what the great old trees had to give him, a physical craving would override any spiritual appetite still unfulfilled, the pangs of an empty stomach reminding him of the practical need to eat dinner. There was nothing to eat in the mountains. The only animals he saw on his walks were a few scrawny chipmunks, some birds, all kinds of bugs, and small frogs. There were some acorns, a few berries here and there, but nothing else of edible substance. The reality of supper always coaxed him into leaving his tree-of-the-day to return to Dartmouth and civilization, the same way he used to abandon his rock horse in exchange for Ritz crackers with peanut butter and his mother. Now it was stir fried vegetables with brown rice and a phone call to one of his buddies in town that beckoned him out from the wilderness, the wild world

humans had traded in ten-thousand years earlier, first for the security of farming, and then for the protection money provided. A large
part of Markus felt it had been downhill ever since the origin of ag-
riculture for the species to which he reluctantly belonged. But with
age he'd also come to see that nothing was ever black and white.
Civilization had produced surgery. And he would become a surgeon, an identity for his ego that the wild woods could never have
given him. This was what his trees told him to do when they spoke
up in his dreams. And he listened with wide open ears in his sleep.

Markus came away from his moments with his trees feeling en-
ergized rather than depleted, opposite to the way he'd felt in high
school after being with a girl, or after hanging out with his friends
in town lately. The end results of his human encounters still left him
drained of energy. Not because his girls or his friends consciously
took from him, but because he gave himself so fully to them. It was
the only way he knew how to be, giving others no choice but to
receive what was being offered. So he existed within this repeating
circle, drawing sustenance from time with his trees, then losing this
fuel before it had a chance to settle into his core, giving it away to
the next available recipient because doing this felt so good, so much
better than keeping the energy that the old birch gave him all to
himself. But Markus was finding that neither his classmates nor his
town buddies provided enough of an outlet for the remains of what
he still held inside. So as winter dropped its frozen blanket down
on New England certain seeds of thought began germinating in his
mind, thoughts that would grow into the need for a dramatic shift
in his behavior.

As an unspoken reward for having reached the middle of his
fourth year of medical school the academics eased up a little that
winter, leading to sudden voids of free time Markus struggled to
fill, hours that had previously been booked up, unstructured oases
within his hyper-structured life. And his walks to his trees lost much

of their allure, not to mention their practicality, once the winter storms began to hit. What he eventually turned to for occupying these new gaps in his schedule surprised him, but only after the fact. During the fact of these moments, while exploring the facts of life all over again, analyzing his actions was the last thing Markus wanted to do. The women he wound up seducing during this period of carnal descent were the random recipients of his live-for-the-moment attitude. What Markus began to live for, more precisely, were Saturday nights. Whatever energy he had leftover from the week he devoted to pursuing his sexual desires, leaving love entirely out of the picture. It was a style of living Markus had never attempted cultivating. Until his fourth year in Med School.

In the midst of that final year of his academic prison sentence, as winter began tightening its grip, descending down from Canada, Markus' libido was reborn. His sexuality made itself known to him in a new way, demanding satisfaction through extremity. He complied, because he thought it was what he needed to do. He dropped down into previously unexplored realms of superficial sex, indulging in impermanent dates, chasing bodily satisfaction most every weekend. Sex replaced walking, and he pursued this new activity with the same all-or-nothing attitude that had defined his walking, his studying, his poetry. The only thing in his life besides studying and sex was his still-budding relationships with his friends in town, while other things, like multiple orgasms achieved in multiple positions, began flowering. Sexual encounters blossomed across the blank canvas of his free time. He came with controlled abandon, Jackson Pollack-like, learning sexual skills he'd never properly developed in high school, and not during his years as a poet either.

The New England women he sought out didn't succumb as easily to his advances as the Latin teenagers he'd pursued back in high school. But Markus found that once he put in a little work, minor efforts in comparison to the rigors of his medical studies, these mixed-blood Europeans, with pale, freckled skin and long limbs, came alive in his bedroom with surprising voracity. He made an Irish Catholic girl from Boston belt out the Hail Mary as if she was singing God Bless America. He induced a Scottish redhead to beg him to join her clan, to plant the seeds of a White Mountain branch of the MacTeague line. But Markus soon found himself hooked on one specific type of woman during this time, and began seeking out what he'd later classify as a subspecies of its own, a genetically distinct kind of female, a unique breed. He envisioned these French Canadian women as having originated from some mystical source in the wilds of Quebec, whose ancestors had drifted down into Northern New England and stopped there, feeling perfectly at home in the long winters and coniferous mountain forests of Vermont and New Hampshire.

Markus found these women to be sophisticated and wildly feline at the same time, lovers of fine things like art and chocolate, while also open to whatever form of sexual adventure he could think up. Of all the Quebecois women he came to know intimately during this time, Marie-Claire literally came out on top. She insisted on riding him every time they made love, spouting Montreal slang Markus never asked her to translate, later wishing he had. She thwarted his first attempt to take her from behind, using a leg-lock to twist him onto his back so she could pounce on top of him, where she pretended he was one of her beloved teenage horses. A few weeks into their relationship Marie-Claire admitted to Markus that she couldn't orgasm unless three conditions were met: he couldn't wear a condom, she had to be on top, and she needed to close her eyes in order to envision her favorite horse, a white stallion named Napolean. Markus had no problem complying with any of these requirements.

She was on birth control, some modern version that only required one shot in the arm every six months, eliminating her period. Markus had always used a condom during sex, both in high school and with the girls that had preceded Marie-Claire there in Hanover. He was not a big fan of condoms, but the girls had always insisted he wear them. More than once his dick had shrunk while he tried covering it, especially when it took him some time to figure out which way the thing rolled down. The girls forgave him for these rare instances of male disability, because his regular performances were well above average. But Markus had trouble forgiving himself for these embarrassing failures until he confided in his townie friends, who all confirmed the limitations of condoms. Being married men, they only had distant memories of these latex challenges, and fell back on their regular advice that he just bite the bullet and get married. Sometimes this layer of plastic was so able to separate the most sensitive part of his body from fully experiencing the unique blend of warm fluids it was so eager to immerse itself in that Markus failed to come no matter how vigorously he pounded away. Eventually he gravitated to the ultra-thin varieties of prophylactics, and finally experienced something close to sexual ecstasy. Close, but not quite, a discrepancy in his degree of pleasure and satisfaction he only became aware of after his first round of bareback sex with Marie-Claire.

Indulging in this new kind of lovemaking, undeniably pure, with no man-made barrier inhibiting this ultimate primal connection between two animals of the opposite sex, gave Markus a sexual high like none he'd ever thought possible. Being inside Marie-Claire for steadily longer periods of time, his ability to control himself increased with every session. And that old phenomenon of gravity becoming irrelevant afterwards returned more intensely than he'd ever known it before, even after being with Marisol, who'd been a standout, albeit inexperienced lover. This new kind of sex had the power to lift Markus up and out of himself to a degree his walks and his trees were never able to provide. But there was another layer accompanying these post-coital states of euphoria, some deeper level of union that tugged at the strands of his DNA. While having an orgasm deep inside this beautiful and intelligent woman, his doctor's mind couldn't help picturing his sperm diligently seeking out an egg that wasn't there. His body reacted on its own separate terms, with a pounding heart, rushing blood, and muscles that swelled with strength to a degree exercise had never inspired them to reach. After coming inside Marie-Claire, Markus would be assaulted with a flood of purpose his biology was programmed to produce, the pressing urge to rise up fully into his manhood and become a father.

He couldn't help hearing a few of his own father's words, delivered by the macaw, slip in through recent cracks in the wall he'd been erecting against them ever since that surreal Sunday afternoon in Rupert's basement. It was a powerful feeling, one Markus found himself marveling at, how perfectly nature had constructed testosterone's floodgates, so that once fully opened by the universal key of bare skin sex with a willing and fertile woman, the desire to be a father became instantly all-consuming. And he was also amazed at how this compulsion persisted for days afterward, accompanying his sex-induced highs without grounding them, even while his lover did nothing to encourage the effect that giving open access to the inner reaches of her womanhood, temporarily barren as it might have been, was having on him. Although nearing thirty herself, an age Markus knew had a relatively reliable ability to set off the alarm on that famous reproductive clock most every woman seemed to possess, Marie-Claire never mentioned any desire to have children. In fact she'd dropped more than a few hints to him that she never wanted kids of her own, forcing Markus to bottle up this intense side effect of having sex with her, never mentioning it. As a direct by-product of this suppression he came to view the invention of birth control as a kind of curse, a cruel biological trick designed to maximize pleasure while eliminating the natural end result, and ensuing responsibilities. On the surface, of course, it seemed to be one of science's perfect discoveries, a miracle rivaling penicillin. But Markus came to see this man-made manipulation of his girlfriend's cycle as another factor in his suffering, one more complication in his endless, seemingly futile effort to become a man.

    The ultimate reason Marie-Claire stood out above all the rest of his French Canadian standout lovers was because of her role in what would be the pinnacle moment in his season of sexual adventure. It happened in one of the little red gondolas that climbed to just beneath the summit of a local ski mountain. The couple was learning how to snowboard together, eager to acquire a new physical activity they could share, something other than their bedroom gymnastic routines. Marie-Claire slipped the lift attendant a twenty to let them have the six-person gondola to themselves. She unzipped his snow pants before they reached the first lift tower. She pulled her jeans down below her belt, revealing silk lingerie with a velvet-lined opening for his entry. The warmth inside her shocked Markus, intense in comparison to the frozen plastic surrounding them. The gondola climbed high. Marie-Claire moved slowly, back and forth, opening her eyes from time to time, seeming to abandon her remembered image of Napolean in favor of the view through the scratched plastic windows. Riding Markus, moaning gutter French, Marie-Claire gazed north through a notch in the jagged peaks. He watched her eyes settle on the distant frozen wheat fields of Quebec, her homeland, the place she was crying out to in her ancestors' language while she came, back to back, her back to Markus, his explosion filling her. He filled her with the lust of his genetic code, because he had nothing else left to give.

    Later that night, after dropping Marie-Claire off at home, a quick sting of pain spread through his chest. Markus called her first thing in the morning. After briefly considering asking her if she wanted to make a baby, aware of the certainty of a negative response, he simply ended it on the pretext of his looming board exams. After hanging up the phone he came to the clear recognition that not only had Marie-Claire come out on top in the end, but so too had every woman he'd seduced during this period of promiscuity. They'd all received some final, accidental fragments of his once abundant love, helping him achieve the one goal he now realized he'd been subconsciously pursuing ever since leaving home at eighteen. Markus had finally succeeded in giving all of his love away. But instead of being free as a result he was now trapped in a prison cell of emptiness, a holding chamber he'd constructed for himself over the course of a dozen years, inside which there was nothing to do except wait for death. No tree could replace what he'd lost. Going back to his mother was no longer an option. What a long wait it was going to be. Markus knew from recent experience that neither his walks to his trees nor haphazard carnal pursuits with French Canadian women were going to be successful distractions from the burden of living out the rest of his life in this state of numbness he was slipping into. He began casting about for another side trail of experience that might ease the suffering inherent to moving forward down this professional path he'd set in stone for himself to walk, even if it was becoming more and more like a tunnel each day. Like the Huey Lewis song he'd always despised as a kid, Markus wanted a new drug, one that wouldn't let him down.

Altered States

IT SOON CAME TIME FOR MARKUS to choose a sub-specialty to focus on within the vast field of surgery, one that would lead him into a specific residency. Lacking strong passion for any one part of the body, he went to see the president for advice. Instead of talking inside Frederick's office they took a walk around the quad, two men ambling further into friendship.

"I see you've got a nice spring in your step there, Markus."

"Thanks to that walking stick you gave me. I was walking fifty miles a week there for a while."

"Excellent. I'm very glad to hear that. But is that the only factor behind your exuberant gait?" the president asked, throwing him a sideways smile.

"There are other factors," Markus admitted. "Like a girl named Marie-Claire."

"Ahh. A Quebecois?"

Markus nodded.

"A unique breed, for sure," Frederick added.

"Are you familiar with these French Canadian woman, Karl?"

The president slowed the pace of his walking. He clasped his fingers behind his lower back.

"There were some, yes. In college. I went to St. Lawrence, on the Canadian border. Sometimes I slipped away to Montreal to pursue these slinky creatures, all of them dangerous women to marry. So, hard as it was, I let each one go."

They stopped beneath a great rising maple. Sunlight caught on the pointed leaves. There were narrow black shadows in the shallow crevices of the gray bark.

"I love the trees here," Markus said.

"Me too."

"On my longer walks I would visit some favorite old trees up in the mountains. I made a map of them all. I could show it to you sometime. Maybe you'd like to visit one of them with me."

"I'd love to. There is also something of mine up in those mountains I'd like to show you. But enough about trees and Canadian women - what's on your mind, Markus?"

They resumed walking, more slowly now. Markus let himself feel entirely contained within the pleasant bubble of the moment. He didn't notice any other passing student while they walked, stopped looking at the trees, ignored buildings while trusting his feet to follow the smooth concrete path. Markus was imbued with a calm confidence just by being next to this man he so revered.

"I need to choose a specialty Karl."

"I know. Which fields are you trying to decide between?"

"I want to be a surgeon. I need to use my hands. The trees told me that. But there are so many kinds of surgery. I need you to help me, because I won't make it through residency if I don't find a focus I can be passionate about."

"Yes. You'll have no Ken Gabriel during residency. Only whatever grit lies in the depths of your bowels. But don't worry about that right now. My advice, Markus, is to think back to your days as a poet, when you lived off the passion for your art. A similar spirit will help you make it through."

"It wasn't art I was living off of back then."

"What was it?"

Markus stopped abruptly. "My love."

He wanted to add more, to describe his ongoing existential struggle with this impossible emotion, but held his tongue instead. Markus had been through this many times in his head. There were no words to describe what had happened, the complete erosion of his once substantial reserves of love. At least not any words he would expect anyone to understand, even a good friend. The president turned to face him, walking backwards, grinning, his puffy white hair brilliant in the afternoon sun.

"Well, then, you've made your choice already."

Markus tilted his head, confused. "What do you mean?"

"Where does love originate?"

"Pff," Markus said, shaking his head. "Most poets would say in the heart, of course, but -"

"And they would be right. Focus on hearts, Markus. See what holes can develop in them. Learn how to fix them when they break. And, if you decide to do your training right here, you'll have the honor of working side-by-side with one of my all-time favorite people in the world, Dr. Kathryn Stone."

With his decision to become a heart transplant surgeon now firmly established, both by the president's endorsement and his parents' pride swelling halfway across the country, with board exams still six months away and whiffs of spring in the air to cap it all off, Markus hadn't felt this carefree in years, not since walking away from home at the age of eighteen. Pursuing sex, and the end result of Marie-Claire, had proven too complicated to be the distraction Markus needed. So in order to move forward as a man who'd lost his love, with no time or map for going back to recover it, he turned to his friends in town with the hope that one of them might be able to help him cultivate a new strategy of avoidance. The escape of choice among his earthy Hanover pals was beer, the cheaper the better. Brands like PBR and Coors were sought out simply for their volume-to-cost ratio. When he joined their gatherings Markus would accept a couple beers handed his way, careful not to mention things like his belief that Coors Light tasted like beer flavored water, his preference for local micro brews, or his lack of passion for beer in

general. There was one member of the group who was equally un-
enthusiastic about beer, although for a different reason. Chip Baker,
an electrician, was a recovering alcoholic, one of those rare former
AA members with rehab experience who'd been able to return to
alcohol in moderation. But the key to his unlikely self-control lay in
utilizing another substance to help him maintain a presence at the
parties after his self- imposed limit of two beers had been reached.

Chip liked to smoke pot, and always brought a joint or two of
high octane hydroponic bud to these gatherings. He'd sequester
himself to puff on it periodically, rejoining the drunk group with
a contented smile, sufficiently altered so as not to feel left out of
the party while the Coors kept flowing. Markus would also halt
his drinking around the same time Chip did, but instead of getting
stoned he would turn his focus fully onto his friends, helping Rick
baste his ribs for the third time in the last two hours, or pretending to be fooled by one of Jim's amateur card tricks. Markus never
accepted Chip's sporadic offers to share a joint, aware that getting
stoned would impede his ability to memorize large quantities of
information about the human body, which was his only job during
those years. But now he'd reached the home stretch, and wanted
a new distraction from unstructured time, when he was prone to
dwelling on his state of emotional emptiness. So Markus called
Chip up out of the blue to see if his friend could get him stoned.
The electrician was more than happy to fulfill this request less than
twenty-four hours after it had been made.

Up until that day in his life Markus' only experience with drugs
had been the mushroom trip with Ishmael and a few hits off spliffs
in Northern California. It was fortunate that his only previous encounter with pot had taken place in Humboldt County, California,
the unofficial capital of high quality bud. There the growers had
taken the science of growing weed to new heights. They produced
such high grade, genetically engineered marijuana that if the stuff
had been around in the Sixties, the hippies of the Woodstock era

might have actually had the clarity of mind while high to successfully transform the country in very tangible ways, instead of daydreaming about these transformations while puffing endless quantities of low-grade Mexican schwag and hanging out naked. So Markus had some general idea of what he was in for when he met Chip in a public parking lot behind the main drag in town. They sat in Chip's blue panel van, the kind of van with no windows, a vehicle viewed as totally sketchy unless it was being used by a carpenter or an electrician or a painter. While Markus tried to get comfortable amidst the jumble of lights and extension chords, wires, rolls of black tape, and toolboxes of various shapes and sizes, Chip busied himself packing the glass bowl of a three-foot bong. Markus had seen a few such devices at high school parties, but never up close like this.

"Damn, Chip. That thing won't kill me, will it?"

"Ha! Takes fifteen hundred pounds of weed, smoked in one sitting, to overdose. Fifteen hundred pounds! That's just not humanly possible."

"Okay."

Chip held up a finger. "But you will cough. That I guarantee. Coughing is good. Makes you even higher. Just don't cough into the bong, or the water will soak the weed."

"Sure."

After studying his friend's technique, already altered from the secondhand cloud of fragrant smoke now filling the entire van, an atmospheric condition Chip referred to with affection as "hotboxing", Markus took hold of the bong with two hands. While his friend lit the bowl he sucked in, filling the glass tube with smoke, enjoying the sound of bubbling water. Then Chip pulled out the bowl, and the collected smoke shot deep into Markus' lungs. He doubled over, coughing violently. Chip laughed as Markus righted himself, pounding his chest with a fist.

"Holy shit," Markus coughed.

Chip laughed some more while packing himself a second hit.

Markus was busy trying to negotiate the high taking hold of him. There was no choice but to give in to another version of the floating sensation that good sex gave him. Although he took note of a similar weightlessness to his body, an even more intense indifference to the ground than sex with Marie-Claire had induced, it was what was taking place in his mind that enthralled him. All of a sudden his thoughts did not feel like his own. They weren't originating in normal locations, weren't following the usual pathways. Even the creative corners of his brain, places that had given birth to all the poems over the years, were silenced by the reefer. His mind was suddenly producing sparkling thoughts, random ideas that were both deep and superficial at the same time, delighting him with their wonderful unpredictability, as if someone else was thinking them. At some point later in the day, after Chip had abandoned him to go wire the high school football field's broken scoreboard, unfazed by second and third bong hits that would have landed Markus in the hospital or some equivalent hyper-controlled situation, during the midst of drifting around the quaint Hanover streets lost in a delicious THC-induced reverie, Markus realized what was so appealing about being stoned on quality pot. His brain, although greatly altered, was functioning with relative clarity. His body, although encased in a kind of numbing glow, moved with an almost normal degree of agility. But what was most gratifying of all, beyond these rather pleasant mind/body effects, was a more spiritual kind of impact the reefer was exerting upon him. Markus didn't feel like himself. In fact he felt like a completely different person was somehow inhabiting his body. This phenomenon was so profoundly uplifting that he couldn't help laughing out loud from time to time. He chased pigeons through the park, then joined a horde of little kids splashing in a fountain. He sparked up light conversation with absolute strangers, bought a jazz cd for the first time in his life, and sat for long stretches of time in fixed spots, indulging in thoughts that required no effort from him to come up with, because the marijuana was producing them entirely on its own. He capped off this glorious afternoon by eating a takeout pizza on a park bench before retreating to his apartment, where he listened to Miles Davis while sprawled out on the floor.

He met Chip again the next day for another bong session in the panel van, then proceeded to ask the electrician to score him a bag of his own. Finding himself the sudden owner of an ounce of bright green kind bud, a few puffs of which took him away from being Markus and into being someone he liked spending time with so much more, a detached reveler, a person with no need to give or take, who was simply content observing the comedy of life, even if life was passing him by without anything so concrete as a poem left behind in its wake. It was a blissful, childlike spring for Markus, during which he was stoned for vast expanses of time. Then all of a sudden he had to start studying for the boards. After flushing the last crumbles of his ounce down the toilet, voices of high school health teachers echoing the term "Gateway Drug" in his head, Markus sought out Chip for help.

"I'm off the reefer, Chip, but the coffee's not gonna' cut it. I need something stronger, just for a month or two, to help me get through these board exams. Can you help me out?"

Chip nodded with understanding as he fished through one of his tool boxes, eventually locating an orange bottle filled with blue oval pills.

"Ever heard of Adderoll?"

Markus nodded.

"It's straight amphetamine," Chip continued. "If a person has ADD, it calms them down. If you don't, it's the best drug known to mankind. Better than pure Colombian cocaine. Without these guys," he said, shaking the bottle of pills in his hand, "I wouldn't be able to smoke pot and get my work down. Together, they're just right. The Adderoll should help sharpen you up dramatically. Just as long as you find a way to come down."

"Great. Can you get me some?"

"Here, take these. I'm getting a new batch tomorrow."

Markus sequestered himself deep in the library stacks, claiming one of the holding cells near where his original meeting with Ken Gabriel had taken place. He took to bribing first year students with some of the blue pills, which he quickly discovered were cherished by many of them, in exchange for supplying him with rounds of food and beverages, so he didn't have to break from studying. The amphetamine did have a remarkable effect on the efficiency of his mind, sharpening it with a precision that even the strongest, highest quality latte could never have come close to achieving. And, as a side benefit similar to the pot, Markus didn't feel like himself while riding the Adderoll buzz. He became closer to a machine that a person, hyper-competent, able to remain in the zone of studying for long expanses of time. This speed-induced form of himself was largely indifferent to other people, a distance he found refreshing, as this released him from the pressure of socializing. He brushed off the first-years nonchalantly, not bothering to answer their persistent questions about what they were in for during the next three years.

"You're better off not knowing," he'd say without looking up from his stacks of note cards.

Markus ignored the library staff's offers to help him locate certain hard-to-find volumes. His brain on overdrive told him he could do everything faster than anyone else, even if it was that person's job to do it. The only downfall to this otherwise perfect drug was that it made winding down at night, and finding sleep, extremely difficult. Rather than take Chip's advice to smoke a little pot to decompress, Markus chose the legal relaxant of alcohol instead. Wine worked best, at first a couple of glasses, until soon entire bottles became necessary for him to get to sleep at a reasonable hour. He bumped into the president once during this period, and immediately discarded his friend's concern over his visibly scattered, disheveled condition.

"Just cramming for the boards, Karl."

"No need to cram, Markus. There's plenty of time to prepare in a -"

"Don't worry about me. Soon this will all be over."

"Just be careful, Markus. You don't look normal to me."

"And what is normal, Karl?" Markus spouted defiantly before moving along the winding path leading to the library prison.

It had been weeks since he'd smoked pot. If Markus had been able to pause for a moment, he would have seen how he probably didn't need the Adderoll anymore. But now there was the problem of all the wine he was consuming every night. Recognizing that he'd become locked in a miniature circle of addiction Markus plowed forward, deciding he would give himself the rest of the summer to chill out. By the time the exams came his tolerance for the Adderoll had grown exponentially, so he took the advice of one of his first-year helpers and tried crushing up the little blue pills and snorting them. Flying high, immune to any needs beyond the most basic biological ones, Markus passed the tests easily, partied hard with the classmates he'd been largely ignoring for years, and then crashed into a bodily state of purgatory he could only classify as depression.

The best part of this chemically-induced, not necessarily downward spiral, had been the fact that Markus spent zero time considering the problem of his dwindling love. He was too busy slaughtering the remains of it to realize what he was doing. It felt so refreshing to take love completely out of the picture, to indulge in a degree of freedom he'd never known before. This new indifference toward the emotion that had so tormented much of his existence allowed him to take the plunge he'd initiated months ago, in Chip's blue van, to one final version of rock bottom. Or it could just have easily been viewed as another mountain peak of new experience, depending on the eventual makeup of his still-forming moral universe. Markus loaded up his hatchback with a half-case of his favorite reserve Rioja, a twelve pack of ultra-thin condoms, and his last five Adderolls. He headed for Montreal, and what his online browsing had revealed to be a plethora of very young French Canadian women, most of whom barely spoke English, and were willing to lend him their naked bodies to him for the reasonable price of one hundred-fifty dollars in Canadian currency, at a time when the US dollar was still high. And the fact that these were his mother's dollars (somehow accepting money from Bethany had lately seemed okay to Markus, while her bread, a much more direct form of sustenance, was still out of the question) might have made the borderline sinful mission slightly more doable than it otherwise would have been. He spent three blurry days in Montreal, achieved his goal while convincing himself it was the Adderoll-infused, Rioja-buzzed version of Markus who was banging a nineteen year old escort, and not actually the real Markus, who was simply an innocent tourist hoping to try some crepes and practice his French. While the call girl propped herself up on an elbow to ask him if he was going to want another round, Markus was too distracted by her beautiful youth to even attempt understanding her thickly accented English. A wave of pain spread across his chest. He wanted to know if she'd enjoyed the sex. He wanted to take her out to dinner, and find out about her life, then make sure she had a decent place to sleep. She told him that she had plans for dinner and a night out with a friend, she lived in a nice three-bedroom house outside the city, and was majoring in biology at McGill. This information only sparked an urge inside Markus to want to date her long distance. He squelched this unrealistic desire as best he could, knowing he had to leave Montreal immediately, and that he could never do this again. After over-tipping her he made the long drive back to Hanover, sore all over and sneezing blue snot, knowing that some kind of crash awaited him there.

Summer seemed like a very cruel season to be depressed. Markus was forced to spend large amounts of time simply fighting the urge to get stoned with Chip, or blow a line of Adderoll and then down a bottle of wine, aware the temporary lift these activities might provide wouldn't be worth engaging in them. Facing weeks of open-ended days empty of responsibility, too broke for a vacation and refusing the extended stay back home his mother kept offering, avoiding his buddies in town now that he'd proven susceptible to their workingman indulgences, Markus grew quickly desperate for some kind of rescue, a life preserver cast his way, something other than a new girl to date or a new drug to try. Without these hedonistic distractions he'd indulged in freely over the past year he woke up every day inside a vacuum, more hallowed out than ever, the days long and drawn out. While sequestered within various altered states over the past few months he had been able to convince himself that it wasn't actually Markus Greene who was doing these things, because he hadn't felt like himself while doing them. But now the strong solstice sun wouldn't let him hide from the memories of these actions, recollections that corrupted his previous opinion of himself as a relatively good and stable guy. Suicidal fantasies rose up, shocking him with their persistent offer of a seemingly easy escape from the place he'd crash landed. When his parents came for graduation they didn't notice anything wrong, because he didn't let anything under the surface show. And so the void of these summer weeks stretched out in front of him. Out of desperation he re-enacted some of his walks, paying visits to a few of his trees in the mountains, but halted this almost immediately after realizing with horror that now, while sitting against a tree, he couldn't feel a thing. Markus had succeeded, whether he'd meant to or not, in making himself completely numb to the living world.

The President

THE SUMMER WAS ALWAYS Karl Frederick's favorite season, because he had plenty of time to paint. It was a secret hobby even his wife and daughters didn't know about. Although she never came out and said so, Karl sometimes wondered if his wife had decided his secrecy surrounding his whereabouts during painting sessions was obvious evidence of an affair. Maybe she imagined herself competing with a younger woman who wore perfume that smelled oddly similar to paint thinner. In a way, Karl did treat his hobby like an affair, keeping it hidden from his family and friends for no reason he could specify, never returning home from his studio with any finished paintings to show off, because he'd been working on the same one for decades. Maybe the semi-illicit nature of his painting gave him the edge he needed to get better at it, provided some kind of energizing buzz that added to the vibrancy of his art, allowing him to feel a fleeting kinship with the likes of Gauguin and Van Gogh. As for natural skill, piano playing came much easier to him. Painting was something he had to work very hard at. Karl had been working diligently, mostly during the summer months, on the same creation for thirty years now, a four-sided mural covering the walls of his studio secluded beside a small creek on the trail-less flank of a nameless peak.

Karl hadn't had a plan in mind when he began the painting three decades ago, during his first summer at Dartmouth. And now that the mural was taking on a specific form, he still had no idea what was being depicted on the canvas. He just mixed colors on his palette and applied them with his brushes, never failing to be surprised by the images he created, never questioning their sources even though everything he wound up painting had no connection whatsoever to his own life experience, nor to anyone else he knew. On this particular July day, eager for distraction from his brooding over Markus Greene's obviously poor condition, Karl stood in the middle of his studio, turning in slow circles, taking in the work as a whole. What had evolved over the years could be described as a surreal, abstract map of America. It was surreal and abstract because only certain, very specific features, both geographic and manmade, were represented. What his subconscious had chosen to highlight struck him as entirely random, with no pattern or logic readily available to make sense of it all. Why had he devoted one entire summer to painting a stone monastery perched on a cliff above the Pacific Ocean, while leaving large swaths of the country void of any specific features at all? There was no answer to this question. Karl had never been to a monastery, and had no interest in organized religion, although he would call himself a religious man when asked. The studio was one of his churches, the medical college was the other.

After this round of speculation about the mystery of his ongoing creation was finished, again forming no specific conclusion to explain it, the same lack of understanding he'd experienced every summer for the last thirty years, Karl opened up a wooden box filled with tubes of oil paint, and began mixing a few colors on his palette. He chose black and white and a little bit of sienna brown. By the end of the day he'd made substantial progress on the dog bounding through a meadow that he'd been working on since June. The fact that he was painting a dog surprised him more than his images usually did. Karl wasn't a dog person. He much preferred the aloof independence of cats to the unconditional loyalty of dogs. But there could be no doubt it was a dog he'd fleshed out amidst the bright green, early spring field grasses, some combination of collie and husky, a young, lonely dog in need of two things - a master and a name, in that order. But Karl wouldn't be painting the master. Getting the dog to look right was going to take him all summer.

He'd spent the previous summer painting an animal as well, a winged, wild species, a bird he learned the name of only after filling in its colors. The location he chose for the tropical bird at times perplexed him more than anything else in the mural, yet at other times, like this July afternoon, seemed to fit perfectly. In the world of this painting it wasn't so odd at all to have an Amazonian macaw flying over the northern reaches of the Midwest, somewhere between Chicago and Detroit. Like everything else in the work, including this mixed-breed black and white dog he was trying hard to get right, Karl never questioned the origin of these images. He simply painted them, because something larger and more important than himself was urging him to do so. Late that afternoon, bushwhacking back down the mountain to his car, he was thinking of a certain young woman, specifically the French Canadian brunette who worked as an ultrasound tech in the hospital. Included within his musings about this cute twenty-something was a sense of relief that his two religions gave sin a tiny bit of breathing room.

A Best Friend

MARKUS GREENE, a medical school graduate who'd recently passed the surgical boards with honors, was burnt out. A summer of decompression spread out before him, its humidity-drenched voids of free time looming, idle hours his hands would have to make some use of without turning back to the habits of his recent past. This period of debauchery, which had culminated in the excursion to Montreal and the sex with an escort, had been particularly successful at distracting him from his ominous condition, namely the lack of any feeling whatsoever in his heart. Now this condition was more pronounced than ever before. He blocked out everything from the past. Markus refused his mother's continued offers to send bread and money. He declined the persistent invitations from his town buddies to attend their beer-soaked, red meat-infused weekend rituals. He ignored his trees as they beckoned him from a distance in their gentle, patient way. His walking stick became entombed with cobwebs in a dusty corner of his apartment. Even the president, who had only been a positive force in his life, was added to Markus' list of people, places, and things that were not options as destinations for retreat from the battle lines of trying to restore some kind of order to his existence.

First he let go of the spacious two-bedroom apartment he'd been renting with his mother's financial assistance, and moved into a tiny one-room studio, eager for the discipline such a living space might inspire. After drawing out this relocation as long as he could, accepting Chip's offer of help moving his small amount of furniture while turning down the accompanying offers of bong hits, Markus sequestered himself in the space for days at a time. He recognized the pressing need to make it feel like a home as best he could, simply by existing within its walls, re-reading *Siddhartha*, aware that his upcoming residency would allow him hardly any waking hours at home. Markus did some meditating, perhaps because the deep, never ending silence of his living space reminded him of the California monastery. Around the middle of July, however, the tandem threats of insanity and a deeper depression than the one he was already ensconced in forced him out into the surrounding world. An initial meeting with his future adviser, heart transplant surgeon Dr. Kathryn Stone, loomed towards the end of August. Markus knew he had to lift himself out of the funk he'd slipped into, a slide he had no one to blame for except himself, struggling daily to boost his low confidence by reminding himself he'd graduated med school and passed his boards, huge accomplishments within the spectrum of things to accomplish in the world.

Craving injections of sunlight, no longer drawn to the shadow-cloaked forests of his favorite mountain trails, Markus discovered a few pleasant meadows on the outskirts of town, former hay fields now left undisturbed, available for him to share with bobolinks and butterflies. He spent long midday hours on his back in these fields, finding animals in the clouds like he and Marisol had done a few times. Some days he read a book or a magazine but mostly he just daydreamed, letting his mind wander, his thoughts surfing the soft summer breezes wafting over him. One day, this ritual that brought him such simple contentment, was dramatically broken. Markus was pacing in circles to flatten down some goldenrod so he could have a spot to lie down in the field when he heard a single deep bark. He turned in the direction the bark had come from, and saw the black and white face of a dog peering at him just above the height of the grasses. The dog was staring him down now, releasing occasional bellowing barks that didn't sound confrontational, but weren't particularly friendly either. Markus had little experience with dogs. He'd instigated a brief campaign to get a puppy during Middle School, until his mother squashed the idea with the argument that a dog was a responsibility he was too young for, a burden she didn't want to assume when he left for college. Markus later wondered if his mother simply hadn't wanted any competition for her unconditional love she was pouring onto her only child every day, eventually deciding it was some combination of both. So he wasn't sure how to react to this present situation. Going on an impulse, following one of the dog's borderline intimidating barks, he barked back. The dog immediately broke into a full sprint, heading straight for him. Markus glanced behind him, briefly considering a flight to his car. Perhaps replaying some version of what to do when a bear charged, how running was the worst possible option, he was about to drop down and curl up into a ball to play dead when the dog reached him, still running full speed, and launched through the air, its front paws striking Markus in the chest. He fell to his back, a soft landing on the flattened grasses. Eyes closed, he braced against an expected flurry of bites. Instead his face was tickled by a flapping tongue. He opened his eyes to stare face-to-face with a dog like no other dog he'd ever seen. Its head was divided exactly in half by a line separating black and white, running from the forehead down to the tip of the nose. At first, his vision obstructed by the eager tongue, Markus thought the dog had one bad eye. Grasping its head behind the ears for a round of scratching, an offering even he knew most any dog would not turn down, he realized the eye was actually multiple shades of bright blue. The opposite eye was brown. The dog rolled off him, offering up its thickly-furred belly for more scratching. Markus then noticed two crucial details; this dog was a boy who still had his balls; and he didn't have a collar. He knew the dog was his. This was a fact. The dog had found him. It needed a name. And a home.

For the next month Markus' only focus was taking care of his new pet. He named it Niko, the name rising up like a prayer-song during their first few days together. He bought his new pet organic kibble, which he supplemented with cuts of meat and fish, the protein portions of his own dinners, which had suddenly elevated in quality now that he had someone to share them with. He took Niko on long walks around town, savoring the delight of strangers compelled to stop and pet a dog they all declared to be beautiful and sweet and well-behaved all at the same time. Markus noticed the delight that simply a brief interaction with his dog brought to people's faces, children and adults alike. These first impressions Niko elicited from people were not false ones. He backed them up every day with his almost perfect personality, exhibiting traits Markus recognized from some research he did on the two breeds. The husky side of the dog seemed to remember what it was like to be a wolf, and likely still heard some version of the call of the wild. Tough, strong, and good in the elements, the only fault with Niko's husky half was the urge to run long distances if given the opportunity. The border collie was the helper, all about home and family and the work involved with these kinds of things. The only fault with border collies was a loyalty that could be more intense than some people could handle. But this homebody side of Niko brought him back to Markus each time he caught some scent and took off into the woods, returning quickly to a single whistle and the praise of his adopted master, with that husky smile and enthusiastic border collie tongue.

Markus took Niko to the parks where other dogs were set free to socialize, their masters congregating for some human socializing at the same time. Niko liked to cuddle in the apartment, but also enjoyed his own space. He slept at the foot of Markus' bed, and woke up whenever his owner did, when the dog would climb up onto the bed and curl into the gap of time between early morning and the rest of the day, a soft, furry interlude when Niko dutifully cleaned between Markus' toes with his tongue. Markus reciprocated this service by removing any ticks he could find embedded beneath the dog's thick husky coat, surprised by the satisfaction he found when the pests popped out between his fingernails. By the time his meeting with Dr. Stone came around at the end of August, the evenings already tinged with a hint of fall's imminent approach, Markus had fleeting notions that he might be something close to happy. He hadn't thought about his missing love, or the state of his heart, all month. Niko loved him unconditionally, without demanding any love in return, the way a buddy or a girlfriend would. He only needed to be taken care of, walked and fed and plucked free of ticks. And wrestled with at least once a day. These were all things that, even in his handicapped state, Markus could accomplish. And the end effect on his state of being could only be qualified as something very close to happiness.

Then he met with his future mentor Dr. Kathryn Stone. The meeting took place at Markus' favorite coffee shop in town, a place called Tunnel City. Although they didn't know it at the time, the meeting initiated a series of rendezvous at that location. His first thought after laying eyes on her, after taking in her dirty blond hair tied up against the back of her head, her sporadic freckles, her well-toned body, was relief. Although Kathryn was a recognizably attractive woman, Markus was not attracted to her. She was obviously a few years older than he was, and he'd yet to feel sexually drawn toward an older woman. Even women his own age seemed too old for consideration. It was one of a few elements to his romantic side that could have been labeled traditional. He also liked to hold doors open, to pay for the whole dinner bill, and lead on the dance floor. The important thing was that not wanting to have sex with Kathryn would give this fledgling relationship a good shot at being a successful one, with opportunities to pursue something along the lines of friendship in addition to their professional connection.

"So, why did you choose heart surgery?" she asked him bluntly that first meeting, in between sips of her green tea.

Markus stared into his latte as if the answer was held in the swirls of milk foam and espresso. "Well, I guess I chose the heart because, honestly, I've been sort of obsessed with the concept of love for many years now. So I figured if I worked with the organ love supposedly originates in, I might eventually come to some tangible conclusions," he continued, aware that he didn't want to come off as some goofy ex-poet unable to handle the rigors of a surgical residency. "Which would be a great side effect to what I can only imagine will be an extremely engaging, challenging career."

"I see. So you actually think there is a connection between love and the heart?"

"I do."

Kathryn lifted her eyebrows with skepticism. Their conversation then meandered back to the technical aspects of her taking him on as a resident, but it would come to be the initiation of many future talks exploring this concept, one they each came at from opposite perspectives. During their next meeting less than a week later, scheduled with the purpose of filling out some required paperwork, Markus brought up his dog. Niko was complicating his ideas about love. He wanted her opinion on these complications, shrugging off the notion that they didn't yet know each other well enough to discuss such topics.

"I give him the simple things he needs. A name and a home. Food. We have dinner together. His love is so direct and straightforward. Our version, I mean the love between people, is so much more complicated."

"Not always," Kathryn said.

"More often than not," Markus persisted. "We're already tight as hell, me and Niko, don't get me wrong. It's just, I don't know, being different species, we can only connect on so many levels. His list of passions includes unsuccessfully trying to befriend cats, and rolling in the shit of various farm animals. And my book reading habit bores him incredibly."

"Two people can be just as different from one another and still click, you know. My first boyfriend was a heroin addict. I've never done a drug in my life. We lasted three years. And as far as chasing cats without success, maybe some of your dating adventures could be comparable? You have had dating adventures, I assume."

She lifted her eyebrows again. Markus loved how they already talked like old friends even though they'd just met a week ago.

"And the rolling in shit? What's my version of that activity?" he asked her playfully.

Kathryn tugged at her chin, looking up from the paper- work spread out on the table between them. "That's a harder comparison, for sure. But his shit-rolling is really just a vice. His fetish. I don't know you well enough yet to finish your side of the comparison, but I'm sure a similar activity exists in your world."

Markus felt the hint of a blush taking shape around his collar- bone, and struggled to contain it there, out of sight beneath his blue fleece.

"Fine. You got me there."

Over time he would come to hate the way she was always able to twist his innately melancholic perspectives into positive viewpoints lacking any possible argument against them. When she wasn't around, however, his thoughts would resume following their old pathways, narrow philosophical musings he couldn't help generating even as they twisted his brain into knots that could only be loosened by a bottle of wine and a full night's sleep.

For a few months that fall Markus achieved a state of balance for the first time in his adult life, the foundation of which was a regular paying job. Although as a first-year resident he was barely earning thirty grand for the year, it was enough to cover all his expenses, allowing him to halt Bethany's monthly infusions of cash that had enabled a high quality of living conditions during med school. Markus was raising a healthy, happy dog, facing parenthood-type challenges that he came to view as perfect practice for a future fatherhood. He was able to maintain his friendships with the president and his town buddies even while cultivating a new, deeply satisfying relationship with his mentor.

In the hospital Markus studied Kathryn's every move, absorbing all he could about the intricacies of his chosen field, his hands itching for the opportunity to operate on hearts even as his nerves frayed a little at the thought of one day soon doing what he was only now observing in the OR. Outside of the hospital setting, at Tunnel City or on long walks together with Niko, they built the foundation of a solid friendship one conversation at a time, their words skipping over gaps in their personalities, blanks they somehow knew what to fill with, as if they'd known each other for a long time. Markus had never had a friend like Kathryn. He particularly cherished their weekend outings with Niko, the three of them like a small family, the dog a thread weaving them closer to one another and to the surrounding nature at the same time. Markus even took her to visit his old growth birch tree perched high on a ridge one Sunday in October. Kathryn appreciated the tree, and was shocked to learn it was a white birch, but she lost him when he spoke of feeling its energy. This ability had recently returned to Markus after having abandoned him some months before.

"Don't you feel that little tug, like a miniature gravity?" he asked her while they both leaned against the trunk.

"No."

"Okay. Maybe someday you will."

He was elated to be feeling the pull of his trees once again, aware that the combination of his new dog and his new friend were helping him shed the numbness that had been settling into his bones over the past year. It was on another walk in the mountains, about a month after the birch tree visit, when Kathryn broke some of the spell he'd been letting himself be swept away by that fall.

"You are aware, Markus, that after Thanksgiving things are going to ramp up for you at the hospital," she said, kicking at some dead leaves on the trail. "I mean, your training is about to get very intense, as we discussed back in August."

"I know," Markus muttered, nodding at Niko waiting ahead on the trail, his signal to the dog that it was okay to continue.

"I'm talking seventy, eighty, even ninety-hour weeks in the OR. Sometimes twenty-four hours straight. You've heard the war stories from my colleagues by now, Markus. You're entering three years of slavery, in exchange for an amazing career when you finish. I've been taking it easy on you so far. But the shit is about to hit the fan, as they say."

"I know."

"But Markus -"

"What?" he snapped, sensing where she was headed with this topic of conversation.

"Niko, Markus. How are you going to take care of that dog while also being my resident? You simply can't do both. I won't let you do both."

Markus stopped on the trail. He took the silver whistle out of his pocket, blew into it once, and bent down to one knee. Niko came bounding back along the trail, grinning, landing in his embrace, licking the bottom of his chin. Kathryn stood above them, hands on her hips, a pained expression on her face, like the parent who has to stop a child's good time.

"So I have to choose between keeping this guy or becoming a heart surgeon? Is that what you're saying, Kathryn?" Markus looked up at her. He didn't need to hear her answer.

"Yes."

He'd been aware of the situation since their first meeting back in August, Niko waiting patiently outside the coffee shop tied to a parking meter, allowing pedestrians to stop and pet him and gaze into his enchanting blue eye.

"What about letting your mother take him for a couple years?"

"No," Markus said firmly, the dog cowering under his loud voice. Markus stood up. Niko retreated to Kathryn's side.

"That's not an option. My mother lives in suburban hell. Niko would hate it there. There's nothing like this," he said, spinning in a circle, arms out to either side like a land baron showing off his own personal forest. "No place for him to run. He needs to run, Kathryn. He's half husky for Christ's sake."

"I know he does."

Markus then made a motion like a pitcher throwing an invisible baseball, his sign to Niko that it was okay to take off up the trail. The dog shot ahead at full speed, kicking up dirt and leaves and small rocks as he ran, a one dog team pulling an imaginary sled.

"That's what he needs," Markus said, his voice trailing off as they resumed their walk.

"I know it's a tough decision for you," Kathryn said eventually. "And I'll try to help you with it as best I can."

"Thanks."

Markus could feel some of the old numbness creeping back in, and did nothing to stop its progress.

"At least," Kathryn continued, "if you let your mother keep him for you, he'd still be in the family. It would be less than three years, and then you'd have him back. He'd have this back," she said carefully, gesturing at the trail. "And he'd still be a young dog."

"Yeah," Markus muttered. "And I'd be an old man."

"Oh please."

Niko sprinted back. He circled them, licking at their hands, herding them forward into the future.

Markus spent the following weeks being tormented by the decision about what to do with his dog. There could be no denying the fact that Niko had been helping him recover a few shards of his lost love. When they were together he began feeling remnants of the old desire to reach out and give to others. But when they were out in public he let the dog do the giving, because that was what most people seemed to want anyway. And every week he was forced to spend more time at the hospital, such a cold sterile place, where Markus quickly retreated into his core simply in order to make it through the long shifts under fluorescent lights, surrounded by linoleum and illness and death. Now there wasn't enough time in his studio with the dog, no chance for Niko to resuscitate him with his unconditionally loving tongue, no morning cuddles to warm him up to the day. There was only room for the basics, a quick walk around the block on a leash, one rushed meal, and not enough sleep. It was no way to live, for man or beast. But the difference was that Markus had chosen this existence, while Niko was an innocent animal now being subjected to an unhealthy life, even as he accepted the changes in his patient, good-natured way.

No other decision Markus had faced in his life, from changing high schools to not attending college to choosing heart surgery, had been nearly as challenging as what to do with his wonderful dog, a comrade who'd changed his life in one afternoon. Forcing himself to accept the fact that choosing a normal life had always terrified him, that he would never have the regular kind of existence his buddies in town had, most of whom had dogs and children and wives, right before Thanksgiving and a promised trip home to visit his parents Markus loaded Niko into his car and drove northwest into Vermont. He'd felt a tug from Vermont ever since living in White River Junction, at the end of his days as a poet. The vibe of the Green Mountain State was much different than New Hampshire, although the liberal Dartmouth community was an exception, and could just have easily been on the Vermont side of the border.

Markus exited the highway somewhere between Montpelier and Burlington, then followed back road after back road, each one less improved than the one before, surrounded by hilly sheep farms carved into the base of rolling, forested mountains. Markus pulled over beside a particularly well-groomed farm, where the road had become almost a trail. He opened the back door of the car and Niko climbed out, looking up at his master for direction, his eyes wide open and trusting. Markus held up a palm and folded it in half. Niko sat down. Markus bent down and clipped off the dog's collar. Niko cocked his head to one side, staring into him with the penetrating blue eye, trying to figure out what was happening. His collar only came off at home. Markus bent down on one knee, hugged the dog, and kissed him on his soft forehead. He stood up abruptly, threw an invisible baseball in the direction of the sheep farm, and Niko shot off. Markus then scurried around to the driver's side door, got back in the car, and sped away in the direction he'd come.

He cried during the entire hour-long drive back to Hanover, bellowing sobs that almost made him veer off the road more than once. These wails were interspersed with silent streaming tears, Markus struggling to convince himself that he'd done the right thing, that Niko would find a new master, someone to give him a name and a home just like he had, that it was the most unselfish way he could have handled the situation. He didn't trust shelters, and the random people they attracted for adoptions. Niko belonged on a farm with plenty of woods around it. Farmers were good people. After a night-mare-laden sleep in his suddenly empty one-room studio, after another fourteen-hour day trailing Kathryn around the OR, that old tightening sensation in his chest returned stronger than ever before. He felt his heart retreating into a deep hibernation, encasing itself in an icy coldness he made no effort to resist, a frozen barrier to human connection even his mother's Thanksgiving meal couldn't thaw. Markus knew he needed to accept this hardening of his insides, to embrace it, or else he'd have no chance at surviving the next three years of his life. This time, unlike diving headfirst into med school, Markus wasn't sure letting Niko go had been the right thing simply because it had been the hardest thing to do. But the choice had been made. Now there would be nothing standing in the way of him becoming a heart surgeon. Not his heart, his love, or any living thing.

Vivaldi On Bourbon

SO AT THE EXACT MOMENT he achieved some concrete balance in his life, earning a salary that covered his expenses, cultivating a solid friendship with a good-looking, successful and talented woman, something he'd needed even more than a girlfriend, and raising a great dog, Markus had been forced to give up one of these elements in order to continue moving forward into the life he'd chosen for himself. He couldn't help viewing this as some cruel trick of fate, how he'd been fooled by a higher power into believing a dog and a new friend could restore what had taken so many years to lose. The dog was gone after five months. And his friend was also his boss.

Two and a half years later, from his perspective emerging from deep within the dark bowels of residency, Markus would think back to that ambling stroll he'd taken with the president with the goal of figuring out a specialty to focus on, retracing elements of the decision that led him to where he was, from his boulder to poetry to heart surgery. If it had been his infatuation with the concept of love, and his sudden lack of it, that led him to focus on the organ it supposedly originated in, it was his connection with a certain heart surgeon that became the main factor in his ability to stick out what would be an extremely rigorous three years of training. By the end of his residency Markus' concept of love, at least the kind between humans, was becoming intertwined with his fascination with both the heart and his mentor, Dr. Kathryn Stone. After staggering out from the black cave of resident servitude, suddenly on the brink of the thirty-something years, he would come to view his love, his heart, and Dr. Stone as entities embroiled in a three-way orgy. And, like most orgies, not all parties involved were finding satisfaction.

That first winter Markus struggled hard to forget about Niko, trying over and over to convince himself the dog had been the bridge he needed in order to make it from treading water in the dark seas of addiction and depression to where he was, training with a world renowned heart transplant surgeon. The eminent physician, one of only a handful of female heart transplant surgeons in the country, began inviting him to her house for dinner parties with colleagues, and took him along on her grand rounds in the hospital. The two fell into a classic mentor and apprentice relationship without either one becoming conscious of it. Their relationship had become the most important one in each of their lives. Aside from his connection to the president it was the only real friendship Markus maintained, having let things slide with his buddies in town, mostly because he had no time outside the hospital that wasn't filled with taking care of his basic needs. He could tell Kathryn things he'd never been able to share with anyone else. Their coffee shop meet-ups expanded to glasses of wine after a long shift, lunches out, and Sunday brunches. The walks were over, however, due to a combination of time restraints and Markus' inability to enter the woods without Niko by his side. They indulged in long rambling talks over the phone on a weeknight. The only thing they didn't do was sleep together. They became a two-person platonic family, sharing little things, engaging in conversations where neither one erected any walls of defense. Markus was glad his desire remained largely on the sidelines, although he was finding himself captivated at times by her slender wrists and graceful hands, especially while observing them move deftly during an operation. In their sacred talks, many of which still occurred at Tunnel City, fleeting escapes from the OR, they began divulging the secret details of their distant pasts.

Markus told her about his debilitating shyness, describing the surreal redness of his face during oral presentations, the lunches alone in the high school bathroom. He told her about everything. His mother's potent care enveloping him while he grew up. The boulder. Jake Boletti. Marisol, and the girlfriends that followed her. Life on the road, essentially homeless, living off poetry sales. Kathryn listened well. It was the kind of listening hundreds of dollars' worth of therapy sessions could never have bought. She was the rare type of person who engaged as deeply in listening as she did talking. So Markus tried to do the same for her.

Not used to men who listened, at first Kathryn held her ground, describing the bright, spotlighted parts of her past, things she'd told other guys on first and second dates. But these rendezvous with Markus were something other than dates. So she wasn't surprised when her more deeply buried layers began surfacing during their long and winding conversations. The girl who would become Dr. Kathryn Stone grew up in a house filled with children, but devoid of love. At least the parental kind of affection. She'd been abandoned at an early age, and spent her childhood at an upscale orphanage on the outskirts of San Francisco. The adult oversight had been competent and organized during her sixteen years in residence. Organized and competent, but never loving. Her caregivers, if they could be called that, came there to work, to put in an eight-hour shift and then go home. Kathryn understood this reality at a young age, years before she left the place. The staff of surrogate parents had to save whatever love they possessed for their own children, to be doled out in their own homes. Kathryn never believed in Santa Claus because no one had played the part. So she told Markus she hadn't been able to accumulate the kind of reservoir of maternal love he had. He said he was envious. She said that was a stupid thing to say, that he should feel lucky to have had what he did growing up. He called it a curse. She called him silly. And so on.

Kathryn explained how she'd never expected to be loved. This certainty came along as a part of her lot in life, and she accepted this fate early on. As an adult, conditioned not to expect love, she didn't devote any time looking for it, and grew into a strong, extremely independent woman. She went to UCLA on a full scholarship. During college she waited tables on the weekends and all summer, taught herself Spanish with the help of the Mexican dishwashers, and saved all the money she could for a gap year traveling alone through South America. The year extended into two when she decided to travel to every continent except Antarctica, mastering physical skills in an attempt to get out of her head, to release all the cramming she'd been forced to do as a premed student. She learned rock climbing and yoga, sailing and tango. Not much for the youth hostel social scenes, she usually spent her evenings delving into the classic literature of whatever country she found herself in. She read Borges in Argentina, Dostoyevsky in Russia, Kazantzakis in Greece. Eventually it was time to come back to America. But she was ready to bid farewell to California, and entered medical school in Baltimore, followed by her residency at Dartmouth.

After a decade of intense training, after building up the heart transplant program at Dartmouth from scratch, Dr. Kathryn Stone was nearing the age of forty on a spinster's path. She was hardly lacking in sexual experience, and never lonely, just handicapped. That was how she always labeled her condition, at least to herself. And, now, to Markus. Unlike her protégé, however, she hadn't spent one second pondering the potential relationship between hearts and love. This philosophical issue had no relevance to her choosing the path of heart surgery. She told him that she'd just wanted the most challenging career she could find, since challenges were what she thrived on. When he asked about the physical condition of her heart she stated confidently that her pulmonary organ was a perfectly healthy one. But Kathryn had no proof of this assumption. She was no exception to the rule that when it came to their own health, to the condition of their own bodies, doctors could be notoriously paranoid. So even though she was a heart disease specialist herself, she'd never made the effort to have her own heart, or any other organ, evaluated. Kathryn hadn't been to any doctor besides her gynecologist since leaving the orphanage, because she'd never had anything worse than a flu.

It wasn't romantic love they shared over these years, but something equally intense, a strong connection based on respect and understanding. There was the dual respect of one doctor for another, and the mutual understanding of one suffering heart for another. But they didn't realize this latter commonality until Markus' very last day as her resident. There was a big party. It got late. Both were very drunk, Kathryn on champagne, Markus on bourbon. Perhaps due to this variation in drink of choice, one gave a much sunnier description of the condition they shared. Kathryn used such terms as "vague emptiness", "like missing a limb", and how it felt there was "a hole somewhere deep inside." Markus came from a darker, more dramatic angle. And he wasn't prone to soft clichés.

"I often convince myself I have no soul. That's what it feels like, anyway," he slurred, leaning against a wall. "Like I'm a walking dead man."

"That's just the bourbon talking," Kathryn teased, knowing it was actually Markus talking. She'd been in a similar place at his age, shortly before meeting him, hopeless and despondent. Kathryn was still hopeless, because she'd come to believe hope was simply not an emotion she had the time to entertain. But despondency, no matter one's situation, was a personal decision. One she wasn't going to choose no matter how bad things got. She shared this philosophy with him that night, as she'd done a few times before, but failed to shift his dark outlook on an entire aspect of living, likely the most important aspect. The ability to love. Bringing up the care she'd witnessed him shower on Niko would have only made him feel worse, so she kept that jewel of knowledge bottled up for the time being.

After the party Markus stumbled around the campus, lost in his head, sinking into a depression. Eventually he wound up at the Medical College. He drifted along the pathway that wound past the administrative offices, kicking pebbles, indulging in the dark thoughts being generated by his bourbon buzz. Then he stopped. Piano music was spilling out from a top floor window, washing over him in a soft shower of notes. Markus spun in circles, suddenly elated and free. He sat down on a nearby bench. Looking up at the source of the music, he realized it was coming from the president's open window. Markus was serenaded with piano solos for close to an hour. The president's playing rivaled musicians he'd heard in city symphonies. It was optimistic music, imbued with possibility. He let his ears drink in the notes, savoring them while thinking about the kind of man the president had made himself into, a diverse, multi-tasking man. Markus realized he might still have the chance to become such a man himself. The president had a wife, four daughters, and numerous grandchildren. Being a father had no doubt shaped the man in many ways, molded him into the kind of adult he'd become, the same way it did for so many other dads. Markus saw it all the time, had seen it in Rupert while growing up, that primary role of being the provider, a role most men seemed to go to great lengths to preserve. The president struck him as a rare kind of man, one who'd been able to fulfill his domestic duties as well as hold down a constantly evolving career, all while maintaining an innate vibrancy, a visceral lust for life manifested in his piano playing.

Sitting there on the bench, half-drunk, reveling in his private concert, Markus felt a poem begin to form in his head. He was shocked, blindsided by a string of verses. And he was scared. His fear almost squelched the poem before his mind had a chance to finish it. Flashbacks to his days as a homeless, wandering poet assaulted him. This sudden flow of rhyming lines was terrifying, a ghost of his former self he'd assumed would no longer be able to haunt him. But the stream of piano melodies coursing out into the night air above forced him to let the verses come to life. Looking back on the experience the next morning, while transcribing the poem he'd scribbled onto the back of his hand the night before, Markus was awed by the power of the mind, how it was able to reach back through all the layers of facts he'd burned into the hard drive of his memory over the past seven years, through the muscle memory required for performing surgery, to the dormant, poetic corner of his brain, a part he'd shut down way back before the first meeting with Ken Gabriel. That it was able to reawaken so fully astounded him, and he understood it was the piano that was allowing it to happen.

The poem's crescendo rhythm mirrored Vivaldi's notes. Markus hand-delivered it, written on fine stationary this time, to the president the following Monday. His hand shook as he laid the poem down on the great desk.

"I thought you should have this. After the party, I walked under your window and heard you playing."

The president smiled. It was a hearty smile of satisfaction.

"Your piano did something to me. Opened some kind of door I thought I'd closed," Markus added.

"Ahh, doors never really close, Markus. Even when you try to slam them shut, they just pop back open again when you least expect it."

Markus watched the president look towards the piano as if gazing into a lover's eyes, one he'd somehow been able to hold onto over the decades without losing any other aspects of his life, paying attention to her when he needed her black and white keys, and the sound of her music. The piano was his muse, his mistress. Markus looked up at his framed napkin poems hanging on the president's wall, and wondered if poetry could be for him like the piano was for the president. The only problem was that a man couldn't entertain the possibility of a mistress until so many other things were taken care of, all the practicalities associated with living, like a wife and children, a career. These concrete things Markus still had yet to obtain.

The president shifted his attention to the poem lying there on his desk.

"Should I read it now?" he asked eagerly.

Markus shook his head. He stood up to leave. "Thank you for the inspiration. I think." It was a reluctant expression of gratitude. "You'll probably know who it's about right away."

"Don't thank me. Thank Vivaldi!"

That afternoon Markus bought three Vivaldi CD's. He didn't open any of them, though, because he worried that hearing the music might cause another poetry relapse, and he didn't have time for that. He was a surgeon now.

BETWEEN HANDS AND EYES

I notice your hands
all night
veins bursting
with experience,
hands that know
what a woman needs.

And then your wrists
slender as the rest of you
hiding under bracelets,
wrists that need
what a woman knows.

Finally your eyes
loyal to the child
dancing within,
eyes that see
what a woman wants.

The rest of you
is like the ocean,
a warm mystery,
what lies between
hands and eyes.

The next morning Markus showed up in Kathryn's office at a time he knew she'd be there. He was wide-eyed with terror.

"What's wrong?" she asked him, deeply concerned, reaching an arm around his shoulders as he tried to fidget with every item on her desk.

"I wrote a poem yesterday."

Kathryn backed off, smiling. "What's wrong with that?"

"It's bad. Very bad."

"Why?"

"I can't go back to writing poems, Kathryn. They're like a drug. I forget about all the other aspects of life. There's no time for that now."

Kathryn cocked her head, trying to understand him. "Maybe there is time. Maybe writing poetry can just be one part of your life. And maybe it always has been. It's just been in hibernation late -"

"It can't."

"Let the poems out, Markus. Let them out into the light."

"I can't."

"You can. A poem is just . . ."

"My love. Right? You were going to say poems are just -"

"Your love. Yes. I was going to say that," Kathryn confirmed.

Markus dropped his head. "Well there you go. My point exactly. Poetry dead-ends right there, at the goddamn L word. Even you, Miss Scientist, who doesn't ponder these kinds of things - even you admit it."

"I do. Yes. So fine. Let your love out, then. There. I said it. You've got it all bottled up, all wound up so tight around itself even you can't feel it. But I bet you a million bucks it's still in there, that you haven't lost any of it at all."

"Ha! Well, that would be a losing bet, then. Because it's gone. Vanished. Murd -"

"Write a poem about me, Markus Greene."

"What?" He rocked back on his heels, ducking away from her, utterly stunned by her request. He blinked. "You want me to?"

"I do."

Markus didn't tell her that he already had.

2

THE HEARTS

A Specialty

IT WASN'T AS SIMPLE as just choosing the heart for a specialty to focus on. Cardiologists were heart experts, but Markus had already ventured down the path of a surgeon. Within every medical specialty there were sub-specialties to choose from, tributaries of a still relatively unexplored knowledge base. One field in which these off-shoots were especially uncharted was heart surgery. Techniques for bypass operations were being constantly refined and perfected through experimental procedures made possible by new technologies. Markus assumed that being a heart surgeon was the greatest challenge he could pursue within the realm of surgery. All surgeons played the role of god on a daily basis, but none more dramatically than those operating to save the most important organ in sustaining life. Then Kathryn invited him to participate in a transplant procedure, a profound experience that became his initiation into the rarefied realm of a micro-specialty only a select few heart surgeons ever enter, one in which his hands had the ability not merely to save a life nearly lost, but to resurrect a patient straight out of the clenching fist of death by replacing a dying heart with one still craving life.

Markus became permanently hooked after the first transplant he assisted with, after spending fourteen hours beside his gifted mentor while she choreographed the bloody dance, helping her fearlessly negotiate the knife edge between life and death. Markus gained a perspective on the persistence of the body's will to live that only a transplant team was able to witness. He watched in awe as the patient, a fifty-year old man with a dying heart, was cooled into a frigid coma, suspended on the brink of death into a bodily purgatory that became a ticking clock against which Kathryn and her team raced, no guarantee that ten hours later they'd be able to coax him back to life. A machine replaced the man's heart and lungs, breathing for him, circulating his blood everywhere except into his open chest cavity, a space kept bloodless so Kathryn could clearly see what to join where as she went through the hundreds of steps necessary to attach the donor heart, which waited patiently in the little red and white cooler beside them. It was a heart that two hours before had been throbbing with life even as the body containing it was being voluntarily hurled off a balcony on the 21st floor of an apartment building in Boston. The suicidal man's brain was crushed, but his heart had survived intact, and now had the opportunity to beat for a few decades more inside another body.

Markus accompanied Kathryn on her post-op visits to the lucky recipient, a man completely aware of the fact that he was literally living on bonus time. Markus' poetic, philosophical side was immediately drawn to the mystical qualities of heart transplants. He was hooked by the undeniable notion that he was standing on the doorstep of his destiny, a certainty backed up by his condition as a person without any love left to give, because a heart transplant surgeon had barely any room for a life outside of his work anyway. Markus accompanied Kathryn on every transplant, becoming her right hand man during these grueling surgeries. He liked every part; the moment they got a call about an available donor heart; the helicopter flight to an ER anywhere between northern Maine and Philadelphia; sprinting through the halls of the Dartmouth hospital's cardiac wing to the OR, where the recipient's chest was already open and waiting; all the tense hours that passed like minutes; and the aftermath defined by his exhaustion made irrelevant by the bright shining eyes of a patient reborn into life all over again. On the few occasions they didn't succeed, when they lost one, Markus felt the drain of his body much more. Kathryn coached him through these unavoidable letdowns, lifting him up and out of a potential depression each time, reminding him how the euphoria that came from giving someone a new life far outweighed the sadness of failing to pull off what could only be described as a miracle.

One of these failures changed Markus forever. They'd reached a point where he was doing most of the surgery, while Kathryn kept a watchful eye over his every maneuver. They got a call from Hartford that a six-month old girl had died in a car crash. Her heart was un-marred, a perfect donor for the three-month old boy who hadn't left Dartmouth's intensive care unit since his birth. He'd been born with a dysfunctional heart, one with an irregular beat, and had suffered multiple heart attacks in his short life. Even though their phones rang at three-fifty on a Sunday morning, the two transplant sur-geons were inside the helicopter on the hospital roof just after four. In Hartford they met the parents, who poured out information in sobs while trying to keep pace running down fluorescent hallways. The couple went on about how they'd drastically altered both of their careers in order to focus all their energy on raising their baby girl, how they'd decided she would be their main contribution to the world, a child molded into the best possible adult by their focused care, combined with a rigorous home-schooling curriculum they'd been developing. Markus had no idea what to say in the blur of the moment, knowing any advice he might come up with would only sound cold and detached, or else wouldn't register through the tidal waves of grief they were enduring. The parents followed the two surgeons all the way to the hospital roof. They wanted to climb in the helicopter and accompany their daughter's heart to its destina-tion. Kathryn informed them this was not possible, but it took the strength of a few paramedics to hold the desperate couple back from the chopper as it lifted away, banking sharply to the north.

By six the two surgeons were back in New Hampshire with the infant heart. During the flight Markus had trouble refraining from taking a peek at the tiny organ. Even Kathryn had never laid eyes on such a young heart. In the OR, when it came time to lift it out of the cooler so Markus could begin sewing it into their patient, he couldn't help cradling it in his gloved hands for a few seconds, taking a moment to admire its perfection, the fresh pink color of still-forming muscle. He thought about the amount of love this heart must have taken in during its short life spent showered by the intensely focused care of those parents. Markus was surprised by a fleeting twinge of jealousy. He was strangely envious of this little boy with his chest splayed open beneath him.

"Markus," Kathryn grunted, nodding at the comatose boy. "Let's get it in there, c'mon now, stay with us."

He snapped out of his selfish musings and began the initial steps of the transplant procedure. Both surgeons were aware of the limited prospect for success this time. The small size of the six-month old heart made the operation extremely challenging. They'd agreed in the helicopter, after a quick peek at the tiny organ encased in dry ice inside the cooler, that there would be a ten percent chance for success. And that was optimistic. So neither surgeon was surprised when, ten hours later, they were unable to jump start the transplanted heart back to life. Markus' stitches couldn't hold the miniature valves and aortas in place once the blood was reintroduced, bursting repeated leaks he kept repairing until their window of time was lost, themselves and everything around them splattered with blood. Kathryn had to force him to stop, grabbing his wrists with all her strength.

"That's enough, Markus. We tried our best. Let's sew him back up. Okay?"

Markus let her take the needle he'd been using to unsuccessfully stitch the small heart in place. But instead of asking the nurses for the steel wires he would need to close up the infant boy's chest plate, he took a clean scalpel off his tray and undid all his work with a series of quick cuts. He removed the heart, and placed it back in the cooler.

"Okay, let's close him up."

"Markus," Kathryn said urgently. "What are you going to do with that baby's heart?"

The whole team stood still, waiting for his answer, staring at the cooler.

"I'm going to ask the parents if they want it. Don't you think they might want their little girl's heart back?"

"No, Markus. That's against protocol."

"Fuck protocol Kathryn! Protocol requires us to tell them the transplant didn't take. What if they ask about the heart? I want to at least be able to offer it to them. Maybe having their baby girl's heart back can help them get over the loss in some way."

Kathryn shook her head, lacking the energy to fight him. "Okay fine, Markus. This one time. As long as no one here utters a word about it." She scanned the team, making eye contact with every one of them, waiting until each person nodded in agreement. Then she turned to face Markus. "And what if the parents don't want it? Then what?"

Markus shrugged. He glanced at the cooler. "Then I'll bring it to organ disposal. And that will be the end of it."

"Go," she said, pointing at the swinging OR doors. "We'll finish up in here."

Markus grabbed the little cooler and walked out of the operating room with determined steps. The first thing he did, before changing out of his blood-splattered scrubs, was call the parents. After he told them what had happened they didn't ask about the fate of their daughter's heart, so he didn't share the details, didn't tell them he was holding it right there in a cooler. After Markus hung up the phone he began making his way towards the organ disposal room, located in the basement of the hospital, adjacent to the morgue. The elevator stopped on the first floor, where an ER nurse wheeled in a gurney carrying a long black bag, zipped up, with a white tag on one end. Markus stepped out. He didn't want to share an elevator with a dead body, even for one stop. But while he stood there waiting for another elevator to open years of hypothetical daydreams, abstract ideas he'd scribbled into the same kinds of journals he used to write his poetry in, coalesced into one clear thought. This thought required one specific action, a now-or-never kind of decision. Markus took in a deep breath, held it, and walked out the ER doors, free-falling into the blue dusk of a Sunday evening. Heads turned at the surreal sight of him, green scrubs covered in dark red blood not yet fully dry, both arms clutching the red and white cooler, holding it tight to his chest as if it contained the most valuable treasure in the world. Because for Markus it did. As he walked purposefully toward his car a plan began forming, a set of drastic, extreme actions he vowed to undertake without delay. If he failed, Markus thought, eyes focused down on the little cooler, at least this plan would distract him somewhat from the tedium of living out the rest of life without his love.

Disease

DURING RESIDENCY Markus continued to cultivate his walking habit, and resumed the visits to his trees, while at the same time letting go of his carnal pursuits entirely. His one-room studio apartment in town cost him three-hundred fifty bucks a month. He fed off the disciplined austerity of his lifestyle, the eighty-hour weeks inside the hospital, his home that barely qualified for such a title. His mind saturated, his body drained, he usually returned to his tiny hovel of an apartment needing only two things: food and sleep. Food was usually something frozen warmed up in the toaster. Although he was allowing his mother to send him one loaf of bread a month, which he froze in quarters, one quarter loaf for each week, one slice per day. The bread added a token of warmth to his daily sustenance. It was all he required to endure so many meals alone, shocked by his frequent reminiscing of med school, when there had always been classmates to join for dinner in the cafeteria, human company he'd taken for granted at the time. He forced himself to get used to the emptiness that was becoming his constant companion, what most people would call loneliness, what Markus knew to be his depleted internal reservoir of love. He needed more than what his trees could ever give him. But he was growing more certain by the day that his condition, this disability he'd given to himself essentially by accident, would prevent him from ever finding what he most needed from life. One blessing he was thankful for was that due to the intense discipline demanded by his schedule, sleep came easily any time he chose to lay his head down on the futon mattress in the corner of his one room apartment.

This sparse existence allowed him to stock up a large reserve of cash during his residency, even while earning a lower middle class salary. And Markus wasn't entirely alone in his tiny dwelling. He shared the space with another living thing, a new version of Niko, like a girlfriend, or a child. His heart was there with him. More precisely a dead little girl's heart he'd essentially stolen, and was keeping alive in a fish tank full of blood he regularly hijacked from the hospital, oxygenated by an array of pumps designed for saltwater home aquariums. He fed the heart through an IV tube, organic protein cocktails blended with lizard DNA, a recently discovered technique that encouraged human muscles to regenerate themselves. Markus kept a diligent eye on his prized possession, sometimes even slipping out in the middle of a fourteen hour shift at the hospital to check on it. He watched the heart muscle grow and thrive in the artificial environment he'd created for it. Over time a vision began forming, pieces of a plan that usually revealed themselves during his walks. It arose from the best, least selfish side of him. He vowed that nothing would prevent him from completing it. Because it would make all his suffering worthwhile. Because it was his destiny. To help give those with dying hearts a fresh chance at life. And love. He needed this sense of deep purpose in order to push forward, to believe he wasn't doing any of this simply for himself.

Shortly after completing his residency Markus became a passionate supporter of cardiac evaluations. The source of this sudden passion arose after having an ultrasound of his own heart taken, something the president encouraged him to do, not failing to mention the fact that a particularly cute French-Canadian brunette ran the machine on certain days of the week. Markus hadn't felt any chest pains in a few years, not since his last date with Marie-Claire, but he went through with the scan anyway. Staring at a video screen while leaning close enough to inhale the scent of the young technician's bare neck, Markus saw nothing abnormal on the screen, although he'd only laid eyes on a few examples during his training so far. A few days later, after the president had a chance to review it, the ultrasound image of his heart was sent to Kathryn for her to diagnose. Markus showed up at her office that afternoon. She seemed unusually scattered. The image filled one of the large monitors in her office.

"You see all those black dots scattered about the gray tissue?" she asked him, her voice wavering, lacking its usual strength.

Markus blinked. "Those dark spots weren't there when I saw it in the ultrasound lab on the day of the test."

"Hmm. That's strange. Well, I am able to view it at a higher resolution here. And what I'm seeing is disease. Markus, you have the heart of a two-pack-a-day smoker! This is very serious."

"I only smoked a few joints back in my poet days. And close to an ounce that summer before residency."

"You could have smoked a hundred ounces. What you have is worse than anything a lifetime of smoking can do."

Markus was perplexed. "But what started the disease?"

"Genetics," Kathryn said definitively. "There's no other source for heart disease of this magnitude, aside from alcohol or tobacco or drugs. But all you do is coffee right?"

"I dabbled with another thing that summer before residency."

Kathryn waved a hand at this confession. "Tell me these stories some other time. You inherited a bad gene, Markus. We're working on locating it, but we're not there yet. And it's too late for you anyway. You haven't noticed any symptoms recently?"

"I've been feeling fine," Markus said, growing pale. "What are my options, Kathryn?"

"The only thing you can do is wait until you deteriorate to the point that you need a transplant to survive. And that could take a while. It could take years, in fact. You're not there yet."

Markus started pacing back and forth across her office.

"I couldn't live with another person's heart in my body. Haven't you read all those cases where heart transplant recipients start having the dreams of their donors? I couldn't handle that. It would be a nightmare."

"That does happen, yes. Not always though. And besides, having another person's dreams, or nightmares, is a small price to pay in exchange for still being alive. Don't you think?"

Markus stopped pacing. "That depends."

"On what?"

"On how much you like being alive."

"Don't be so dramatic, Markus. Follow me."

Kathryn beckoned him through a thick steel door and into the inner sanctum of her office, a place Markus had been many times before. They were in the comfortable viewing room outfitted with leather seats, facing a glass wall. Beyond the glass was a high-tech, functional operating room Kathryn used for teaching her students.

"I don't have any decent coffee. Just instant. Folgers."

"I'll take some."

Kathryn prepared their coffee in the kitchenette at the back of the viewing room. Markus tried to settle into the space. She brought the coffee over in Styrofoam cups. They sat down next to each other.

"I've seen so many others like you, Markus. More every year. Healthy people, with dying hearts."

"Makes sense. I know what's happening to them. It's the same thing that's happened to me."

"What?"

"Their hearts are decaying from a lack of love. Simple as that."

Kathryn brushed his comment aside with her free hand like it was a pestering fly.

"Contrary to what the poets want us to believe, Markus, hearts and love have nothing to do with one another."

"How do you know?" Markus probed.

"Call it woman's intuition."

Markus sighed. "I'm not a poet anymore," he said, his voice distant.

"I know. And you made a wise choice to give that up. You're going to be a wonderful surgeon. Besides, poets are usually broke."

Markus shrugged. "I've met some broke surgeons too. But, like our president says, we can take excellent vacations."

Kathryn laughed loud, almost spilling her coffee. "He does say that, doesn't he?"

"I won't be taking any vacations with my extra money."

"No? So what are you planning to do with all that dough you're about to start making?"

"When I'm finished, I'll show you."

His voice wavered with these words, when it should have been strong. Markus stood up and left without saying a word. A key detail underlying the purpose behind his project had suddenly changed. He still wanted to help his future transplant patients in a way no surgeon had ever been able to. But if he was to accomplish this goal, he would now have to help himself first. To initiate that process he went straight to visit the president at his office. Karl seemed to be expecting him. Markus explained how he'd just seen the images of his diseased heart.

"So does this confirm that theory of yours Kathryn told me about?"

"That my heart is decaying from a lack of love?"

The president nodded.

"Yes," Markus continued, pacing in front of his desk. "I have to admit, back in the spring of my fourth year, I smoked an ounce of pot in about six weeks, followed by amphetamines and alcohol abuse for another month, followed by - well, that part is kind of irrelevant."

Karl was shaking his head now. "Takes a lot more abuse to damage the heart of a man your age. Must be in your genes, Markus. Unless . . ."

"Unless my theory is true," Markus spouted. "Right? There's no history of heart disease on either side of my family, Karl."

The president stood up. His tone deepened. "Maybe you are right, Markus. Maybe losing your love is literally killing your heart."

Markus stopped pacing. "There's no maybe involved. I know it is."
The two men faced each other across the vast desk. "Maybe hearts and love are connected," the president said.

"I know they are!" Markus shouted.

"But that doesn't matter, does it? All that matters is you need a new heart. Period."

"I do, don't I."

"Only thing to do," Karl said, sitting back down, "is wait for yours to get -"

"I know. Kathryn told me. I have to wait for it to get worse."

Markus gradually began to inherit some of Kathryn's heart disease patients, who were all awaiting transplants. As she'd trained him to do, he held extensive pre-surgery meetings with these patients. They were sad, dying people, sagging inside their bodies. Many had unhealthy habits. All of them, as far as Markus was concerned, had lost most, if not all, of their love. They'd been worn down by their own lives, becoming pale, wheezing creatures living on borrowed time, ghosts occupying bodies that no longer felt like their own. They all had hungry eyes, eyes starving for what Markus might be able to give them, a second chance at living. A rebirth, a clean slate that could erase what is was they'd lost. They needed him to fix all the damage they'd inflicted upon their hearts through various methods. Markus didn't consider genetics much of a factor at all. His diagnosis was that love was the only issue involved.

As the months passed, Markus came to firmly believe that the black spots in these diseased hearts had little to do with a faulty gene. Nor did they develop due to the carcinogens from cigarettes, or the ravages of alcohol or drugs, things so many of his patients confessed to having had abused over their lives. Instead these blank spaces, even in the hard drinkers and heavy smokers, were just the places in the heart that the patient's love used to occupy. Before it was given away. Or taken. Or most often these empty spaces had never been filled by parental love in the first place, as they'd been designed by nature to be. Hearts that never knew love as a child, and were never able to find it in time as an adult. Markus developed the theory that in unhealthy people with heart disease, carcinogens and toxins simply became placeholders occupying the space where love should have been. In people like Markus, without a genetic predisposition to heart disease or any bad habits, there was only the empty space, miniature black holes, vacuums consuming themselves with every beat. Holes he'd created by his own doing.

Sitting there in front of her demonstration operating room one day, Kathryn listened to her protégé's theories. Her eyes first widened in kindergarten wonder, then narrowed with scientific skepticism.

"So you're saying love is physical? That some kind of substance fills up these cavities in healthy hearts?" she asked.

"Yes. I'm saying exactly that. The physicists have proven thoughts are holographic, that they occupy actual physical space in the brain. So why wouldn't it be the same with love, occupying space in the heart? I just haven't been able to determine exactly what this substance might be beyond the combination of muscle tissue, blood, and electrical currents already there. Maybe that's all it has to be. It's the same kind of question about the physical location of the soul that philosophers have argued about for centuries. After measuring the weight of bodies just before and after death, many came to agree that the human soul weighs 21 grams. But how much does a person's love weigh?"

"These questions aren't made to have answers, Markus," Kathryn said. She forced a smile. "Love and science don't mix. They're two different species. Unable to mate. That's why we have poetry. And art -"

"Screw art," Markus huffed. "We're scientists. Maybe love and science can be like horses and donkeys? Ever think about that?"

"Ha! All that pairing can make is an infertile mule," Kathryn spouted playfully.

"Well at least mules are alive. And I'm sure they have sex too. Just because it won't lead to offspring doesn't stop an animal from trying to mate. Or trying to experience love, so to speak."

"Mule love?"

"Sure. Why not? I should tell you, Kathryn, that I make it a priority to hold pre-surgery meetings with every one of my patients, just like you taught me to do."

"Good, Markus."

"Yeah, sort of, except my meetings are different from yours."

Kathryn crossed one leg over the other. "In what way?"

"We don't spend much time talking about specific heart disease issues. You know, health habits and symptoms, these kinds of things."

"No? So what do you discuss in these meetings?"

Markus stood up. He began pacing back and forth, negotiating the space between rows of seats, his shoes sticky from wads of gum left behind by bored students.

"We talk about love," he confessed.

Kathryn closed her eyes, as if this simple action might be able to erase what he'd just said from her memory. Markus maintained his pacing while he elaborated.

"I developed a series of questions I can ask to determine the amount of love an individual patient possesses. I came up with a scale. People like you and me would score near the bottom. The Dalai Llama would be at the top. And so would my mother. So would most mothers, I think."

"How do you know I'd be at the bottom?" Kathryn protested. "Because I'm not a mother? Ask me these questions of yours!"

Markus held up a palm. "I can if you want. Some other time though. Seriously, Kathryn, every heart disease patient I've had so far scores in the bottom 10th percentile, proving my theory that -"

"Their hearts are dying from a lack of love. I know your theory."

"Wild shit, huh?"

"If you believe it."

"I do believe it."

Kathryn stood up and made her way towards the door into her main office, shaking her head, wearing a half-smile Markus couldn't see.

"Let me know when you start experimenting," she said over a shoulder.

"I will."

Markus' Hearts

THANKS TO HIS DISCIPLINED AUSTERITY during residency, Markus was able to save up the cash to afford a down payment on a house, with plenty left over for the substantial project that had been slowly taking shape in his mind. He gave in to the pull Vermont seemed to have on his spirit, and after a few excursions deep into the Green Mountain State he found exactly what he needed. It was a centuries' old farmhouse just outside the small town of Waterbury. The house was classic New England, squat and sturdy, with a front porch and an attached barn. Hay fields surrounded it on all sides. When taking breaks from his dramatic ground-floor renovation Markus would head out the back door with his walking stick in hand. Beyond the pastures he wandered into the fifty-thousand acre preserve that was Camel's Hump State Park. It was an ancient forest, cool and dark, cloaking the massive mountain. He scaled the peak once a month, becoming intimate with the pleasant trail, indulging in the diversity of the landscape, miniature streams coursing through fields of ferns, old-growth birch trees twisting towards the sky, a tiny pond perched high on the mountain's shoulder, exposed ridge lines leading to an open summit garnished by mosses and lavender tundra. Native Americans named it *Tah-Wak-Be-Dee-Ee-Wadso*. The Saddle Mountain. Markus thought the name fit much better than Camel's Hump. Or Crouching Lion, as the settlers had called it. Because when he sat on top of the peak his thoughts would arch back to his days riding the boulder in Grosse Pointe, pretending the big rock was a horse. Now he rode the greatest stallion a man could ask for, with a view of a hundred miles in every direction, galloping across all of Northern Vermont. And part of this view contained a certain sheep farm, one Markus wasn't yet ready to pay a return visit to, aware that someday he would.

Less than a year after their alcohol-infused discussion about the connection between love and heart disease Markus drove his mentor, and best friend, to his old farmhouse outside Waterbury. Kathryn had requested a tour of his recently completed project, so he was bringing her to his house for the first time since the day he'd moved in. It was a sunny Saturday afternoon in September. The New England air was crisp and cool. The mountain resembling a whale's tail rose in the western sky, a constant beacon guiding Markus towards home. After many minutes of silent driving across the undulating landscape of the Green Mountain State, Kathryn spoke up.

"So I never asked - why Vermont?"

"Part of me just figured that if I get busted someday, Vermont might take it a little easier on me. But really I just like the way it feels over here a lot more than New Hampshire. There's more light. And more farmers." Markus sighed with contentment as they rolled up his long gravel driveway. "It's absolutely gorgeous, isn't it?"

Once out of the car he flung his arms up into the air and spun in a circle, opening his palms to the vast sky, to the sloping green fields surrounding his house, and finally to the peak with its high domed summit of large boulders rising high above the pastoral scene.

"It is very beautiful, Markus. Even to a city girl."

"Well I'm a suburban boy. But if I'd grown up here, I might have turned out sort of normal."

"You're normal enough." Kathryn nodded at the low white house with chipping paint. Red wooden shutters were closed tight over every first floor window. "Are you going to show me around or not?" she asked.

"Let's go!"

The side door of his house led into a dark, musty mud room, the kind of entryway often found in old New England farmhouses. A space for the kids to kick off boots, hang coats, drop mittens.

"Seems normal so far," Kathryn joked.

Markus had his hand on the steel handle of a thick wooden door. Beside the handle was a built-in combination lock. With his free hand he typed in an elaborate code. The deadbolt released with the sound of metal sliding through metal. Markus pushed the heavy door open. A suction sound enveloped them as they stepped into darkness. Markus reached down and found Kathryn's hand.

"This is a very special moment for me," he said. "Thank you for being here."

She squeezed his hand. Markus flipped on the lights, illuminating the vast space, the entire first floor of the sprawling farmhouse. Every interior wall had been removed. The four remaining walls were blanketed in stainless steel. Powerful lights were embedded in the plastic ceiling. The floor was polished white marble. An operating table occupied the middle of the space, flanked by all the requisite accompaniments: IV stands, moveable spotlights, racks of stainless steel tools, sterilization sinks, an EKG machine, waste disposal buckets, cabinets filled with syringes and rubber gloves and anesthetic drugs, racks of slippers and scrubs, an open-air shower, and a bank of screens and keyboards. A heart/lung machine on wheels lurked off to the side, loaded with dials and switches. Hoses and wires hung off it in loops. A circular saw with a diamond studded blade, specially designed for cutting through a person's chest plate, rested on a shelf at the base of the machine.

"This is amazing, Markus," Kathryn said warmly.

"You like it?"

"I do. You did a great job with the design. Any surgeon would be happy to operate in here."

"Thanks, Kathryn. That means a lot to hear."

The scene was another version of one Dr. Stone knew well. She spent half her working hours in operating rooms not unlike the space she was now standing in, except the structure housing this one was a two-hundred fifty year old farmhouse instead of a modern-day hospital. What then caught her attention was a row of mini-fridges lining the far wall. In one corner a cylindrical black tank was suspended up high on a platform. Clear plastic tubes filled with greenish liquid spread out from the tank, across the back wall, and down behind each mini-fridge.

"Of course I have some questions," Kathryn said, heading across the room. "First of all, what's in all these little refrigerators back here?" she asked him over a shoulder.

"My hearts."

Kathryn froze in mid-step. "Excuse me?"

"My hearts," Markus answered again. "Go take a look if you want."

"Oh God. What have you done, Markus."

Kathryn continued forward slowly. After reaching the mini-fridges she knelt down, opened one, and gasped. Inside the tiny fridge, the kind of appliance normally found in hotel rooms, filled with snacks and shot bottles of liquor, were a few large glass jars. Each jar contained pieces of heart tissue floating in clear viscous liquid. And each sample appeared to have come from distinctly different sections of the muscle Kathryn knew so well. The contents of one fridge was different from all the rest. It had only one jar, in which floated a complete heart. It was fairly small. Kathryn guessed it to be around the size of a normal seven-year old's heart.

"Markus Greene?" she called out, using his last name the way a scolding mother would.

"Yes Kathryn?" Markus hadn't moved from his initial position just inside the door leading in from the mud room.

"I think you have some explaining to do."

Markus walked towards her. "I will explain. But can I trust you Kathryn? To keep this all a secret, between you and me and nobody else? Ever?"

Kathryn closed the door of the mini-fridge holding the young heart. "You can, Markus. I promise."

"I need more than a promise. I need you to swear on the Hippocratic Oath."

"What?"

Markus knew the pledge every doctor made as a part of initiation was the one thing his mentor held sacred above all else in life.

Kathryn closed her eyes. She held one palm up vertical between them. "I swear on the Hippocratic Oath to keep your secret a secret." She snapped her eyes back open. "Now tell me what the hell is going on down here."

Markus smiled. "Okay. But we should go upstairs before I do."

"Why?"

"So you can be sitting down while you listen."

The upstairs of Markus' farmhouse had little furniture. The floors were wide wooden planks, with gaps of space between the boards. There was a soapstone wood stove, lots of hanging plants, and large pillows in various corners.

"Welcome," Markus said, making his way into the kitchen area.

Kathryn wandered around the mostly open space beneath a low ceiling. She ran the tip of a finger across bookshelves in search of dust, scanned above for cobwebs clinging to the overhead fans. She found the place to be remarkably clean, especially for a bachelor. There were no dishes in the sink. The kitchen's tile floor wasn't sticky.

"Do you actually eat in here?" Kathryn asked him.

"I do. I'm a modern man, Kathryn. I can cook AND clean up after myself."

She shook her head. "What a catch."

"Yeah. The both of us. On the surface, anyway. Too bad our insides are so screwed up."

"Speak for yourself," Kathryn teased.

The joke fell flat. The afternoon had already begun to alter the nature of their relationship, adding a new layer of weight. And it was only three o'clock. Kathryn wandered into the living room. Markus occupied himself in the kitchen making them gin and tonics.

"I'm pouring us a couple drinks," he announced.

"Oh, so I need to be sitting down AND have a buzz on when I hear this confession of yours?"

"Yup."

Kathryn was standing in front of the panoramic rectangular window in his living room. The only things occupying the spare room were a futon, a television set, and a DVD player. There wasn't even a coffee table. The futon looked old. It was sunken in the middle.

"Maybe I'll just sit on the floor," she said when Markus stepped into the room carrying two clear, bubbling drinks in his hands.

"Oh stop," he said, handing her a drink. "Cheers!"

"Cheers. I guess."

Markus nodded at the futon. "Have a seat. I need to pace while I talk."

"What if I have to pace while I listen?"

"Funny."

Neither one of them smiled. Kathryn sat down reluctantly. She took a long sip of the strong drink.

"All right, I'm ready. Fire away."

Markus paced back and forth in front of the long window, glancing repeatedly at the dark-green, hulking mountain he knew well. From this close up angle it looked less like the graceful tail fin of a whale, as it always did on the drive up from Hanover, and much more like the notorious dromedary it was named after. But right now this custom view of his backyard mountain failed to ground him like it usually did. Markus felt like an actor on a stage delivering a monologue to describe past actions taken by a fictional character he was playing, some crazy deranged surgeon from a surreal Borges novel. As he told his mentor and best friend the details necessary for moving his endeavor forward, Markus realized he'd yet to come to moral terms with what he was doing. All along he'd been telling himself that the beneficial ends would justify the nefarious means he was engaging in to reach them.

"All right. So, do you remember that one transplant call we went on, to retrieve the heart of the six-month old baby girl who died in a car crash?"

"Of course. How could I forget that one? If only the helicopter had gotten us back an hour sooner we could have had a shot at saving that little boy . . ."

"I know. We were so close. Well, remember you handed the cooler to me after we found out the recipient had gone brain dead?"

Kathryn nodded. Her nodding evolved into a shaking head and closed eyes as she guessed the first part of his confession before he stated it.

"I never brought that baby's heart to organ disposal."

"You brought it home, didn't you? To your lab down there," she whispered.

"I did. I've been feeding it ever since, growing it to full size. I've been successful with a technique that utilizes lizard DNA to encourage muscles to grow. Have you heard of that?"

"Yes, I've read about it. And what about the sections of heart tissue in the other fridges?"

"I've taken all of those from the original - they are the building blocks of pure hearts destined for the patients you've given me. They'll never know the true source of their new hearts, Kathryn. I'll have to get good at lying by the time they're ready. But before I can even think about constructing complete hearts out of the requisite parts, I'll need to bring the first one to life. Make it beat, I mean. Once it reaches adult size, which should only take a few more months of hydroponic feeding."

"You really think you'll be able to do that? That's not a realistic expectation, Markus. What about the four-hour rule?"

"That rule is for hearts in coolers, not for one growing in a jar of plasma, a living muscle. Everything I'm doing hinges on being able to get that heart to beat. The muscle tissue is growing fast. It wants to live, Kathryn. I mean, it's living now. It wants more than life. It wants to beat. When the time is right I'll need to spark it into beating. That will be the hardest part of all, for sure. But if I succeed, it will be my heart, a vessel full of pure love. A fresh start."

Markus was pacing faster now, watching his bare feet as they strode back and forth down the same wide floor board. He stopped abruptly, and turned to face Kathryn. She was staring at him. Her eyes were wide with a combination of disbelief and terror. She spoke in a hushed, urgent voice.

"And all those other pieces you've got? I still don't understand -"

"Like I said, they all came from the original, six-month old heart. I cut a small sample from every component of that infant's heart. Using basic cloning techniques, I've been able to get those pieces to grow towards full, adult-sized versions on their own."

"But then what?"

"Then I have to combine the cloned components into completed hearts, each with the potential to beat. I'll have to stitch all the parts together into a whole."

"Are you out of your mind? How are you going to build a heart from scratch? That's only been done in science fiction stories, Markus. Frankenstein kind of stuff."

"I'm sure it can be done. I'm going to experiment until I pull it off. If we can build hearts out of man made parts, plastic and wires, then why can't we build them out of the real parts? Actual ventricles and aortas?"

Kathryn let her head fall into her hands.

"What?" Markus asked, speaking to her hair. "Now you think I'm crazy. I knew I shouldn't have told you about any of this. I should have kept it all to myself. But I couldn't, Kathryn. Being the only one was killing me. I'm sorry . . ."

Kathryn spoke into her palms. "I'm not sure what to think anymore."

Markus swiveled on one foot to face the window. He wanted to be up on top of Camel's Hump instead of in his living room. He closed his eyes and imagined himself on the mountain. He could picture the pristine forests well, fern and moss-cloaked, primordial, spontaneous brooks bursting from the ground, arteries and capillaries of newborn water flowing down into the valley surrounding his farmhouse, joining the Winooski river, and eventually the sea. It was a strong, confident, brooding mountain, with a summit that could shift in an instant, oscillating from a throne piercing the sky above the Northeast Kingdom to the last seat on a wind-whipped ride straight into the apocalypse. The mountain gave him the strength to ask her the question, even as he expected to be hit in the back of the head with her glass full of melting ice and sliver of lime.

"Would you consider doing the first transplant operation for one of my hearts? The baby girl's heart?"

Kathryn slowly rose up off the futon. "To put it into you, Markus?"

"Yes."

She walked over to him. "I'll have to think about it. Long, hard thinking. There's the legality issues and -"

"I know. You can just say no right now."

"I'm not going to say no right now. But I'm not saying yes, either."

"Fair enough."

They stood together by the long wide window, looking out, sharing silence.

"It's hard," Markus said eventually.

"What you're doing? Of course it's ha -"

"No. I mean being alone, Kathryn. A bachelor. Without a family of my own." He nodded sharply at the floor. "Maybe I wouldn't be doing any of that crazy shit down there if I had a wife and children." He turned to face her, squinting back sudden tears.

Kathryn held her eyes on the view out the grand window, gazing at the domed mountain her apprentice loved so much. "When you're like us, Markus, alone I mean, you have the chance to find a different kind of family. A spiritual family. A group not bound by the blood and guts of marriage and genetics, but by a different connection entirely. Bonds not defined by titles, or even geography. These are what I call our people. We have the freedom to find them, you and I, and call them our family. To grow because of our relationships with them."

"Don't you grow with a spouse, and your children?"

"Yes. But in a different way. You just can't have both, I guess. Many folks have neither. It's important to remember that."

"Have you found your people?" Markus asked her.

"Some of them. You never stop finding them, even if years go by between one and the next."

He whispered his next question, almost afraid to ask it.

"Am I one of them, Kathryn?"

"Of course you are."

Markus pondered the concept of his people for some time. Believing in Kathryn's theory gave bachelorhood a whole new light, allowed him to see his situation from an entirely new angle.

"But what about the lonely times," he asked her, an almost desperate tone underlying his words. "The Sunday mornings. Saturday nights. Shit, the whole goddam weekend. And dinners. What about all the dinners alone, Kathryn? How do we make it through all the fucking dinners?" He was shouting now.

"You just do, Markus," Kathryn said calmly, placing an arm around his shoulders. "You pick up the phone and call someone. Take a long walk. Volunteer. But you surely don't feel sorry for yourself. Got it?"

He faced her. They were close enough to kiss. "Yes. I got it."

Markus started pacing the room again, slowly this time, calmly.

"We're the lucky ones, Markus. There are a lot of miserable married people you know. Being married and being alone are each different kinds of hard. Both are equally hard, maybe. But if you can master loneliness, eliminate it from being any kind of threat, you'll be all set. And you'll find your people. And be happy."

"What if you're the only one I've found so far?"

"What about Karl?"

"Is he one of yours?"

She nodded.

"Then I guess that makes him one of mine."

"I think it does."

During the drive back to Dartmouth each doctor thought hard about the other. Markus thought about Kathryn's discipline and focus, how she was driven yet playful, with that girlish giggle she unleashed at the slightest provocation. People loved her laugh so much they often tried harder than normal at being funny just to elicit one of her giggles, instigating a circle of happiness, giving birth to the glow Kathryn shared readily with those around her. There was a brightness to her green and yellow eyes that belied so much more than intelligence. She had a spark, and anyone at least half awake would notice it, would be drawn to it like a moth to a porch light. But she always moved so fast only a few got close, those who happened to be existing on the same rhythm, the same pace with which she was moving through her life at that given moment in time. Or series of moments. Or years. Markus had been moving along with her for years.

Kathryn was thinking how she'd known Markus for seven years now. He was certainly one of a very select group. One of her people. But he was taking his obsession too far, letting the healthy parts of his genius be over-ridden by the manic side, the side hooked on extremity. She could only hope that he would be okay in the long run. Kathryn grounded part of this hope in her knowledge of where Markus came from. His mother. Kathryn had met Bethany at his graduation from medical school. She knew that, in the long run, the offspring of such a strong woman would have no choice but to be strong himself. Even if one day he would have to go back to her and rest for a time as her only son again, basking in the spill-over of Bethany's substantial love for however long he needed it, in order to locate a balance point between genius and mania. But there was also the problem of his sick heart to consider. He needed a new one. So did it really matter where this new heart came from? By the time they arrived back at the hospital Kathryn had already made up her mind. If Markus could finish growing that baby girl's heart to adult size, and then jump start it to life somehow, she would transplant it inside him. Because she loved him, and wanted to give him a shot at loving her back. But she still hadn't bought into his wild hypothesis, firmly believing that any success Markus might have at restoring his supposed lost love would not come from this transplanted heart itself, but from the placebo effect it might have on his hope. Without hope, Kathryn knew, there wouldn't be enough fertile ground inside him for her own love to have a chance at taking root in there.

The Beat

ALTHOUGH KATHRYN HAD DECIDED to perform the operation on Markus, to transplant the little girl's heart into his chest in exchange for the diseased one wasting away inside him, following their meeting at his farmhouse there was a period of great distance between apprentice and mentor. Whereas before they would talk at least once a day, usually meeting up for lunch or an afternoon coffee, now they hardly spoke at all. Markus was spending every waking minute of his free time outside the hospital in his home operating room, doting on his prized heart. He constructed cocktails of all-natural proteins from wild-harvested seaweed and fish oil, injecting them straight into the growing muscle, and into all the cloned parts developing in separate fridges. He played Mozart for it on Sunday afternoons. He read *The Giving Tree* out loud to his heart. Markus almost went so far as inviting his parents for a visit, so he could introduce them to his future heart while it was still in plain sight, but ultimately rejected the idea.

When he wasn't pampering the original heart Markus was working on techniques to fuse all the growing pieces of the other hearts into complete organs. They had all reached the proper size, thriving on the twice daily feedings of his liquid protein cocktails. He spent long nights experimenting into the early morning hours, trying different methods of building a complete heart out of these cloned parts. Sewing all the requisite components - ventricles and aortas and capillaries and valves - together into one complete organ, using stitches that would dissolve over time, was the easy part when compared to the final challenge of bringing these finished products to life. As a surgical resident, Markus had practiced sewing up all kinds of tissues, and had acquired the delicate touch every surgeon needed in order to succeed. The touch of a pianist, or a painter.

He was able to build three complete hearts in less than six months. Three mini-fridges were emptied of their shelves. Each of these now held one large jar. Each jar contained one heart. It was now time to bring the original heart, which had reached adult size, to life. There were no manuals to consult on how to accomplish such a thing. He'd decided early on that the key would likely be to use some combination of oxygen and electricity, the two requirements of living hearts. But how much of each should he use, in what ratio should he combine them in order to inspire this homegrown muscle into making that first tentative beat? How many joules of current, and for how long? Should he give it pure oxygen, or the more diluted form a person's blood naturally provided to a normal living heart? Every night he was awed by the notion that he was now playing a kind of god more than he ever had before during his young surgical career, trying to give life to a muscle that had taken millions of years to evolve. These thoughts sometimes overwhelmed him, often threatening his ability to go forward. But he kept going forward, aware now that going backward was not an option, and that it never had been even when he'd indulged in the tempting illusion of a retreat. By cutting himself off from retreating to his mother and her bread, Markus had eliminated the option of trying to go back to retrieve what he might have lost. Moving forward, mapless, loveless, and blind, was the only possible direction. Death was the other option, and that was going to happen eventually no matter what he did. So a nothing-to-lose attitude came to define him during this time spent exploring these uncharted realms of heart transplant medicine in his farmhouse operating room.

Markus set up a medium-sized fish tank on top of his operating table. He filled it with blood hijacked from the hospital, circulated it with pumps, injected it with various quantities of oxygen using the heart/lung machine he'd bought used from a Mexican medical supply company. The machine was designed to simulate the actual heart and lungs of a living person. Remembering his father's design for lighting the macaw cage, he installed flood lights in the floor so he could see into the viscous red liquid well enough to locate the heart he would be submerging inside the fish tank. For the electricity source to jumpstart the organ his instinct was to use a defibrillator, the machine with shock pads that were placed on a patient's chest during cardiac arrest. But without a body he couldn't see how the pads would be able to transfer electricity into his floating heart. After enlisting the help of his friends in town, Markus soon found out that Chip's wife needed surgery for a hernia, and the self-employed electrician didn't have health insurance. So Markus performed the relatively simple procedure for her in his home operating room, and bartered this service with Chip in exchange for help channeling the current produced by the jumper cables, as they'd nicknamed them in Dartmouth's ER, into the kinds of micro-wires Markus would be able to attach to his heart submerged in the fish tank filled with blood.

What followed was a string of long, dark nights. Markus blasted eighties rock, Metallica and Guns & Roses, drank shots of high-end bourbon, and shocked his floating heart with electrical current all night long. He varied the rhythm of these shocks, trying out different frequencies, from once-a-half-second jolts that simulated a beating heart, to once a minute, to a few times an hour, to one jolt over an entire night, and everything in between. This electrical experimentation went on for weeks. It was the darkest time of Markus' life, darker by far than his lonely lunches in the high school bathroom. He'd show up at the hospital bleary-eyed and haggard, partially hung over, sleep-deprived. His performance in the actual hospital OR slipping, Kathryn tried to intervene more than once, the same way one might with a drug addict.

"I'm almost there," Markus would plead with her every time. "I'm so close."

"The only thing you're close to is going insane, getting arrested, or both."

"I just need a couple more nights," he would beg.

Sometimes Markus would find himself distracted by the heart itself. He stared at it for long stretches of time, taking in the sight of his future heart suspended in the lit-up blood, a virgin heart, one that had never known loneliness or fear, the pain of rejection or the burden of grief. It was a pure heart, organically grown, raised under the persistent attention of Dr. Markus Greene. It was the one thing he needed. The only thing he needed. A fresh start that would bring him back to square one, filling him with the pure love that unlucky little girl had possessed, like he'd possessed for so many years. Before giving most of it away, then consuming the leftovers for himself in order to survive his training, and make it to this moment now at hand.

And then it happened. Markus almost didn't notice that first beat, causing him to wonder if maybe he'd missed others before. He was taking a break from inducing the last round of shocks, pouring himself a shot of Woodford. *Sweet Child Of Mine* was blaring across the operating room. What first caught his eye was a series of circular ripples spreading across the surface of the blood, like those made by a pebble tossed into the middle of a pond. He pressed his face to the glass, peering closely at the pink, illuminated heart. Markus reached over and clicked the current back on, into the last rhythm he'd been using, one shock of twelve joules every ten seconds. What he saw then stole his breath. He dropped the shot glass on the tiled floor. Shards of glass and bourbon splashed across his slippers. He was transfixed, awed by the surreal sight of this newborn heart, carefully raised to adult size by his own two hands, suddenly pulsing with beats, hungry for life, drinking its fill of oxygen-infused blood. The heart/lung machine beeped wildly, announcing it was no longer needed to keep this patient alive. He turned off the machine and detached the electric wires from the submerged heart, which maintained its steady beat, confirming his success. Markus dashed over to a counter along a far wall to grab his cell phone, almost slipping on the spilled bourbon. He dialed Kathryn's number. When he got her voice mail he dialed again, over and over until she finally answered, her voice weary.

"Markus? What's going on, its four o'clock in the -"

"I did it."

"What?"

"I've got it beating right now. My heart is alive. It's time for the transplant. How soon can you get here?"

"Oh God, Markus."

"How soon, Kathryn?"

"I'll be there in thirty minutes."

"I love you."

Transplant

THE FIRST THING Markus did to prepare for his transplant was change the music in his stereo system from eighties rock to the Mozart symphonies he normally played for his cherished heart on Sunday afternoons. He checked on the blade of the saw that would cut through his chest plate. He took the clamps that would hold his chest apart out of a drawer that hadn't been opened since he'd placed them in there two years ago. Then he said a prayer. It was a quick spontaneous prayer, a token offering of words to a god he couldn't actually picture, choosing to visualize his childhood boulder, and the summit of Camel's Hump, the closest places he'd found to a church. After the prayer he stripped to his boxers, then painted a straight line in iodine down the center of his chest, a guiding stripe Kathryn would soon follow with the saw. He lowered the fish tank carefully to the floor, terrified the heart might stop beating. It was crucial for this newborn heart to stay alive until the last possible second, when Kathryn transferred it into his chest. The longer it stayed beating outside Markus the better chance she would have of reviving it once she had sewn it up inside him. Unable to wait any longer for his surgeon, Markus made sure the door to the lab was open. Then he climbed up on the operating table, inserted the IV needle into a prominent vein in his arm, and began the flow of anesthesia that would knock him out for the next 6 hours, at which point Kathryn would dose him again with the powerful cocktail of drugs.

Markus woke up on the operating table twelve hours later. He slowly lifted himself up on an elbow. A dull pain permeated his torso. He heard the door to the outside close. A car started up and pulled away. He was all alone. Most of the operating room was dark. Candlelight flickered from the top of the heart/lung machine, splashing just enough light for him to inspect the steel wires that were holding his chest plate together. He spent a moment admiring Kathryn's stitching job, tracing the exposed wires with the tip of a finger. He then placed a palm on the left side of his chest, just above his nipple. All his life Markus had avoided feeling any evidence of his heartbeat. He dreaded those times early on in med school when he'd been forced to take his own pulse, reluctantly pressing two fingertips into the corner of a wrist, forcing himself not to visualize his actual heart, pretending the wrist belonged to one of his future patients. And he'd never once placed a palm on the upper left side of his chest, like he was doing right now. Markus had let a couple girl-friends rest an ear there to listen, but asked them not to report what they'd heard, not to share the particular nature of his heart's beating. This avoidance stemmed from a notion he couldn't shake, one the random stings of pain originating in that corner of his chest likely contributed to, a strong belief that if he ever felt his own heartbeat then it would promptly stop.

He wasn't having these kinds of thoughts now, sitting upright on his home operating table, bathed in the light from candles lit by his surgeon and best friend. Instead he wanted to get to know this new organ in his body as if it was a girl he'd decided to pursue a lifelong relationship with. The marriage kind of relationship. So Markus let his palm rest there on his bare skin for some time. His new heart pounded vigorously in his chest, throbbing with life, pushing out into his hand in a perfect, half-second rhythm. He smiled. The next few days would be like a honeymoon while they got to know one another better. When he finally swung his legs down off the operat-ing table and took his first tentative steps forward, powered by the virgin pulmonary organ now living inside him, Markus waited to see where his legs would take him, what decisions his brain would

make with a new heart suddenly part of the decision-making equa-
tion. All he could think about was Kathryn. He wondered where
she'd gone, why she'd left him alone. He wanted to kiss her, to hold
her tight against the fault line of his fractured chest.

Leading up to the surgery Markus had assumed his personality
would change in subtle ways following the procedure. He'd heard
enough stories about transplant recipients having to get to know
themselves all over again, adjusting to new kinds of thoughts, getting used to dreams populated by strange people they'd never met.
But his new heart had only spent a few months in another body.
And to Markus, having that baby girl's dreams would be an easily
tolerable side-effect in exchange for feeling himself infused with love
once again, overflowing with his former need to share himself with
so many people. Or, maybe, with just one person this time. Markus
stumbled through the candlelit operating room towards the door.
He wanted to be outside. The old Markus would have wanted to
be out- side right now too, he thought. He pushed his way out the
two doors and emerged into the night. He looked up at the stars,
taking note of the distinct feeling the star-filled sky was giving him.
It was an unfamiliar emotion, a kind of optimism he wasn't used
to. If Kathryn or his mother had been there to ask him to define
this strange emotion, he would have searched his vocabulary for
a proper word. Markus did this anyway, even though no one was
asking him to. The word he settled on to describe what he felt was
hope, something he'd once thrived on, but had since gotten used to
living entirely without.

The last time Markus could remember a similar feeling, a hopeful
mood consuming him, had been while hiking through the woods
with Niko and Kathryn, acknowledging a kernel of hope that the
scene was a preview of his own future family. Before those fleeting
moments of bliss he had to go all the way back to his afternoons
spent riding his boulder in his patch of backyard forest, hoping
without any rational reason to that the giant rock would transport

him away from the suburban hell he was trapped in. Niko was gone, and the boulder never did move, teaching him the lesson that imagination was much more important to his long term survival than hope would ever be, that there was nowhere to go during those years except back inside the house to curl up into the womb of his mother's care. This hopeful imagining led him to writing poetry. Writing poems led him to become a doctor. And becoming a heart surgeon had led him to this moment, gazing at the stars with the same eyes he'd always possessed, contemplating thoughts of eternity with the same brain he'd always had, breathing the crisp night air with the same pair of lungs, while feeling the moment with a new heart. A hopeful heart, one hoping to find a recipient for his newborn love growing stronger with every beat. A love that remembered his dog.

Busted

FOLLOWING THE HEIGHTENED MOMENTS bonding with his new heart beneath the stars Markus became quickly over- come with fatigue. Acute pain radiated out from the split down his chest as the anesthesia began leaving his system. He had to lie down, but wasn't sure if he could make it up the stairs. He needed to see Kathryn, or at least call her on the phone. Why had she left him alone after the procedure? This question haunted him. She must have left as soon as he had showed signs of waking up. He assumed she'd wanted him to have time alone with his heart. This thought made him smile, caused waves of warmth to fill him, coursing out to his extremities. His skin seemed like barely enough of a barrier keeping his blood inside. He made it back into the house and located his phone, sat down on the operating table, and dialed Kathryn's number. She answered after half a ring.

"Hi Markus."

"Hi Kathryn. How did the operation go?"

"Very smooth. When I put your new heart in it practically attached itself. Everything lined right up perfectly. It was a breeze, as far as a transplant can be, anyway. How are you feeling?"

"I feel great. I mean, there's a ton of pain. Everything hurts. And I'm exhausted, like I need to sleep for days and days."

"You do. That's totally normal."

"I know."

Markus laid down on the operating table. He curled up in a fetal position, cradling the phone against his ear with both hands. The candle light spilled over him. "I want to see you. I need to see you," he said.

Her voice went cold and distant. "That's not going to be possible, Markus."

"What do you mean? You can't come back over here?"

"No. Not now. Maybe not ever."

"Why?"

"Because you love me."

"I do. Is that a problem?"

"It wouldn't have been before . . .but now it is. You have the heart of a little girl. I need the love of a man."

Markus went cold. He shivered. Goose bumps spread across his skin. He struggled to sit up, groaning from the all-consuming pain. "What are you saying Kathryn? You're the one who always told me how love and hearts are separate, how they have nothing to do with each other -"

"I know, I know. But while operating on you I changed my mind. I held that little girl's heart in my hands for some time before I put it in your chest. I felt her love. Literally, I mean. Specifically. I saw her eyes. I saw her parents. I felt the triangle of family love they'd all shared, contained in that heart. It's strong and good and pure, just like you wanted. It's your heart now, but it's not your love, Markus. It's hers. It was hers, I mean. That poor little girl's love. I don't know. Anyway, I have to go back to sleep. I work in a few hours. Goodbye."

Markus let the phone drop off the edge of the operating table, heard it crash apart as if the floor was miles away, as far away as Kathryn's voice had been. His new heart pounded anxiously now, driving him off the table and up the stairs. All he could think of was the view in his living room. His mountain. The climb upstairs sapped the last strength from his legs. He crawled into the living room and over to the window. On his knees, facing the mountain, he watched Camel's Hump await the day's first light. His pulse slowed. Warmth returned to his skin, smoothing away the goose bumps. He loved the mountain. He loved Kathryn. He loved his mother and his father, the president and Ken Gabriel. And it wasn't that little girl's love. It was his, emanating from his core, intertwined with his spirit. How was he going to prove this to Kathryn? Markus looked to his favorite mountain for an answer, which took its time to reply, and in doing so gave him the answer he already knew. Time.

As the newborn sun struck the eastern flank of Camel's Hump, Markus felt the urge to sleep begin to overtake him, but he feared the dreams that sleeping might produce. The sight of the majestic mountain absorbing the day's first light imbued him with contentment, allowing him to begin looking forward to whatever dreams his new heart might inspire, thinking of that sweet little girl now. Maybe he would even take a nap that afternoon. He always remembered his dreams after a nap. Once dawn had established itself he got back up on his feet and brewed a pot of French press coffee in the kitchen, trying to begin the process of killing time until his first opportunity to see Kathryn, avoiding the bottle of morphine pills in the bathroom, choosing to feel all the pain as long as he could. Pouring the rich brew out of the glass pitcher, bending down to inhale the aroma, Markus was happy that his new heart hadn't altered his deep appreciation of coffee. He glanced at the clock on the microwave. The digital yellow numbers read 6:48. Soon his mother would be taking her first break from baking and he could give her a call. But then his heightened state of morning bliss was blatantly interrupted.

At first the sound was so far in the distance Markus thought his ears were tricking him, inventing muffled siren sounds due to the exhaustion permeating his body. But as the unmistakable noise of police sirens grew steadily louder he knew not only were they real, but that they were approaching his house. He walked over to a corner of the living room. Peering out a side window overlooking his driveway, his new heart pounded at the sight of three police cars, lights ablaze, pulling to a stop on the gravel. His amygdala tried to kick his exhausted body into fight-or-flight mode, releasing the floodgates of adrenaline into his bloodstream even though he was physically unable to respond. Markus silenced this biological reaction as best he could, knowing he couldn't run, that fleeing the situation was not an option. This was the deep trouble Kathryn had warned him about. He made a quick decision to meet the police outside before they had a chance to knock on the mud room door. He couldn't imagine they had a warrant to enter his house, and didn't want to offer them a complimentary peek at the thick inner door leading into his clandestine operating room.

Fueled by blind adrenaline Markus went into his bedroom, stepped onto the small porch, and walked down the wooden stairs into the backyard. He'd never thought of it as an escape route, although it could have been one. There would be no escape for him this morning. He forced himself to round the corner of the house, where he found three officers knocking aggressively on his mud room door.

"Can I help you gentleman?" The calmness in his voice surprised him.

One of the officers took a step towards him. "Are you Dr. Markus Greene?"

"I am."

The policeman reached for a pair of handcuffs that were dangling from his belt. The other two officers surrounded Markus, each taking hold of an arm, bending his arms behind his back. Markus felt the cold metal tighten around his bare wrists. This tactile sensation of steel clamped around bone was one final, ultimate confirmation that he wasn't dreaming. The words everyone had heard in the movies, that famous string of sentences no one ever wanted to hear in real life, barely registered.

"You have . . .remain silent . . .you say will . . court of law . . ."

All Markus was thinking about was who he would call when he got to jail. Should he spend his one phone call on Kathryn, or his mother? He didn't want to call either of the women in his life. His mother would be too overwhelmed by such terrible news about her only child.

And his relationship with Kathryn was suddenly in a state of total flux. So after a long ride in the back of a police cruiser he landed in a holding cell with a sliding glass wall inside a prison north of Burlington. Markus turned down the chief warden's offer to use the phone.

"You don't even want to call your mother, Doc?" the big scruffy man asked. The nickname would stick. Markus would be known as Doc to everyone in the jail from that moment on. "Even convicts usually have mothers that give at least a couple shits about them."

Markus shook his head, defeated at a battle he'd created for himself, a war he never should have been fighting

"My mother only cares about her loaves of bread. They replaced me a long time ago."

It was a lie, the first one Markus had ever told in his life. But all rules had just been thrown out the window. The guard surprised him by sniffling back what could only have been an accidental tear or two.

"That's the saddest fucking shit I've ever heard in all my years in here. Damn, Doc. Even the murderers we book wanna call their moms. Unless that's who they murdered. But those aren't even people in my book. We've never had one of those in here."

Markus let loose a dark chuckle. "I'm not much different from them. Sometimes I wonder if I'm human myself."

The guard wrinkled his thick brow. "I thought you landed in here for stealing body parts or something."

"Eh, that was just the end result of a murder I committed a long time ago. But there's no evidence for that crime."

"Who did you kill?" the guard asked, his voice now hushed and eager.

"My love."

Markus wound up calling his mother a short time later, mostly to please the guard, who remained visibly disturbed by his lack of elaboration about this mysterious murder. Eventually Markus asked him for two quarters, and was released from his cell to use the pay phone in a dark corner of the cold concrete booking room. Bethany answered after a couple rings. She was crouched in her giant mixing bowl, working on a mechanical problem within the oily bowels of the great machine.

"Mom, it's me. Markus."

"Oh, hi honey. How are you?"

"I'm in jail."

"I see." Bethany took in a long, deep breath, exhaling it slowly before speaking again. Her tone was all business. "How much is the bail?"

"Fifty grand."

"Rupert will take care of it. Hold on, let me call -"

"Mom, I have the money. That's not a problem -"

"Save your money for the lawyer. Rupy!" she screamed.

Markus pulled the receiver away from his ear for a moment.

"Mom!"

"What?"

"Don't you want to know what I did?"

"Actually no, I don't. I just want to get you out. And give you a hug. There will be plenty of time for you to tell me what you did. Later. If you want to. But not now."

"Okay, Mom."

"I love you, Markus."

"Thanks."

What followed was the longest night of Markus' life by far, longer than any night spent on a park bench as a homeless poet, or cramming for an exam until dawn, or in the OR for the fifteenth hour of surgery. This night was longer than all of those nights combined. Everything was cold and hard, concrete and metal. Frantic at being confined, he threw himself at the sliding glass wall holding him in the cell. When this action drew no attention he stuck his head deep into the toilet in a lame attempt to kill himself, knowing he lacked the conviction to do so while blowing air bubbles in the scummy brown water. His thoughts continually arched back to that nothing-left-to-lose feeling that had led him into this situation, eventually settling on his season of debauchery after med school. Now that life had finally forced him to slow down, giving him ample time to look back on some things, it was then that Markus realized his months spent tunneling downward through addiction was the one time he actually was losing some of his love. Up to that point in life he likely hadn't lost much any it at all. And what a mess he'd made of everything now. What an absolute mess.

Rupert and His Bird

BETHANY TOOK MONDAYS OFF from baking. Usually she just rested, her body weary from the physical toll of the work. In the afternoon she might pay a few bills, or try to book a new customer while sipping iced tea beside her backyard oven, sprawled out on a chaise lounge chair. Later on, back inside the house, she would research a new recipe, study how to bake a new kind of bread. Sourdough rye was her next challenge. Her baking bible was a book called *Soul Loaves; Authentic Techniques For Artisan Bakers*. The author, of course, was Pierre Lufont. But on this late summer Monday Bethany decided not to retreat into the safe oasis of her mentor's words, chose not to resume her study of rye, the successful baking of which Pierre had told her required the precise calculations of a scientist married with the intuitive touch of an artist. It wasn't that she was intimidated by this challenge. She was actually looking forward to mastering rye, anticipating the day she would ship a finished loaf overnight to Paris, so he could sample it and either confirm her success or inform her she needed to try again. Bethany would never serve a new style of bread to her customers without her mentor's final approval. While learning pumpernickel, that dark German bread, soft and dense with a subtle seed crunch, it had taken three loaves shipped across the Atlantic before she'd been able to win the Frenchman's endorsement for moving it into regular production.

Bethany decided to put the rye off for another day. For some reason she didn't even want to eat dinner with her husband, the one routine of marriage they'd been able to maintain throughout the years. Although she didn't cook anymore, Bethany still enjoyed sharing dinner with Rupert, takeout he picked up on the way home, or one of the frozen entrees she ordered online and stored in her walk-in freezer. But she didn't share Markus' belief that happiness came down to whether or not there was someone to have dinner with. It wasn't happiness she felt while eating a frozen lasagna across from Rupert, but rather the simple contentment that came from engaging in a longstanding routine.

Not sure why she was doing this on her only day off, Bethany got up from her lounge chair and built a fire in her oven. Soon she had a raging bonfire going in the back of the adobe dome, feeding wood in through the open hatch door, her eyes gleaming at the sight of coals building up into a towering mound. Sweating from the exertion and the heat beginning to radiate off the rustic oven, she began peeling layers. Bethany took off clothes until there was nothing left but her underwear. Drenched now with perspiration she only wanted to sweat more, to take the feeling of elation she got on regular baking days to an entirely new level. Acting on pure impulse Bethany climbed into her oven. Her bare knees pressed into the burnt cornmeal encrusted on the great slab of stone. She crawled towards the fire, its glow seducing her, the red coals throbbing like a primordial heart. It was the momentary epicenter of her personal universe. She sat down cross-legged in front of the flames, bowed to worship the heat, then tipped her head back to thank the oven for providing all those loaves, for holding her in this moment. Her pores exploded while she cried out inside, silently screaming for relief, begging the cosmos to ease Markus' suffering.

While baking inside her oven Bethany transformed from mother to martyr, finally and fully leaving her past identities behind, the roles of wife and mother, environmental activist, friend and boss and baker. Inside the hollow dome of earth she oscillated between nothing and everything, emptiness and fullness, grief and joy. Her experience inside this spur-of-the-moment sweat lodge culminated in her belting out Madonna's *Like A Virgin*, screaming the lyrics at the top of her lungs. Upon finishing the song she ripped off her soaked bra and panties, tossed both into the flames, and climbed out of the oven. The late summer air was thick with humidity. Moisture clung to her skin. She faced the back woods. The sky was gray-black, cloud covered. Her eyes focused on the tops of the trees. They seemed to shimmer with white light, a subtle glow extending just beyond the outline of their collective canopy. Bethany smiled. The trees were calling to her. So she walked towards them, eager for the tiny forest's embrace, knowing that a previously unknowable piece of her son awaited her in those woods. She literally bumped into this fragment of Markus' childhood when she stumbled into his boulder. She climbed up on top of the great rock and daydreamed herself through the rest of the night, until dawn reminded her of reality, and the fact that she was already hours late for that day's round of baking. While riding Markus' boulder straight into a Tuesday sunrise, Bethany made the abrupt decision that she would move to northern New York, to some small Adirondack town in the middle of nowhere, maybe by a lake, where she would set out to build the largest wood-fired baking oven in the country, a giant dome one hundred feet in diameter, rising ten feet high in the middle, constructed out of a combination of imported Hopi adobe and local brick. And its construction would be overseen, of course, by Pierre Lufont.

Her husband remained back in Michigan during the work week, where he occupied the unsold house, clinging to his subterranean palace, declaring over and over to the macaw how he'd always planned on taking his last breath in the basement lair. Rupert figured it was the best possible place he could die, ideally while watching the 1985 Super Bowl played on repeat in three dimensions, Jim McMahon dancing on his coffee table, dodging Patriot linebackers while driving the Bears to victory. He dreaded the thought of spending his final days in that shack his wife had insisted on moving to, where he now went most every weekend. Rupert often shared this nightmarish notion with his cherished pet.

"That house is in the middle of nowhere," he'd regularly complain to the macaw.

"Buwahh, the boonies. Crazy Mad Baker, bwok."

Rupert was growing deeply jealous of his beautiful bird. While he forced himself to dutifully head to the Adirondacks every Friday, the macaw got to stay behind over the weekend, kept well-fed by a digitally controlled food dispensing system, entertained by a 3D documentary on the Amazon playing in repeat, surrounding the spoiled bird with tropical plants that turned the ceiling into a jungle canopy while kindred, plumed avifauna flew past his cage. The macaw relished his weekends spent in a simulated version of his ultimate paradise, predator-free, with no shortage of dried mango strips. His owner continually reminded him of his luck. Rupert doted on the macaw during his weeknights in the basement. He would take his cherished pet out of the cage to mist its wings with water, to comb its tail with a toothpick, talking to the bird the whole time about topics ranging from his crazy baking spouse to his day at the office. And occasionally he brought up his son.

"Buwahh, The Convict."

Rupert couldn't get the bird to stop using this title when referring to Markus, even though the macaw had only heard his owner utter it once, when Markus had first been arrested.

"His name is Markus. My son is a doctor."

"Doctor Greene. Buwaaah."

"That's better. Thank you."

"Thank you." The bird scratched its cheek with a claw. "Friday Rupert leaves. Buwah. Friday goodbye Rup -"

"It's only Tuesday," Rupert grumbled.

The bird cocked its head, as if trying to calculate how long he had to wait before his depressing owner would turn the jungle on and leave him alone with the flocks of parakeet avatars.

"It's not Friday yet. Christ, am I really that bad? You'd better watch out, or I'll bring you to Saranac Lake and leave you with the Mad Baker one of these days."

The macaw beat its wings against the bars of the cage, visibly disturbed by the sound of that name.

"Buwaaaah, glad she's gone. Buwah. You and me. Father and son. Bwock."

"That's right," Rupert confirmed, lowering the bird back into its cage. "Just the way we like it. But you're not my son."

Rupert drifted to the other side of the room and made himself a scotch and water. His father's paintings, lurking in a trunk inside a nearby closet, called out to him more than they ever had before. His dad seemed to be gloating from the grave, happy that his artistic gene had reappeared after so completely skipping a generation. Rupert's greatest fear had come true. Markus had without a doubt inherited this unpredictable section of DNA, a unique code Rupert believed to program not only the urge to make art, but also the homosexual tendencies that had led his father to abandon the family for a life with a man, a history Rupert's entire existence had been spent trying to erase. But all he'd done was perpetuate this erratic gene through his own son.

Drink in hand, he sat on the couch. Took off his shoes. Rested his white-socked feet on the glass table. Rupert then closed his eyes, letting his memory arch back in time to the moment his wife had announced her desire to move to the Adirondacks. He could see it clearly, could hear every word. They were standing in her walk-in cooler. Fans buzzed in his ear. She had asked him to step in the frigid room so her staff wouldn't hear what was being said.

"I want to move to northern New York. To a town I found on the maps called Saranac Lake."

"Why?" Rupert asked. For the first time he was surprised by a new development in his wife's constantly evolving career. "I don't see why that's necessary. You have a customer base here. You have all the equipment you need -"

"I need a bigger outdoor oven to bake like I want to. A much bigger oven. That's just not a possibility here."

"There's more room out back. We can expand the yard if you want. Take out all those trees -"

"That's not an option. I promised Markus we'd never cut those trees. Those woods were his special place. His boulder is out there. It's a magic boulder."

Rupert rolled his eyes, unable and unwilling to comprehend the idea of magical rocks.

"There are other reasons, too," Bethany continued that day.

"Like what?"

"Like how it's nice to see the stars at night sometimes. There are no stars here Rupy."

"I've never known you to be a stargazer, Beth. Even in your younger days. You never mentioned the stars when we were dating."

"I used to watch them when I went up north. For hours. The stars were so sharp and clear up there, the way the sky is supposed to look at night. Now I want to see them like that every night," she stammered, stomping her foot down like a frustrated child.

Rupert narrowed his eyes. "This is about that Frenchman, isn't it? Lupont?"

"Lufont. No, it's not about him. Pierre lives in Normandy. With his wife." She averted her eyes, focusing on a heaping mound of buttery croissant dough cooling on the stainless-steel table next to them. "He will be helping with the oven, as a consultant, just for a few days."

Rupert crossed his arms. "I see."

"Rupy please, we've made it too far for you to get jealous of some French baker." She huffed out a deep breath. "Listen, I'll tell you the real reason behind my decision. I need to be close to our son."

Rupert closed his eyes. "Our son is in prison, Beth."

"That's exactly why I need to be close. He needs visitors. I can visit him twice a week, on my days off from baking. We can smile at each other through the plastic window, talk about nice things while I try not to cry. I have to be close by, or he might not make it out of there. He doesn't need me to be his mother again. But he does need me to be his friend. This is just something I know without a doubt. Okay?"

The bluntness of this final statement, supported by matriarchal intuition, boxed Rupert into a corner, and took away any argument against his wife moving to the northern Adirondack outpost of Saranac Lake.

Following his wife's relocation, if anyone had asked him, Rupert would not have declared himself to be happy. He wasn't depressed either. He was existing in a kind of limbo, spending large amounts of energy trying to adapt to mid-weeks void of the domestic side of his existence, which had been relatively constant for the last thirty years. A few years later, looking back, he would come to realize it was the macaw that kept him going during that time. The bird with a thousand word vocabulary filled the double void left behind by the departure of Bethany and Markus. His son's exodus from the parental nest hadn't fazed Rupert much at all. Outside of a few months during two baseball seasons they hadn't been very close. And all children left home to make their way in the greater world. It was an ancient ritual, a natural phenomenon that replayed itself over and over in the history of families around the globe. Rupert had been happy for his boy, certain the world-at-large would wear him down quickly, that within a few months they'd be hearing about college applications being filed with urgency, Markus' adventure as a wandering poet becoming his version of the gap year some of their friends' children were taking in between high school and college. But this single year became three, more like a crevasse or a canyon than a gap, the kind of proverbial crack he and Bethany always promised Markus they wouldn't let him fall through. Then something along the lines of a miracle, a divine intervention, ushered him straight into medical school. But even heart transplant surgeons weren't immune to slipping. And there were always cracks to fall into no matter one's place in the world. These things happened. Bethany had positioned herself in a place where she could help catch him before he fell too far down. There was nothing else to do now except wait for things to play out.

The first few weeks after his wife's relocation to her Adirondack camp were the most challenging period of time in Rupert's life up to that point. He promised her six weeks on her own to settle into the sprawling former hunting lodge he'd bought her, in cash, before initiating their plan for him to visit two weekends a month. Those weeks without his wife book-ending his every day were more challenging than any sports battle he'd waged in high school and college, harder than the academic slam of Harvard business school had been, more difficult than working in feed lots and slaughterhouses for two years after his MBA, getting his hands dirty on the ground levels of the industry he planned on dominating. Rupert had achieved all his major accomplishments, athletic and academic and business, by the age of thirty. Now here he was nearing sixty, too old for a mid-life crisis, and too young for death.

Bethany's exodus from Grosse Pointe had an immediate clarifying effect on Rupert, as if the lack of her daily presence was a kind of pill, a drug that allowed him to see things he'd never let himself acknowledge. Most of these visions occurred in traffic jams, the one place where life forced Rupert to slow his constant forward momentum. Over the years he'd developed methods to combat the evening rush hour (he went to the office so early in the morning that traffic was irrelevant), holding conference calls with his most eager young managers, ingesting a series of cd's on investment strategies, studying sports news on his blackberry and making corresponding decisions about his fantasy teams. Suddenly lacking the destination of his wife pulling him towards their house after another twelve-hour day fulfilling his role as the family provider, the log jams of traffic on the ten-lane freeways became extremely challenging for Rupert to endure. He stopped scheduling conference calls, turned off the stock advice cd's, and let his fantasy football team slide into last place, enduring his employees' shock over his sudden lack of dominance in that arena of the office's coffee break culture.

During one particularly grueling Friday evening rush hour Rupert hit a kind of breaking point. It was so bad that even ESPN Radio couldn't soothe his restlessness. Encased in the black leather and mahogany interior of his Lexus, wondering if there were always this many horns blaring around him during other identical traffic jams he endured most every day, crawling forward a few feet at a time, the only thing he wanted to do was put his car in park and climb out of its suddenly false version of comfort. Maybe an eighteen wheeler was about to plow into him from behind, crushing him and a few others to death? Maybe it was safer, and far more interesting, to walk home? And then he was struck by thoughts of his son. His thinking hit him out of the blue because it came from a shifted perspective, an altered viewpoint that was allowing him to see Markus in a different light. Rupert was focused specifically on his son's form of courage, a trait he'd never before applied to Markus. It was a strange version of bravery for sure, but Markus' leap from home, car-less and penniless, had perhaps taken more guts than anything Rupert had ever done. And then to survive for over three years selling poetry, homeless by choice, had been an extremely courageous way of grabbing life by the balls, exactly what Rupert had always told his son to do whenever he was given a brief window through which to offer up a little jewel of fatherly advice. His son had done these courageous things in his own original way. And then, regardless of his current troubles, had gone on to become a heart surgeon of all things, instilling Rupert with a permanent swell of fatherly pride he'd never dreamed of experiencing. Overwhelmed by guilt at having not allowed himself to slow down and try appreciating Markus' slow development into manhood, he almost did act on his urge to get out of the car and walk home. But Rupert's practical side, the ultimate foundation of his personality, had not been worn down enough by these weeks spent living alone. However he did maneuver his car into the breakdown lane and then proceeded, illegally and to the sound of many angry horns, to the next exit.

Once off the highway Rupert found himself driving through middle-class neighborhoods he'd never been in before. His GPS guided him to a pet store, where he bought over one hundred dollars' worth of treats and toys for his macaw, vowing he would spoil the bird as much as possible, hoping this could be some kind of penance for the lack of attention he'd given to his son over the years. Rupert stood at the counter filled with dried fruit strips, hanging swings, and miniature mirrors, a hint of tears in the corners of his eyes that he refused to allow to develop any further.

"You must have a lot of birds," the clerk said casually while ringing up all the toys and treats.

"Actually I only have one bird. A macaw."

"Oh. Lucky macaw!" The clerk paused, holding a bag of sticky seed sticks under the scanner. He must have noticed some kind of fragile quaking beneath Rupert's voice. "Is everything okay, sir?"

"Not really," Rupert admitted, surprising himself with his honesty. "Being a father is a tough job, kid. One I may have completely failed at. I've never failed at anything."

The twenty-something cashier resumed ringing up the purchases, nodding with understanding. "But that job isn't over yet, is it?"

Rupert cocked his head, considering this notion. "Maybe not."

The kid was right. Maybe there would be more chances to get fatherhood right down the road. A short time later, while Rupert struggled to follow the guidance of the overly nice female voice coming from his GPS, his traffic-jam induced revelations were still playing out. Now he was dwelling on the one true father-son talk he and Markus had ever engaged in, when he'd had the macaw deliver his speech on finding happiness as a man through the dual avenues of money and sex. In hindsight, not only had the method of delivery been a cowardly one, but the content had been misguided as well. Maybe there was more to being a man than doing whatever it took to obtain the security these two basic commodities provided, then holding on to them for as long as possible, because losing these essential elements of manhood would be a kind of death. After forty years as an adult, Rupert found himself realizing what his wife had likely known all along, that there were many shades of life in between the black and white, many kinds of men and women, many ways to be a father to a son. A husband to a wife. He was trying hard to dodge the doubt now stalking him, some brief and cruel summary of his existence as nothing more than a hard-working man who'd allowed people to enjoy quality hot dogs at baseball games for a fair price. After finally making it to the familiar grid of his neighborhood streets, having survived the spontaneous break in his regular commuting routine, Rupert found himself consumed with one overwhelming hope. He hoped that Markus would someday give him another shot at a father-son kind of talk. Before it was too late for them both.

The Convict

KATHRYN WAS THE FIRST to visit Markus in jail. They sat on opposite sides of the scratched plastic window, talking on black phones. Static buzzed in the spaces between their words.

"How are you even sitting up right now?" she asked him.

"Adrenaline, maybe. I can't feel a thing." Markus leaned forward. "Did they confiscate my hearts?"

Kathryn nodded. "You had to be stopped, Markus. You know that, right? You were going to kill yourself if you didn't slow down, especially after the operation, something I never should have - maybe you had to wind up in here to realize how out of balance you'd gotten."

"Christ, Kathryn. How can you say that? You sound like you're on their side." Markus closed his eyes, shook his head slowly. "I invested so much in those hearts."

"I know, Markus. I am on your side. Of course I am. But you got what you wanted. Your new heart. I didn't tell them about the transplant. That's still our secret. How does it feel?"

"I'm still trying to get to know it. But what you said on the phone yesterday, about not wanting what I have to give you."

"I'm sorry, Markus."

She placed her palm on the wall of clear plastic. He met it with his own palm.

"I'm just scared," Kathryn continued. "It's like you had some kind of emotional lobotomy, and I have no idea what to expect from you now."

Markus nodded. "That makes sense. I'm scared, too. But excited at the same time. Kathryn?"

"Yes?"

"Remember when you asked me to write a poem about you?"

"Of course I remember."

"I already had written one. My old heart came up with the words, after that party, while listening to Karl play his piano. Now my new heart is telling me to give it to you. So, when I get out of here, the first thing I'm going to do is give you that poem."

They simultaneously lowered their hands from the thick plastic between them. Kathryn's eyes grew wet.

"I'm not sure when I'll be posting bail," Markus mumbled.

"Why?"

"'Cause I don't want to go home. And there's nowhere else to go."

"Markus. That's just silly. There are plenty of places to go."

"Like your place?" He forced a smile that didn't last. "It's not so bad in here, actually. They call me Doc. And I kinda' like the head warden. We've been playing chess late at night. Except he might still think I'm a murderer."

"Jesus, Markus."

"It's just a little misunderstanding I haven't bothered to clear up."

Kathryn looked around, taking in the grimy cold setting. "Listen, just promise me that when you do get out of here, that you'll rest. For however long it takes. Until you get better. Whatever that means."

"I'll have no choice. My hearts are gone. And I'm on indefinite leave from the hospital."

"You need a lawyer, Markus," she said with urgency. "You need to get the hell out of here. This is no place to rest."

"I don't have a lawyer."

Kathryn stood up. "I'll lend you mine." She pulled out her cell phone and called her lawyer, Andrew Robinovitch, a Lithuanian Jew.

Then came an unhealthy visit by his mother the next morning, one that would have ended in a screaming argument, with Markus shouting his blame at her, if he hadn't asked her to leave almost immediately. Markus posted bail later that day after Robinovitch urge him to do so, making it clear that lingering in jail when he was a practicing surgeon, one with more than enough cash on hand to post bail, would be severely detrimental to his case. The first place Markus went wasn't Kathryn's house. He went to visit the president in his office. Markus sat across from Karl, shaking with nerves while awaiting the man's judgment, a verdict he took more seriously than the one a jury would be giving him someday soon.

"Do you have anything to say in defense of yourself, Dr. Greene?"

"I got distracted, Karl. Simple as that. The quest for love became my only siren, luring me to a crash landing, a kind of death. But I think I'm healed, resurrected thanks to this new heart. And maybe that's all that matters."

"Well, doing hard time will sure matter, to you and to our institution. Let's put all metaphors aside - my advice is to forget about poetry and love, Markus. There are other things in life beside these two."

"Like surgery?"

"That's your job. I'm talking about art. My piano-playing and your poem-writing are the same thing. Forms of creative expression. You need to find another one. And soon. It might be your only salvation, in case you lose your license to . . .anyway just look at Picasso if you want a good example. The guy gave up painting at the pinnacle of his career, and became a sculptor for the rest of his life. A goddamn brilliant sculptor!"

"I didn't know that."

"It's true. You can do the same thing Markus. Love is worth pursuing. But by definition it can never be permanent. And the only way to deal with the terrible tragedy of impermanence is to create art. That's what I believe, anyway. I wasn't always a pianist, you know. It wasn't the piano that seduced me away from surgery."

"What was it?"

"Painting." The president stood up and rounded the corner of his desk, heading for the door. "Follow me. I want to show you something."

"Karl?"

"Yes Markus?"

"Before we leave I need to copy that poem I gave you. The one about Kathryn."

The president smiled. "No problem, Markus. Just make sure you invite me to the wedding."

"We haven't even gone on a date yet."

"I think you two started dating, whatever that means, a long time ago."

Five hours later the two men were miles inside the White Mountain National Forest. They'd followed no recognizable trail to reach their destination, which was a log cabin standing next to a small brook on the trail-less flank of a nameless peak.

"Didn't Robert Frost have a cabin like this in the mountains of Vermont?"

"He did," the president confirmed. "Why do you ask?"

"No reason. Just heard a piece about it on NPR a few years back."

"Never mind Frost. What I've basically done is the same thing Gauguin did," Karl explained. "The guy spent years painting the walls of his jungle house in Tahiti. It was his final masterpiece. Except I'm not going to burn this thing down while I'm inside of it, like he did."

"That's good to hear."

"Yeah. What a waste. No one was ever able to admire his ultimate expression."

"I think it's kind of bad ass. Like Salinger writing fifteen novels after Catcher In The Rye, and locking each one up in a safe forever."

"They were both morons. What's the point of art if it's not shared with others?"

"So you've spent years painting the inside of this cabin, but nobody sees it."

"You're about to see it. I'm going to share it with you, right?"

Markus nodded. "Has Kathryn?"

"She was the first. After my wife, of course."

"Of course."

For the first time Markus wondered why he'd never laid eyes on the president's wife. He brushed aside the thought. Neither man attended cocktail parties, the most common situation for meeting the spouse of a colleague.

"Did you know I was outside your window that night, listening to you play Vivaldi?" he asked.

"Of course I did. Saw you stumbling from a mile away! I can't play like that for no one. Christ, a man needs an audience to play Vivaldi, whether it's one person, or a thousand. Same thing with Mozart."

The president beckoned Markus to follow him into the cabin. Moving closer to the building Markus noticed that the outer walls looked like they'd been hewn by an ax. The sides facing out were rough and knobby. They gray wood, old and dry, was ornamented with petrified mazes made by long dead bugs. Markus ran a hand along the outside wall as the president opened the only door.

"This wood seems like it's 150 years old," Markus commented. "At least! Where'd you get all these ancient hand-cut beams?"

"Long story," the president said under his breath, obviously unwilling to elaborate.

"Okay."

Inside there were no windows. An oil lantern hung from the ceiling like a rustic chandelier. The president struck a match and brought it to life, illuminating the square interior. All four walls were blanketed entirely in painted canvas. The scene was a three-hundred sixty degree mural with four corners. Markus turned in circles, trying to absorb it all. He saw a great lake, and the tall cylindrical towers of a downtown city building. He saw a suburban mansion with a boulder in the back woods, a stone monastery by the sea, and a domed peak rising above a white farmhouse. There was a black and white dog sitting in a field. Flying above it all was a single blue and yellow macaw, painted in pastel brightness against a billowing cloud.

"These are all parts of my life. My dad has a pet macaw that looks just like this one!"

"I know."

"Karl. What the hell is going on? I haven't told you about any of these things!"

"No, you haven't. I painted them all before they happened. I didn't know what was going on until recently, when you wound up with that dog I'd painted a few weeks before. So I've come to believe that a true painter, and like true surgeons there are few, gets to play with the strings of fate, Markus. He paints something he wants to see become reality. And if it's painted well enough it can be real. The fact that you're here, over thirty years after my first brushstroke, proves this painting is not so bad after all!"

"Not bad? It's a goddamn masterpiece Karl."

The president shook his head. "No it's not. You're the masterpiece, Markus. This is just paint on a wall. Just one man daydreaming in oil."

"But you're not going to burn it down, right?" Markus asked with urgency.

"Of course not. You'll have to decide whether to torch this cabin or not. Because, when I go, she's yours."

Markus' eyes followed a series of streams descending from the domed mountain, joining in the distance to form a long, emerald green river that culminated in a moonlit waterfall spilling down towards the floor. An old bearded man piloted a small boat on this river, heading upstream.

"Who's that?" Markus asked, pointing at the character he couldn't place in his life.

"Someone you haven't met yet. He studies rivers. I don't know anything else."

There was a tiny pond above where the streams started, high on one side of Camel's Hump. Markus knew that pond well. A group of people were gathered beside it in a small meadow.

"A party?" Markus asked, pointing at the group of tiny painted people.

"Must be. Don't ask me, though. I just move the brush, and paint what comes. You have to actually live it."

"I am."

During the hours they spent hiking back out, hacking their way along the overgrown game trails, bushwhacking through the forest, neither man spoke a word. When they finally neared the road, the faint rush of traffic penetrating the forest, the president spoke up.

"Just tell me one thing, Markus. Going back to our conversation about love."

"What do you want to know Karl?"

"If you think that you gave your love away, why did you keep copies of all your poems?"

"I needed them to make money. To survive."

"Exactly. Love is survival. And you're still alive. So, by simple logic, you still have your love. You've always had it." They stood beside the car now. Neither man wanted to get in, to leave behind the mountains for the town.

"I think I'm going to start painting," Markus stated eventually.

"That's the best thing I've ever heard you say," the president said.

"But first you have to give Miss Stone that poem. And then take her on a date."

"That first task will be easy. The second one I'm not so sure about."

"Eh. Just keep asking her until she says yes. That's what I did with my wife. The true keepers never give in easily. Kathryn's been holding out her entire life!"

"And so have I."

White Dancing Coyote

BETHANY KNEW THERE WERE REASONS she'd felt drawn to the northern Adirondacks beyond the proximity to her incarcerated son and the chance to build the largest wood-fired bread oven in the country. Those first weeks she spent at the lakeside compound allowed her to immerse deeply in the setting, taking note of a previously dormant side of herself begin to emerge. The crazy loon calls reverberating off the surrounding mountains woke up some wild part of Bethany she'd tasted during those weekends alone on the Upper Peninsula. Without Rupert swooping down every night, grounding her from the yeast-infused highs of her baking days through his programmed needs for dinner and conversation, she was able to begin coming unmoored from her lifelong marital duties. Bethany initially thought she would be spending most of the month rejuvenating the old log-cabin style house. It had been a former retreat for the Rockefeller family, then a fishing and hunting lodge for many years before being abandoned for almost a decade. So the structure certainly needed a lot of work. But the domestic activities, dusting and sweeping, setting up the kitchen, buying curtains and linens and rugs, failed to hold her attention like she thought they would. The things that grabbed her were outside.

Bethany took her time preparing the site where the oven would be built. Pierre was due to arrive a few days before Rupert, thus avoiding any overlap between the two men. While clearing the large circle of ground near the rocky shoreline of the lake, Bethany let herself be distracted by the natural vibrancy of her new home. She was captivated by the towering, old-growth spruce trees. Their thick

THE COMMODITY OF LOVE   187

trunks and evergreen canopies gave off a warm feeling of protection.
She followed little trails along the forested shoreline of the lake,
stopping on rock outcroppings to take in the constantly shifting
scenes, the large lake proving to be far more entertaining than television. Ospreys dove to snatch squirming trout in their claws. Pairs
of loons, mated for life, patrolled the little bays they called home.
The layers of mist born from the water's surface rose up to cloak
the forested ridges, collecting around the mountains until joining a
passing cloud. Bethany took all of this in as deeply as she could. She
passed these days in a state of waking bliss, gliding through her new
life in a condition of permanent peace.

The only thing that threatened her almost constant state of reverie
were thoughts of her son. This unavoidable motherly concern assaulted her at night, inhibiting her ability to revel in the coyote calls
slipping in through open windows. Any mother would be devastated
to have a son charged with a felony. The charge, although odd and
extreme, was not a heinous, life-ending kind of crime. But when
she'd visited Markus in the jail there had been something about the
look in his eye that had worried her deeply, accompanied as it was
by a body language portraying total surrender. Bethany forced herself to hope this was only the temporary effect prison was having
on her son's outlook. This blind faith allowed her to move forward
into the new existence she was cultivating here in Saranac Lake, a
third life she'd never expected to find, an ultimate incarnation of her
spirit that motherhood, and then bread-baking, had led her into.
When her son showed up out of the void a few months later this
unwavering belief, with no proof she should have been believing it,
was confirmed. Markus arrived as a weakened version of the man
she knew he'd worked so hard to become. But there was something
about his posture and the slight kick to his step that proved he had
something definite to live for, which her intuition told her was likely
a woman. So Bethany cooked for him every day, returning to the role
of mother for a time, however long he needed her to be one.

188 ❧ I. ALEXANDER OLCHOWSKI

After returning from his visit to the president's log cabin painting studio Markus went straight to Kathryn's house on a quiet Hanover side street. She wasn't home, so he slipped the poem under her front door. Frustrated that she was playing so hard to get after all they'd been through, he made an abrupt decision that the best thing he could do to give himself a shot at wooing her would be to follow the advice she'd given him as closely as he could. It was time to rest. And he couldn't think of a better place to do so than northern New York, at his mother's compound on Saranac Lake, a place he'd yet to lay eyes on. So Markus drove up there that night. He almost left a message on Kathryn's phone asking her to check on his house from time to time, but there was no need to bother her with such a request. It wasn't like he had plants to water, or a cat to feed. Markus still hadn't been back to his farmhouse since being arrested. It would be some time before he would be able to handle the depressing sight of all those empty fridges.

So he spent a full season resting in the pine-scented air of Saranac Lake, soaking in the peace and quiet of the remote setting. Before bed every night he asked his mother what was for breakfast, and always approved of the menu. He ate her bread every day. Having already lost so much of his identity, Markus figured he had nothing left to lose when he decided to join one of the ceremonies his mother had recently taken to hosting. The leader was a Lakota elder who'd come all the way from his reservation in South Dakota. For the entire first day he had all sixteen participants tying prayer bundles, little pieces of fabric filled with tobacco and attached in series to a long string. He instructed them to focus all their attention onto each bundle, to affix a specific prayer to every tiny sack of tobacco. Markus felt completely out of place amidst all these middle-aged women, women pursuing new paths into new stages of their lives. But the Native American, wearing all black, with a black cowboy hat adorned with hawk feathers, kept smiling at Markus. His left eye was noticeably larger than his right. Markus looked into it a few times, transfixed by the brown textured depth of the man's pupil. When he looked away he would see a flash of images, wide sweeping grasslands beneath a piercing blue sky. An eagle. A teepee. He'd never traveled west of the Mississippi, and was starting to wonder if something he needed to find was out there, an ancient kind of truth held by this medicine man's homeland.

On the second day, lightheaded from twenty-four hours without food, the women and Markus helped gather wood and stones for the following evening's sweat lodge ceremony. Bethany was on cloud nine, and wore an almost constant smile. She was revered by the women, all of whom viewed her as both a friend and a hero, a matriarchal warrior who led by example. Her son was another story. Markus followed her around like a lost sheep as she collected dead wood and large stones. She intentionally avoided the easy-to-find rocks along the lake's shoreline, as they might hold water, and therefore be prone to exploding inside the lodge. Bethany did the collecting, while Markus did the worrying.

"Don't people sometimes die in these things, Mom?"

"Only if the ceremony is not approved by Great Spirit, honey."

"What does that mean?"

"Usually, if the leader of the sweat is not qualified, or has bad karma, Great Spirit will make his disapproval known. Sometimes that results in a death. But don't worry - White Dancing Coyote is a good man, with strong medicine. We will all be safe in the lodge tomorrow night. Just remember to pray, and pray hard. The hotter it gets, the harder you pray."

"But I don't even know how to pray," Markus admitted. "I mean, I've never done it before."

Bethany stopped her harvesting. She cradled a bundle of dead sticks in her arms.

"Yes, well, we weren't exactly a religious household, were we?"

"Nope."

Bethany gazed at the blanket-cloaked sweat lodge rising in the distance, its shape mirroring the round adobe oven on the other side of her lakefront compound.

"Your father's religion was his work. And I put all my faith in you, Markus."

Markus dropped his head. He kicked at the ground. "And look at me now - a complete failure!"

"Pff! You're not a failure, Markus. You're a surgeon for heaven's sake."

"I was a surgeon. Now I'm a felon."

Bethany shrugged off this fact. "Then you have something specific to pray for in the lodge. But I've been wondering about one thing."

"What's that?"

"What did you do during all those hours you spent in the back woods behind our house?"

"Mostly I sat on a boulder and made up stories. I pretended it was a horse. Or a boat."

"I know that boulder! I found it after I did my first sweat lodge all alone in my bakery oven one Monday afternoon. When I came out, naked and dazed, I was drawn right away into your woods. I still call them that - your woods. Because they still are. And I bumped into that great rock!"

Markus smiled. "I would ride out of the neighborhood on my great stone horse, away from all the houses that all looked the same, pretending I was a cowboy."

Bethany's face wrinkled with doubt. "Were you riding away from me too? Away from your overbearing mother?"

"Maybe. But I was probably just galloping away from myself. I was so goddamn shy, Mom. Those days were very long. Every single one of them was long. For years and years."

"I know."

"You guys were good parents. Dad . . .he tried. I always knew that. I guess I just wanted freedom. I didn't like suburbia. Those woods, eh, if you could even call them that, they were my favorite escape. And that rock, along with a little imagination, was my form of transportation."

Bethany scratched her chin. She looked up at the clouds. "I never really liked Grosse Pointe either. I was too busy with you, and then with my baking, to even realize how much I felt trapped by all those endless neighborhoods. All the damn pavement. It's so nice to be here, to smell the forest, to breathe fresh air. Isn't it?"

"Oh yeah. I got hooked on this kind of setting in Vermont. We should climb Camel's Hump sometime." Markus was surprised by the excitement creeping into his voice.

"What's that?"

"My favorite mountain. It's out behind my house. I guess you could say it's my new boulder."

"All right, then. We'll go Saturday morning, after the sweat lodge. You'll be the guide!"

"Okay, Mom. Sounds good."

Rupert called that evening. After a short conversation with her husband, Bethany called Markus to the phone.

"So mom tells me you guys are going to climb some Hump Of The Camel mountain?"

"It's called Camel's Hump, Dad. Yeah, we're thinking of going up there Saturday. Why do you ask?"

"Well, it sounds pretty nice. I've just been thinking, doing a lot of thinking since . . .you know."

"I know, Dad."

Rupert couldn't refer to the recent, tragic death of his macaw in specific terms. The event had shaken him more than anything else in his adult life had, including hearing the news that his son had been arrested for felony organ trafficking. The computerized feeding system failed during one of his long weekends in Saranac Lake. When he returned to Grosse Pointe on that Sunday evening for another week of work, Rupert found his cherished pet rigid on the floor of its golden cage. He held a backyard funeral the next morning, a ceremony no one in the neighbor- hood attended, since there was no new entertainment gadget being revealed this time. He didn't go into work that week until Wednesday. His employees called the house repeatedly to make sure he was okay. After mourning all week, contemplating religion for the first time in his life, spending hours sobbing on the phone with Bethany, Rupert announced his semi-retirement to the Board Of Trustees at Scoreboard Franks that Friday. He made a short speech admitting the need for more time in the boonies with his wife, revealing their nickname for Bethany for the first time outside the walls of his house, to someone besides Markus.

"My macaw, I never actually named him, but that doesn't mean I didn't . . .well . . .love the little guy. He was like a second son, really." That was when the tears started forming. Rupert had never cried in front of anyone, not even Bethany. "We used to call my wife the Crazy Mad Baker. A little inside joke between me and the bird. And my son. We were right! Bethany is a crazy mad baker. But in a good way. And I'm still crazy mad in love with her. So today I'm letting you all know that I'll be spending more time in a little town in the middle of nowhere called Saranac Lake."

The Board accepted his decision unanimously. Rupert spent that weekend immersed in his mourning, finally cleaning up the cage, staying in his basement for three days straight, taking breaks from his depressing task to watch replays of the Chicago Bears' entire 1985 season in three dimensions.

"One thing I was thinking," Rupert told Markus over the phone, "was that maybe I could give another father-son talk a shot, since I sort of cheated the first time anyway, letting, you know . . .do the talking."

"I know."

"And, also, you're a little stuck right now. Like last time. Only different."

"Last time I wasn't a felon."

"Exactly! So I'm flying out there tomorrow. I was thinking that maybe all three of us can climb that Camel Hump thing. As far as your old man can make it, anyway. I'll try my hand at another father-son talk, the kind with a capital T, and mom can add her perspective. Whatever the heck you call the angle that woman is com -"

"All right, Dad. See you tomorrow. I'll pick you up at the airport. Just email me your flight info."

"Will do."

"Oh, and make sure you bring your bathing suit."

"Why? It's too cold to swim in that pond your mother lives on, isn't it?"

"We're doing a sweat lodge ceremony tomorrow night. A Lakota medicine man is here right now. They call him White Dancing Coyote."

"Oh. I see. Can I handle a sweat lodge?"

"Sure. You just sweat. And pray, I guess. Don't worry, I've never been in one of these things either. Just figured it's got to be easier than taking a med school exam. Then on Saturday morning we'll hike The Hump."

"Sounds like a plan, son."

"I can't wait, Dad."

So all three of them entered the sweat lodge at dusk that Friday evening, squeezing in with the group of half-naked, middle-aged women. Markus was the only one wearing a shirt. He hadn't told his parents about the clandestine transplant, and likely never would, so he had to hide the evidence of it. The darkness inside was punctuated by a pile of red glowing stones piled in a sunken pit, creating a primal light source that seemingly floated in the all-encompassing blackness. Sounds and sensations wound together; the hiss of steam; heat burning down their backs; earthy aromas of sweetgrass and sage smoke; Lakota prayer songs chanted over a low steady drumbeat. Thump. Thump. Thump. Thump. They all prayed out loud, first one at a time, and then together. They thanked ancestors and wild animals, Great Spirit, the sun and moon, the Four Directions, earth and sky, blood and bone, water and stone. The medicine man brushed them with the wing of a golden eagle to help their prayers take flight.

When it was all over Rupert was the last to emerge from the lodge, staggering up to the bonfire, eyes bloodshot, dripping sweat off every angle of his body. His face was radiant, glowing. It wasn't just a smile he wore. The closest word to describe his expression, Markus thought to himself, was pure joy. His father seemed happy to be alive.

"Hallelujah. That was absolutely amazing! I saw a white light. I died, I think, and then came back. And I saw Him!"

"Great Spirit?" Markus asked playfully.

"My macaw," Rupert stated. "He's in the Amazon. His heaven."

Bethany was standing close beside her new mentor, the master who'd so swiftly replaced Pierre Lufont's position in her life. The old Indian adjusted his balls, reaching a hand up and under his elk skin loin cloth.

"I should have sewn a pair of nice cotton briefs inside these things," he joked, elbowing Bethany in the bicep with his free arm, chuckling.

"They warned me you were a dirty old man," she teased.

"Only because we need a way to come back down to the ground. This old coyote is descended from a long line of Lakota medicine men. Staying grounded is my daily challenge. And yours, too."

"Why is it mine too?" Bethany asked, transforming into the eager student.

"People like you and me, the healers, if we get too serious it can all break down. Things become too overwhelming. You've got your bread. I've got my cigarettes," he said, locating his pouch of tobacco where it rested by the fire. He started rolling up a smoke.

Markus drifted over towards his mother. "Dad had quite the time in there huh?"

"He sure did. I thought he was going to pull a muscle in his throat while saying that prayer."

"More like shouting that prayer," Markus said. "Didn't know the guy had it in him."

"Honestly, Markus, neither did I."

He was about to tell his mother the decision he'd made inside the lodge, but instead kept his new plan to himself. No one else needed to know about it. No one would understand. Even he didn't fully comprehend the source of this idea, only the certainty that he must follow through on it soon.

The next morning the nuclear family trio hiked in silence for hours up the eastern side of Camel's Hump, all three reveling in the well-designed trail that meandered its way through the untouched forest. Markus wondered if his father was saving his promised talk for the summit. He preferred to get it over with, so he brought up his latest news while they took a break beside the small pond high on the mountain's shoulder.

"A couple of days ago I was contacted by a prospective transplant patient. The president of Dartmouth Medical College, a good friend of mine, gave him my number. He called me from Peru, the location of his current project. The guy's a seventy-two year old aquatic biologist. He's actually kind of famous. They call him Water Man. In certain scientific circles, anyway."

"So this guy needs a new heart?" Rupert asked, gazing with visible apprehension at the distinctive rounded rocky summit looming above the tranquil pond.

"He does. Along with a replacement liver. I guess he did a bunch of hallucinogens in the Amazon years ago, and did permanent damage to his liver. I'm not even sure he has heart disease. It might just be a natural deterioration from age. Either way, he's got one of those Lexus health insurance plans through National Geographic. They'll cover whatever any doctor orders."

Bethany spoke up for the first time that day. "They do say seventy is the new sixty," she joked.

"Exactly," Markus confirmed. "If I install one of my hearts inside him, this Water Man will have another twenty good years at least. He told me how he has a couple more rivers to study. The Mekong was one that he mentioned. I think that's next on his list."

"But son, didn't you lose your license to practice as part of this mess?" Rupert asked.

"In New Hampshire, yes. But Vermont has yet to take any action. And I've still got my operating room at home. The only problem is they took all my hearts."

"What hearts?" Rupert asked.

"That's a very long story, Dad. Read about them online. It's all there, I'm sure. The whole goddamn saga."

"But Markus, I've read every single article that's come out about you. None of them have mentioned any other hearts besides the one you stole out of the hospital."

"Hmm. That's strange. I had three of the most amazing home-grown hearts you could imagine, all cloned from that original one I took, hand-stitched and ready for transplant until they locked me up and confiscated them. I made those hearts from scratch!"

Markus grew sullen. The task of rebuilding something akin to his previous stable of pure hearts was a daunting one, especially now that his actions would be monitored very closely.

"Markus, please, don't do it," Bethany pleaded. "You've already lost enough."

"Let me talk to the boy," Rupert said.

"I'm a man, Dad," Markus corrected him.

"Okay, son. I'll buy that. But can we clear one thing up right away?"

"What's that?"

"Are you gay?" Rupert asked bluntly.

"Rupert!" Bethany spouted, shocked.

"No, Dad. I'm just wired a lot different than you are. Different than most guys I guess."

"Fair enough. Now, where were we -"

"Wait - if we're getting everything out on the table, I have to admit, I'm a Tigers fan. And I have been for many years now."

Rupert released a deep, defeated sigh. "That's fine, son. I'm over it already. I'm used to suffering as a Cubs fan all alone."

"Ok good."

"So," Rupert continued, "it sounds like operating on this Water Man would give you back some of the confidence you seem to have lost. Speaking of confidence, isn't it time you found a woman to marry? Maybe all of this mess wouldn't have happened if you were a married man, working on a family of your own. After all, the Greene line stops at you, Markus. Not to put any pressure on you or anything."

"It's okay. I've just been waiting to find my love."

"Maybe love isn't all that romantic, even when you do find it," Rupert quipped.

Bethany slapped her husband on the shoulder. "Of course it is!"

"What I mean when I say my love is exactly that," Markus explained. "I've been trying to locate my own true love, inside of myself, before I found one woman to give it too. I know this doesn't make much sense to you guys, but stealing that heart was part of this. I'm just going to leave it at that."

A silence followed. It was the kind of philosophical idea that didn't have a place in Rupert's worldview. Trying to be a good father, he worked hard at squeezing it into one of the cracks in his lifelong belief system, tiny fissures that had developed since the death of his macaw.

"Well, have you found it yet?" he asked, hanging on his son's answer with surprising intensity.

"I have, Dad. I just took the long road, like you said. Had to lose it all before finding it again."

"I think we all might do that," Bethany added, using the sage-like tone she'd been cultivating since moving to the wilderness.

"Well, then, there's no more time to waste, is there son?"

"No, there isn't. Except the woman I want to love is playing extremely hard to get."

"Maybe you should write her a poem," his mother suggested.

"I already did. Gave it to her right before I came up here. Maybe I'll do a painting for her next."

"Are you a painter now?" Rupert asked.

"Not yet. But I'm going to start learning. I think I need it. And a friend of mine might be able to teach me. He's a master, in the ultimate sense of that word."

Rupert stopped abruptly on the trail, which was now a steady incline of large stone steps.

"I'm glad to hear you would be interested in such a thing. There have been some in our family that possessed the gift for brushing paint on a canvas."

"Really? Who?" Markus asked eagerly.

Bethany shot her husband a look that implored him to stop there. Rupert ignored her.

"Your grandfather. And his father too."

"Do you have any of their paintings?" Markus asked.

"No. Your grandmother . . .never mind."

"So did the painting gene skip over you, Dad?"

Rupert shrugged. "Must have. I just never had the urge to try. Or the time."

Now Rupert had his own look for Bethany, a nonverbal message in the secret language of marriage that Markus didn't want them to translate for him.

"Maybe we could learn together," he proposed.

"We could," Rupert agreed, without missing a conversational beat. Bethany and Markus shared a glance of surprise over his new spontaneity. The trio continued marching on towards the summit in silence.

"So I can't help asking - who is this woman you're in love with?" Bethany asked eventually.

"My mentor, Dr. Kathryn Stone. You met her at my graduation from med school."

Bethany kicked at a root, and dropped her head. Rupert winced.

"I don't think she's the right one for you," Bethany said, gravely serious now.

"Why not?"

Both parents held ominous expressions, their shift in mood contrasting sharply with the overall vibe of the day up to that point.

"What's up guys?" Markus prodded.

Rupert turned to his wife, giving her the floor. She closed her eyes.

"Dr. Stone turned you in for stealing that girl's heart, Markus," Bethany said solemnly.

Markus was beyond shocked. "How do you know?"

"It's been all over the papers. And the television."

"I haven't been reading the papers. Or watching T.V."

"I know."

They were in a spot called Wind Gap, a high, forested rift between The Hump and another large summit to the south. Markus refused to continue onward to the pinnacle of his beloved mountain. He urged his parents to make the final climb to the summit without him. He told them that he couldn't be up there in his current state of mind, knowing it would forever taint the special place Camel's Hump held in his heart. Or, more accurately, in his memory, because his new heart hadn't altered his charmed memories of the dramatic summit, the most sacred place in his world. He didn't need the escape of it right now. No. He needed Kathryn, hugged tight into his still-healing chest, enveloped in the love spilling out from his heart once again. His love. He returned to Saranac Lake with his parents, passing up an opportunity to stop at his farmhouse, eager for a little more rest in a place where he had no personal history to drag him down.

Markus Jr.

A WEEK AFTER THE HIKE Markus drove himself from Saranac Lake to Hartford fueled by a clear purpose, acting on the concrete decision he'd made in the sweat lodge. He was going to come clean, and then apologize. If his parents were right about all the news coverage his case had been getting, the parents of that dead little girl must certainly know what he'd done. The media had even nick- named him Dr. Franken-nuts. He hadn't called ahead to tell them he was coming. The couple was all smiles when they opened the front door of their tidy suburban house in West Hartford. They led him into the kitchen. There was a portable crib resting on a table. Tucked into the blankets was a baby boy no more than six months old.

"We named him Markus Jr. After you, Doctor Greene," the mother announced.

"You named your baby after me? Why? I've done a horrible thing! I came here to confess to you guys in person, to beg your forgiveness."

"What horrible thing?" the father asked.

"I had your daughter's heart transplanted into me," Markus blurted. "To restore my love. This was a very selfish thing to do, so I came here to apol -"

He had to stop speaking because the mother was taking hold of his head in both hands. She stood up on her tiptoes, and stared into his eyes.

"Honey! Come here!" she called out to her husband, who came swiftly to her side.

"What are you doing Ma'm?" Markus mumbled helplessly.

"I see her! Look, David. Our little girl. She's living inside you, Doctor Greene."

The husband nodded with absolute certainty. "I do. There she is," he said, pointing into one of Markus' brown eyes.

The couple backed away a few steps. Markus blinked.

"We named our new baby boy after you, Doctor Greene," the mother said. "Because you tried to keep our daughter's heart alive, even if it meant breaking the law. And you succeeded. She is alive. Inside of you!"

Markus looked down at his feet. He had to let them believe in this fantasy, one he didn't completely disagree with. Their daughter was living on through him, in some way no one would ever be able to measure, her DNA intertwining with his own during every heartbeat. But he wasn't who they thought he was, and wanted to make that clear.

"I won't be a surgeon much longer. New Hampshire has already stripped me of my license to operate. And the other forty-nine states will likely follow soon."

"You'll always be a surgeon," the mother said.

"That's right," the husband confirmed, crossing his arms to finalize the couple's firm opinion.

And Markus decided to believe them.

After leaving their house, instead of heading back to Saranac Lake for more down time like he'd planned, Markus drove in the direction of Dartmouth. But he didn't exit the highway at Hanover, realizing there was no place there for him to go there, forcing himself not to consider a knock on Kathryn's front door as an option. And neither was crashing like a bum at the president's house. So he continued on into Vermont, suddenly craving his own bed. When he finally arrived back home for the first time in over a month, he took a moment in the driveway to admire the bright stars. Then he went into the house. He had the urge to take one look at the operating room before going upstairs. Once inside, the shining space illuminated, he saw that nothing was changed. He couldn't help walking over to his row of mini-fridges, surprised they were actually still there. He opened them all, just for the hell of it, thinking they might need to air out a little. What he found inside one of the refrigerators shocked him so intensely he placed a hand on his chest to make sure his new heart hadn't pounded itself loose inside him. It was one of his hearts. And someone had been feeding it. Markus knew right away who it was.

He wondered briefly about what had happened to the other two, deciding they must not have survived the gap of time between his arrest and Kathryn's first secret visit to his basement operating room. He would ask her about them the next time they spoke. At least he still had one heart, although there would be no time to use it for cloning any new ones, not if this Water Man was really going to come for a transplant. Shrugging off the knowledge that he would have to start his project all over again from scratch, Markus went upstairs to scribble down the poem that was already writing itself in his head.

OUR TIME

> ticking time ticks forward in
> little pushes
> think-think, make-make
> something
> all the nows of every moment
> are a forceful fight against

> Real Time

> backsliding oval time that
> feels good on the fingers

let's control
we, you and me can shape it
malleable
from the tick-tock torture
into aaahhh
long, lifesong second laughs
and endless
      spiral
          putty

3

WATER MAN

The Ese' Wa

THE ESE' WA PEOPLE, inhabiting the banks of the Rio Tambopata in the Peruvian Amazon, were the mixed descendants of mestizo settlers and the Ese'eja indigenous people native to the area. They maintained some of the old ceremonies and rituals of the Ese'eja, but had also developed new ones, as well as their own distinct language. They lived on the upper reaches of the Tambopata, where the Andes gave way to jungle, water-soaked forests swallowing the stone. Their villages were far enough away from the jungle city of Puerto Maldanado to never encounter tourists. Only the occasional scientist would venture beyond the remote Tambopata Research Center and into their territory. The Ese' wa's most recent ceremony was a celebration that took place during a 48-hour span of time following the longer rainy season. They smoked dried coca leaves and danced, sang songs and drank fermented cassava root, actions performed to honor the White Water Man. He was their Jesus, a modern day savior who'd materialized just in time. The centerpiece of the ritual was a life size effigy of Dr. Jacob Pearlman they'd constructed out of bamboo and twigs and some clothes the scientist had left behind more than thirty years ago. An entire generation of Ese' wa had grown up since the 1970's, when Jacob came to live in the village, but the ceremony was maintained with strict allegiance to its original form, one that had been passed down by the elders. The men sang songs honoring his bravery and intelligence, praising their gods for the gift of his visit. The women's songs were more wistful in tone, the eldest among them yearning for another chance to impress him, one especially more fervently than all the others, while the younger girls expressed hope for his return, and with it a shot at a fruitful courtship with the man who'd rescued their river before they were born into the jungle along its banks.

Na-oosh. The water in a river. The Ese' wa had many words for water. *Oosh-wa* were raindrops. A rainy season forest swamp was simply *oosh*. A man was *doh*. So they called Jacob *Na-oosh-doh*. The Water Man. He took the time to learn their language while also learning their river, aware he couldn't know one without the other. A few weeks after his arrival Jacob had his own palm-thatched hut, which he'd helped construct, and could communicate basic information with the Ese' wa in their tongue. One day the *ama*, the chief, called Jacob into his palatial dwelling in the center of the village. The large, squat man was seated beside a fire of glowing coals. His torso was painted in an array of red and black patterns. A single jaguar tooth hung from his neck. His long black hair fell in a thick braid down his back. A simple piece of fabric woven from vicuna fibers covered his groin. Jacob approached the ama tentatively, taking a seat on the offered stump. He'd yet to adopt the Ese' wa's clothing. He wore his khaki cargo pants, vented fisherman's shirt, Teva sandals, and a wide brimmed hat. Jacob took off the hat and placed it beside his feet in a gesture of respect.

"Anoh, Ama," he said. "Anoh, Na-oosh-dah."

They passed the *chongo*, a clay pipe, back and forth a number of times. Jacob enjoyed smoking the dried coca leaves. They gave him a clear buzz, jolting his mind awake like a shot of double espresso. Eventually the ama placed the chongo on its altar beside the fire. He proceeded to tell Jacob that, in the eyes of the elders, it was time to offer him a *woo-dah* of his choice. Jacob quickly realized that he was being told, not asked, to pick one of the village's available teenage virgins for himself. She would be his local wife, his *lum-woo*. She would live in his hut, and prepare his meals when he returned from his long days on the river. He and Sandy, the mother of his son, still weren't officially divorced, but explaining this to the chief would have been impossible. There was nothing he could do but accept the offer. Anything else would have been worse than rude.

"Asanti, Ama," he said, bowing.

The chief rose to his feet, eager not to waste any more time. "Va aya," he said. Go outside. "O woo-dah tick-tock."

Jacob scrunched his brow as he stood up, curious about the source of the chief's word for waiting, obvious proof that he was not the first westerner to spend substantial time with the Ese' wa. He would ask the chief about this another time. Right now he had to go and choose himself a woo-dah. Because time was ticking.

The Tambopata

OVER THREE DECADES LATER, having reached his 72nd year on the planet earth, Dr. Jacob Pearlman found himself pondering various one-liners that might be etched on his tombstone. Lately he'd been having trouble taking a deep breath. And then there were the chest pains he was trying to ignore. But no one lived forever, and he couldn't think of anyone who knew him well enough to come up with a few accurate words worthy of being carved forever in stone as the final bookend to his life. And there was also his long-held opinion that the permanence of stone was an illusion. A person only had to glimpse the Grand Canyon to understand that rock was no match to water's enduring effect over time. But someone would likely want to memorialize him in stone words, believing in their finality even if Jacob never would. That an entire lifetime could be summarized by a sentence or two struck him as absurd. Jacob had come to terms with his mortality decades before, after ingesting aya-huasca in the depths of the Peruvian Amazon, a place he'd recently returned to at the request of National Geographic. New data from Nasa satellites made a case for the Amazon overtaking the Nile as the longest river in the world. Jacob was to make a firsthand visit to the great river's original source high in the Andes. Summing up his life in one sentence was eluding him every time he tried to come up with something. But this morning he felt a specific sentence begin to emerge. The words seemed to rise up from the glacier-born water rushing over boulders below his thatch-roofed hut, the same one he'd inhabited, along with his teenage lover Inez, thirty years before. *IN WATER HE FOUND THE TRUTH.* He wrote these six words down on a page of his research notebook, closed it, and turned his attention to other things.

The sun, already hot, was rising up over the snow-cloaked Andes, signaling the end to dawn, Jacob's favorite part of the day. Thirty years ago Inez would have been stirring to life in the other room. He downed the last of his coca tea, reminiscing about his indigenous wife. Like some other Ese' wa girls, an odd curving bulge of bone extended out from her lower back. She was able to satisfy his attraction to this feature, something concrete to hold onto during what had been some inspired lovemaking sessions. But neither Inez nor the chief had volunteered to share what they knew about this strange phenomenon. It was as if some ancient appendage had stopped fully developing somewhere along the ancestral line. Eventually, unable to contain his curiosity, Jacob had paid a visit to the village shaman on the outskirts of the community, along the thin line between civilization and wilderness. The shaman convinced him to take the ayahuasca, and the hallucinogen showed him, among many other things, how there was a distant link between women like Inez and the mystical pink river dolphins of the Amazon River, an evolutionary crossover his scientist's mind was at first unable to fully believe. Until the day of his departure, when Inez proved its validity.

He could see from his little front porch how the daylight was changing the river's color from sandy brown to a more emerald hue. Jacob folded his hands atop the leather-bound journal. If water had led him to the truth, he was thinking, then the truth had led him, ultimately, back to the Amazon. Would this be his last river, a final intimate union, one more climactic journey from outlet to source? Every river he'd come to know over the course of his career, from the Nile to the Ganges, the Mississippi to the Yangtze, had led him back here, to this land teeming with caimans and jaguars, smiling natives, and the restless ghosts of Inca kings. And every woman in his life had led him to this state of acute loneliness. He would never know what it was like to have a life partner. That security and comfort of routine love, day after day, year after year. It had been a fair trade, with some loneliness inherent to the deal. But this was his first time on a great river without a local woman sharing his space, smoothing out the rough edges of his days on the water. His mind arched back once again to Inez, how he used to feel the heat of her gaze on the back of his neck while he focused forward, on the view of the ancient river below, where he would watch his woman scoop up buckets of its green-brown water. Then that cool silky liquid would be flowing down across his bare shoulders, massaged into his still taught skin by her strong and tender hands. Then, after the bath, Jacob would venture out into the day.

There would be no bath this morning, but the day still called him into action. He was supposed to be making his way towards the newly revised source of the Amazon, a glacial stream spilling off Nevado Mismi, a peak high in the Peruvian Andes, making the Amazon now the world's longest river in addition to being its largest. But Jacob had detoured up the Tambopata, once again off the route he was supposed to be taking, for a visit with his old friends. He needed a rest. There was something very wrong with his heart. He was spending most of his days downstream at the famous clay lick, a giant wall of orange mud that attracted thousands of macaws from all over the jungle every morning at dawn. Jacob had taken to perching in the camouflaged blinds above the lick, which National Geographic had used for a photo shoot of the spectacular event a few years ago. Great flocks of multi-colored birds, not only macaws but parrots and parakeets of all kinds, descended upon the cliff from various corners of the vast tropical rain forest. Something about the birds helped him forget about the pains in his chest. The macaws, practically stunning enough to survive off their beauty alone, had an undeniable optimism about them as they busied themselves sucking the salt out of the clay. Thinking about his son also helped him ignore the chest pains. Before leaving the cabin he would tap out another email to Eddie on the satellite cellphone he was still trying to figure out how to use. Jacob was certain that once the kid got a taste of the rivers he'd be permanently hooked. It was in the Pearlman genetic code. Rivers ran in Jacob's blood, so he must have passed this on to his only son. He had to at least find out.

During some of his more reflective moments alone on his rivers Jacob sometimes liked to daydream about aliens. He would imagine that if they did exist, and had discovered the earth, then they were probably observing humans with absolute confusion, and perhaps disbelief. He wondered if they might be thinking that homo sapiens were made up of numerous sub-species. There were the bankers and lawyers and doctors, the car mechanics and professors, athletes and carpenters. And there were the scientists. Jacob pictured himself as being part of a specific sub-group of scientists, one of a wide-ranging band of eccentric nerds spread out around the globe, consumed with the task of cataloging and documenting the ill-effects being imposed upon the planet by their fellow humans. Although Jacob didn't start out his career with such work in mind, his research had evolved to focus primarily on the degradation of rivers as a result of human activity. These activities occurred not only on the rivers themselves, upstream and downstream and everywhere in between, but on other continents as well, transported by the clouds, dropped in the rain. Pollution, like the nature it polluted, was all connected. That was how he'd come to know the Ese' wa people three decades before, when he'd veered off course from the main branch of the Amazon to pursue a band of illegal gold miners who were roaming the upper reaches of the Tambopata, greatly damaging what had been a pure and untarnished ecosystem.

Jacob was proud to belong to this cohort of colleagues he'd invented to make his career feel less isolated, and figured that if these curious aliens actually did lump people into categories, they might respect, and maybe even feel sorry for, scientists like himself. He still couldn't help the fleeting flashes of mid-life crises he was far too late to indulge in, nagging thoughts that told him it was pointless to be documenting the deterioration of the natural world, that the group of humans he should belong to instead were the ones engaged with inventing solutions to the problem of too many people, the windmill builders and solar panel designers. But these moments of doubt were few and far between. He was able to avoid feeling guilty because during the first half of his career the rivers had been so much healthier, the planet so much cleaner than it was now. To be studying them all for his job had been living a dream come true. Pushing paper in an office cubicle was Jacob Pearlman's version of hell. Only recently had things reached the crescendo of a crisis. All the rules were changing. Climate change was affecting everything. That was where Eddie came in. His son could pick up where he was leaving off, with the chance to live a purposeful life helping to save the world's greatest rivers, to resurrect them from the dead. Jacob could teach him everything he knew before he died. The only problem was that his son was a stock trader on Wall Street. And if Jacob didn't get a new heart soon, he wouldn't be around to pass along anything onto the kid beyond the six words he wanted carved on his own tombstone.

IN WATER HE FOUND THE TRUTH. But truth was not Jacob Pearlman's ultimate goal. He always wanted what the rivers gave him. Freedom. This was the most important thing in the end. Freedom, for Jacob, was the ultimate precursor to happiness. But after a lifetime spent pursuing these aqueous avenues of liberation, his spirit suddenly felt constrained. The source of Jacob's sudden confinement was the paternal burden in his head. He was being steadily consumed by an overwhelming internal pressure to ensure his legacy would continue on through Eddie, that his body of work would keep growing after his physical body was gone. And Eddie was the key ingredient in this plan. But there was so much to do before that could happen. First he had to get a new heart, the one waiting for him in northern

Vermont. If he recovered, a big if at his age, the ultimate challenge would then loom. His son would have to be extricated from the life he'd constructed for himself to inhabit, an existence built out of raw materials Jacob could only view as tenuous: the glass and steel of the skyscraper headquarters of Goldman Sachs, the brick and drywall of his Westchester mansion, the eight-year, dead-end relationship with his college girlfriend. It would all crumble over time. Jacob's carefully chosen words, the Rio Tambopata, and the world's most powerful hallucinogen would be the trio of catalysts to make his son's world disintegrate faster than it otherwise might have. He just had to convince the kid to fly down here.

His original study of the Amazon had progressed from mouth to source. It was the direction Jacob had chosen to study every river since his first, the Mississippi, which culminated in a chemical stew spilling into the Gulf Of Mexico. This strategy enabled him to get the most polluted, depressing end over with so he could finish his journey in a place of relative purity, where there was never any need to test for man-made chemicals, where he could spend ample time catching enough fish for a worthy feast with the locals. Jacob's work day on any river usually drifted towards a conclusion in peaceful silence, content with the wandering of his own mind. And today this meant slowly shifting his thoughts from the Tambopata to Inez. She was still in the village, hadn't married, and was barely fifty years old. It was a natural mental transition.

Jacob rebuilt her out of memory every day, wondering how long he could go without visiting her hut, knowing she would take him in her arms. Like every woman he'd been with over the course of his life, she was a human extension of the river he was currently studying. Her eyes reflected the burnt emerald colors of its depths. Her movements in their bed had the strength of its swift current. Her personality was complicated, shifting from the purity of a source to the complex muddle of an outlet, containing rapids and pools and everything in between. Her liquid voice washed over him during the hours of night, allowing him to feel as if he'd never really left this river at the end of the day. At least this was how it had been all those years ago.

Today, just before leaving his hut for a boat ride down to the clay lick, he finally received a reply from Eddie after weeks of messaging him. *Hi Dad. Good news. I'll be in Lima in three days.* Jacob let out an uninhibited holler of pure joy, then made his way down the great set of stairs to his research boat tied up along the bank. He descended the stairs faster than usual, his entire being consumed with the imminent appearance of his son. The village chief, a son of the former chief who'd given Jacob the name Water Man, was waiting for him at the bottom of the stairs.

"My son's coming, Chief! I don't even know what he looks like," Jacob said in between deep breaths of humid air as they climbed into the boat. "Haven't seen the kid in years."

"So it will be a great surprise for you then, yes?"

Jacob turned to smile at one of his loyal friend, an allegiance that had been passed down from one generation to the next.

"Yes, it will. My son will be as much a surprise today as he was on the day of his birth, when his mother squeezed him out onto a muddy beach on the bank of the Mississippi. I half expected him to resemble a catfish more than a person."

The chief chuckled. "I hope you do not expect him to look like a fish this time."

"True. I expect him to look like a man."

Eddie

EDDIE PEARLMAN considered himself a survivor. He'd survived the pressures of Harvard Law School, had endured the stress of building a Wall Street career within the bowels of Manhattan, and had lived through the traumatic repercussions of September 11, 2001. But lately his spacious, well-appointed office on the 53rd floor of the Goldman Sachs building, a space that had always felt safe to him in a way his suburban house in Westchester never did, was no longer a haven from life's frequent storms. After scaling the first few rungs it had been a relatively easy climb to reach this plateau, one version of ultimate American success. All he'd had to do was endure a couple years of eighty-hour work weeks, engage in some blatant ass-kissing in a few board room meetings, and sacrifice a few long Sunday afternoons playing golf. Eddie despised golf. But these were such small prices to pay for the guaranteed security of being a company man. Now all of a sudden this towering building didn't feel like it was made out of steel and concrete, but constructed instead out of the same vaporous cyber-documents of credit derivatives he and his colleagues had been emailing around the world in pursuit of massive profits. His home away from home felt less stable than a house of cards.

His father had been trying to get in touch with him for weeks. This was a rare thing for two reasons. Dr. Pearlman didn't believe in the culture of the world his son had given himself over to, and the man rarely had access to email or a phone. The famous aquatic biologist shunned technology, a habit that only added to his allure among the scientific community, as well as the average reader of National

Geographic. But lately there had been an email or voice mail message almost every day. Eddie's father was worried about him. News of the global financial meltdown had even reached his remote outpost above some tributary of the Amazon. Today Eddie decided it was time to reply. He'd been putting off a response until he felt able to muster something positive for his dad to hold onto. Earlier that morning, while being driven to his office in a shiny Lincoln Town Car, he came up with a spontaneous plan of action. He would jump the sinking ship of Wall Street, accept one of the CEO's generous severance packages, and go someplace where the money might be consid- ered a small fortune, some Caribbean beach front locale, a mellow place where he could open up a little bar, and learn how to surf. The first thing Eddie did upon arriving at work was email this decision to his father. Before leaving his office that evening to head upstairs for a late meeting with his boss to announce his decision, a reply appeared in his inbox. *Come to Peru. I need an assistant.* It was such a shocking invitation that Eddie kept refreshing the browser on his laptop. The words came back each time, the dark blue capital letters indicating the request was not being made lightly.

Eddie got up from his desk and walked over to the wall of floor-to-ceiling windows. He gazed out at the maze of towering buildings, their window lights making an abstract pattern, giant rectangular fireflies frozen in mid-flash. His focus was drawn through a gap between a set of skyscrapers to a view of the Hudson, gray and wide, contained in the straight concrete channel, making its steady way to the sea. His father had never done one of his famous river profiles on the Hudson. For the first time in his life, Eddie wondered why. He thought he had an idea. It wasn't the fact that the river wasn't long enough, or interesting enough, to warrant his father's time and effort. Dr. Pearlman had no doubt avoided the river because it would have brought him too close to his son for comfort. The old man must have changed, Eddie thought. Or maybe not. Maybe their reunion had to take place on Jacob's terms, in some strange land, with his mistress of the year at his beck and call, and an ancient river close by to absorb their silences, to wash away the gap of space between them, and provide an illusion of closeness.

Eddie had to force himself into the elevator. The ride up to the top floor office of the CEO seemed to last many minutes, when in reality it was no more than twenty seconds. He tightened his tie, wiped a scuff mark off the tip of a shoe. He couldn't help feeling like the Armani suit he was wearing was a kind of second skin, that when he took it off later he would be like a newborn baby, clueless and vulnerable, unsure of how to move back out into the world. But that was later. For the moment he still had the suit on, was still a mid-level banker with the Wall Street giant.

The elevator stopped at the twenty-second floor with a ding. The door slid open. Eddie walked up to a winding polished counter occupied by one of his boss' three full time secretaries. The other two had gone home for the night.

"You must be Eddie," said the cheery blond woman with black glasses.

"I sure am, Ma'am."

She beckoned towards a great, polished wooden door that was cracked just slightly open. "He's expecting you. Go right on in."

"Thanks."

He took in a nervous breath as he stepped up to the door, pushed it open, and walked in. Basil Rogers, a man Eddie had only met in person once, rose up from behind a large mahogany desk. His bushy white hair contrasted sharply with his tan face. He reached out a hand. Eddie stepped up and shook it, hard and long. Basil grinned.

"I like a man with a good strong hand shake. Please, take a seat."

Dropping back down into his swivel chair, the CEO gestured at one of the two leather sofa chairs facing his desk. As he took a seat, Eddie glanced around the sprawling office. It seemed barren, with many blank gaps on the white walls, empty spaces on the floor where there should have been furniture.

"Used to be a lot plusher in here, Pearlman. I had to sell a lot of the décor recently on Ebay so I don't get grilled by congress, like that poor sap over at Merrill with the antique trash can!"

"Good idea, sir," Eddie said.

"So what can I do for you?" Basil clapped his hands with the question. "I know you didn't schedule a meeting to hear me complain about my interior decorating issues."

Eddie could feel his palms sweating as doubt flooded his mind. There was nothing to do but leap forward.

"I would like to take one of the buyout settlements you're offering."

Basil nodded slowly. He leaned back in his chair. His nodding gradually evolved into a shaking of his head.

"You're one of our best and brightest, Pearlman. I never expected you to volunteer to jump ship. What are you going to do?"

Eddie coughed into a fist. Even as he said the words he didn't believe they were coming from his own mouth.

"I'm going to Peru. To help my father on the Amazon River."

Eddie stood up, prepared to leave. There was nothing else to say.

"Well, I'll be damned!" The beaming Irishman rose out of his chair, circled his great desk, and slapped Eddie's upper back. "That's the best thing I've heard in a long time."

"It is?"

Basil took a step back. He cocked his head to one side, taking in the sight of his now former employee, assessing what he saw.

"Tell me though, kid, why do you have the fear of the devil in your eyes?"

Eddie looked down at his feet. It took him a great effort of will to look back up and stare the powerful man straight in the eyes.

"I thought this company was going to be the foundation of my whole life, sir. But today I couldn't feel the floor of my office under my feet. It's like everything I've ever believed in is crumbling to pieces all around me."

"Well, to be honest, it is. You're making a great decision to get out while you can. Me, I'm a Lifer. And in all my life spent climbing up this giant ladder, I've never seen it this bad. But I am the captain, so I have to go down with my ship. Take the money and run, Pearlman. Go hang out with your pops on the river, and stop looking like a jaguar's going to eat you. Because even if one does, that'd be a damn good way to go out!"

Eddie cracked a smile. He reached out a hand for a final firm shake. "Thank you, sir."

Basil winked. "Your check is in the mail, kid. Now get on outta here, and don't ever come back!"

The changes in Eddie's life began immediately. He no longer had a personal driver, what had been his most recent perk. So his girlfriend picked him up outside the Goldman headquarters shortly after his meeting had ended. Hannah was nervous behind the wheel, navigating her little Honda through the streets of Manhattan. He figured she was wondering why he'd asked her to come get him instead of having his driver take him home. Eddie had planned to cut all his ties in one fell swoop that evening, but he wanted to wait at least until they got out of the city to break up with his girlfriend of eight years. He breathed with a secret, silent relief that she hadn't taken him up on his suggestion of being a stay-at-home fiance, something he'd proposed after his latest raise. Hannah was a full-time social worker. She enjoyed her job. So he wouldn't be hanging her completely out to dry. He looked at her hands clenched tight around the steering wheel as she drove them up Madison Avenue.

"I can drive if you want," Eddie proposed tentatively.

"I've got it."

"Okay."

"How was the meeting?"

"Oh, fine. The CEO is quite a character. Goofy Irish guy named Basil. I'd never said a word to him before today."

There was a long silence as Hannah focused on making the turns required to get them onto the Triborough Bridge.

"And what was this meeting about?" she asked.

"I'll tell you when we get home."

Something in his voice must have given him away. Her jaw clenched. Her eyes narrowed. The car sped up through the thick traffic now enveloping them.

"Just tell me. If you wait, I might crash."

Eddie believed her, and spoke up quick. "I quit today. Took one of the half-million dollar severance packages being offered by the company. On Monday I'll clean out my office. Done. Goodbye."

Hannah eased up on the gas pedal. Her face softened. She turned to him with a soft smile.

"That's great news, Eddie. What are we going to do? Travel Europe?"

Might as well get it all over with, Eddie thought, his eyes glancing down at the air bag sign in front of him.

"I'm going to Peru, alone, to be my father's assistant. Alone."

His girlfriend pulled over into the breakdown lane. The car shook as the traffic whizzed past.

"Get out."

Her voice sounded like it belonged to an entirely different woman from the one Eddie had been with for the past eight years. He reached into the back seat, grabbed his briefcase, and dutifully climbed out of the little car. The hatchback disappeared quickly into the rushing stream of cars, leaving him standing there in his black Armani suit breathing exhaust fumes.

Eddie Pearlman certainly didn't trust the average New Yorker enough to hitchhike his way home. So he walked the seventeen miles, all day and through the night, arriving at his Westchester driveway around eight o'clock the next morning, his clothes frayed and dusty, his leather shoes scuffed and tattered. He wasn't surprised to find the house empty, and most of Hannah's things gone, includ-

ing her Siamese cat. After searching the house, he dropped his briefcase on the marble kitchen counter, sat down on a bar stool, and
cried. Eddie's tears had many sources: self-pity, guilt, doubt, regret,
fear, and the throbbing pain in his feet. He tried to think of something he could do to calm himself. He thought about calling his
mother, or his old college buddy Pete, but decided he wasn't ready
to talk to anyone. He pulled his blackberry out of his suit jacket
pocket. The little device had grown to become a kind of security
blanket amidst the hectic shuffle of his life. When traveling for work
he slept with it lying on the pillow next to him in the hotel bed.
But his G-mail inbox account didn't provide him with the usual
peace of mind. Checking his stock positions held no allure. He put
the phone down on the cold counter. Grabbed the remote to the
kitchen T.V. Turned it on. The channel was set to CNBC, his favorite network. The streaming blue and white stock prices and the pun-
dits' loud voices, things that usually never failed to soothe him, now
only added to his inner panic. He clicked off the screen and stood
up. His house was striking him as a giant a maze of empty cavernous
space. He spent the next few hours pacing about its entirety, mutter-
ing to himself like a crazy person, finally heaving his body onto one
of the guest beds that had never been used, where he passed out into
a deep, nightmare-laden sleep.

The first thing Eddie did when he woke up late that afternoon
was masturbate. He thought of Hannah the entire forty-two seconds it took him to come. Then he indulged in a long, hot shower.
Downstairs, he again located his Blackberry. This time he went
straight to a travel site, found a one-way ticket for Lima that left
on Tuesday, and purchased it with the corporate Amex Basil hadn't
asked him to give back. Then he cut the credit card up with scissors,
made himself a toasted bagel with cream cheese, and ate it. Feeling
slightly comforted, Eddie reached again for the phone, and called
his mother.

Father & Son

GIVEN THE WIDE-RANGING, adventurous life he'd led, most of his acquaintances assumed that Dr. Jacob Pearlman had little in the way of a daily routine. Those who'd known him closely, however, mostly women indigenous to the rivers he'd studied, were aware that he stuck to a strict regimen every day he was on a job. Jacob always woke before dawn, an actual time that varied a great deal based on his location in the world. He would get out his round orange cushion and meditate for about twenty minutes, doing his best to let go of every thought that rose up into his mind, most of them having to do with freshwater resources. Then he would do forty minutes of yoga. It was something he'd once done with vigorous exertion, but his practice had evolved over the years into more like an extensive session of stretching. While daylight broke his woman would be preparing a pot of whatever local tea was available, which he'd drink on whatever porch he had while going over his charts and notes for the upcoming day of research. In the evening Jacob liked to have one strong drink, something unique to the locality, arak in Egypt, rice wine in China. In Peru it was a clay mug of cassava beer. After dinner he liked to enjoy a cigar with a good view of the stars. Then it would be time for making love. Finally he would lie in bed reading, usually his favorite magazine *Aquatic Explorer*, until sleep carried him off into his dreams. Jacob had been moving through his life this way for most of the past forty years, until he invited his son to come visit him in Peru. He couldn't wait to tell Eddie some of his stories. These tales began with the Mississippi, which he'd nicknamed Twain's River. They ended, at least for now, here on the Tambopata. But Jacob was determined not to let this be the end of his career. He would need his son and a new heart, in that order, to ensure this wish came true.

It was a two-day journey by boat to pick up Eddie in the jungle outpost city of Puerto Maldonado. Like his college road trips had once done, a multi-day river trip never failed to inspire his mind to roam. With the chief there, who'd insisted on accompanying the scientist, Jacob had a pair of ears available to take in his musings. His most common subject, of course, was the rivers he'd studied all over the world. And although it hadn't been his favorite one, a distinction still held by the Amazon, the river he most often brought up was the Mississippi.

"That river has more soul than a lot of people I've known," Jacob announced on their first morning of travel. "Starts out all crisp and clear, still lookin' like the headwaters Lewis & Clark paddled in, full of rainbow trout, swelled by tears from the ghosts of Lakota squaws. She finishes muddy, infused with jazz and Cajun spices, giving dirty brown birth to rice paddies and shrimp farms and the jazz-playing descendants of slaves. Yup, Twain's River is as diverse as the United States herself."

The chief was obviously fascinated by Jacob's words, barely half of which he understood. The next afternoon, on the way back upriver Eddie proved to be much less enchanted about his father's rivers. Especially the Mississippi.

"My son grew up in the bayou," Jacob informed the chief. "Swamps not a whole lot different from these jungles out here."

Jacob was making an initial foray into deeper subjects beyond the practical small-talk during the airport pickup and the logistics of getting back on the river. His son did look more like a man than he'd had a few years earlier, the last time Jacob had laid eyes on him, at Eddie's graduation from law school. But that wasn't saying much. Eddie still had the look of a college kid who hadn't ventured outside his comfort zone much at all. Until now, maybe. At least he was making the effort.

"Must have been some kinda' neat childhood growin' up in those bayou swamps, eh Eddie?" Jacob continued.

"I hated those swamps," Eddie stated, tugging at his Polo shirt, trying to keep it from sticking to his skin dampened by the humidity. "I couldn't wait to get the hell out of there so I could take a breath without sucking in a bunch of mosquitoes."

"Ahh," Jacob said, linking his hands behind his head. "So you wound up in New York City, where you can't take a breath without sucking in a bunch of smog."

The chief chuckled at this, drawing a sharp glare from Eddie.

"New York City is in the past now, Dad."

"Good. That's where it belongs. A man can be shaped by many places. I was molded into what I've become by the currents of so many rivers. Twain's River taught me how to feel, son. A big city can't teach a man anything except how to close himself up. How to build walls to seal off his insides from all that chaos."

Eddie fired without warning. "Did the Mississippi teach you how to abandon your family too?" he asked.

Jacob leaned over to place a hand on his son's shoulder. "No. The river had nothing to do with that. If anything, the Mississippi was telling me to stay. Your mother's a great woman. I gave her up in exchange for the life I've had. My career. It was an equal trade. A fair bargain. And I haven't spent a whole lotta' time looking back. Until now, that is."

"What do you see now?" Eddie asked, laying his free hand on top of his father's.

"I see Twain's River in you, son. The Mississippi made me a man. Even before I met your mother. That strong Midwestern sun baked my skin into something more like the texture of a crawfish shell. I lived on raw catfish and rainwater for weeks. Got robbed at knife point by a couple of escaped convicts in a rubber raft just south of St. Louis. Gave 'em everything except my data. They wanted that too, who knows why, maybe they thought they could sell it for something. Slashed my arm from shoulder to elbow. See the scar?"

Eddie moved over for a close look at the battle wound.

"How'd you get out of that one, Dad?" Eddie asked, his interest in his father's past suddenly perking a little.

Jacob grinned with pride. "Popped their silly raft with a fishing hook. The bastards could barely swim!"

"Sweet."

"It was pretty sweet, son. I was about the same age as you are now, maybe a little younger."

"Hmm."

"Did your mother tell you how that saga ended?" Jacob asked.

"No, Dad. She never really talked about you."

"Oh. Well she was the nurse who stopped the bleeding in the ER until the doc could stitch me up."

"Sounds romantic," Eddie said sarcastically.

"It was, actually. So when your mom came back to check on me, after the doctor was finished sewing me up, I asked her out," Jacob said with obvious pride.

Eddie was looking off into the jungle, trying hard to seem uninterested.

"She said yes, of course," Jacob continued, unprompted. "The day after she took out my stitches, I took her out on Twain's River in my research boat. At night. We had a candlelight dinner on the water. Under the stars."

"Catfish?" Eddie asked dryly.

Jacob shook his head. "Steak."

Eddie released a frustrated sigh.

"What's the matter, son? You don't want to hear about our courtship?"

"Mom already told me more than I ever wanted to know."

"Oh did she? I thought you said she never talked about me. So what would you rather talk about then?"

"Your rivers."

"Great subject! Fire away, son."

"Well, what made the Mississippi your favorite one?"

Jacob crossed one leg over another. He ran a hand through his white hair.

"That's a good question. Perhaps there are a few reasons. It was my first river. My virgin expedition. It's America's river. And I'm an American. But looking back, maybe the best thing was that aside from that encounter with the convicts, my life wasn't being continually threatened, not by diseases or poisonous creatures or armed guerrillas, like it has been ever since."

"Makes sense," Eddie said.

"And Twain's River's got soul, son. That's all there is to it."

"Does the Amazon have a soul?" the chief asked.

Jacob smiled. He uncrossed his legs, tapping one foot on the floor of the boat. "Oh yes, it sure does. Maybe the most soul of them all, Chief. Just so damn mysterious. And ancient. Twain's River had a spirit I could wrap my brain around. This river . . ." Jacob paused, shaking his head, knowing the chief was aware they were only on a tributary, unsure of what his son knew at this point. These were details he planned to fill him in on back at the hut.

"The Amazon is more complex than I'll ever understand, at least in the years I've got left, anyway. It's the longest and largest, stretching from the Andes to the Atlantic, traveling through so many layers of history, transcending the boundaries of time."

Jacob and Eddie's nights above the Tambopata, chatting together on the porch, began extending well past midnight. Each started gradually letting down his guard, allowing the other a clear view across his interior landscape. Of course Jacob's inner vista stretched out much farther than his son's, its nuanced features layered with the mysteries of abandoned, forgotten cultures, its invisible topography defined by the greatest rivers of the world. The details of Eddie's youth painted the picture of a spirit molded largely by his effort to pursue a life that was a polar opposite of the one his father had chosen, a subconscious quest that was only becoming clear to him as the scientist revealed its details out loud. While talking with his father, Eddie began to realize that if stability was a religion, then the life he'd been living in New York made it appear like he was one of its most steadfast devotees. Over the course of his years as a twenty-something he'd built up a small fortune, and owned a house in an affluent Westchester neighborhood. He and Hannah had recently celebrated their engagement after eight years together. There had been plans for a wedding, two kids, and a dog. He'd been taking evening classes working towards his MBA. His only vice, which he'd learned to indulge in with moderate extremity after the workday, was a penchant for strong liquor.

"Well it seems like you've got your whole life figured out already, son." Jacob said one night. "Congratulations."

"Not really, pops. I quit my job. My fiance left me. I actually have no idea what the hell I'm doing." Eddie confessed. "All I know is that this river, just being here, is doing something strange to my system," he continued.

"Ha!" Jacob shouted, clapping his hands. He got up to join his son, placing an arm around his shoulders. "You're catching the virus, son. Just wait until we head upstream towards the - "

Eddie pulled away. "What virus?"

Jacob laughed deeply. "Don't worry, it's not malaria you've got, but rather a tropical version of the same bug I caught all those years ago on Twain's River. I call it the River Sickness. Trust me, once a big river's gotten into your blood, you're done. I've seen it happen to every one of my assistants over the years."

"I can't believe I gave up my life in New York - my house, my career - Hannah! What's going to replace all those things?"

Jacob smiled. "Those things were an illusion, son. Only the rivers are real. The sooner you accept that freshwater is the religion of your future, the better off you'll be from here on out. I want to hand my life over to you. When the time is right. When we're both ready."

At the end of these long nights spent bonding with his son, Dr. Jacob Pearlman would lie in bed thinking about the Nile. It was the last river he'd been on. More precisely his late night thoughts usually centered on Cassandra, the Arabian concubine he'd been with during most of his two years in Africa, a woman who'd convinced herself she was the descendant of Hatshepsut, one of ancient Egypt's greatest female pharaohs. Jacob caught himself wistfully reminiscing about the love they'd made on most nights, how Cassandra had implored him to give her a child, certain this would fulfill some strange prophecy about a return of Hatshepsut's line and a new Egypt ruled by her offspring. This had seemed far-fetched to Jacob when compared to Inez's connection to river dolphins, and there was no shaman to help reveal its validity. He didn't resist her request, however, spraying her insides with the haphazard seeds of an older man, while thinking about his son Eddie. She'd told him how she possessed a fertility rivaling the surrounding rich soils, a fecund femininity capable of giving rise to an empire of a bloodline. And this was why Jacob was now thinking of his Cassandra, as a woman more fertile than the Nile River basin itself, even though after two years spent being intimate with her she hadn't become pregnant. Because now he wanted another child. One more son, just in case Eddie went back to his old life without accepting the bait he planned to offer him. By the time he was on the Nile, shortly after turning sixty, he no longer craved a sexual release every night like he had for so much of his life, and was beginning to see this particular kind of freedom as a gift. It allowed him to feel something for Cassandra that he could only classify as love. And he convinced himself the stinging pains that sometimes coursed through his chest afterward were simply a side effect of this complicated emotion he was just learning how to feel.

But after no new life had taken inside her by the time he'd finished his work at Lake Victoria and was sent back to the Amazon, he felt new levels of concern and responsibility over the outcome of the young man who was still his only child. The lovemaking they'd shared along the Nile, as Jacob looked back on it, had been some of the best of his life by far. They'd had an unspoken agreement that Cassandra would take on the majority of the effort involved with sex, usually mounting him for long periods of diligent riding, while he kept her mind amused with his rambling thoughts. She was able to please herself multiple times a night, learning to express her orgasms in purring, full-body shudders. Jacob's pleasure would build up over successive nights, finally erupting in a once-a-week explosion that left him gasping for air, and wondering if his heart had stopped. He accepted that was how sex had to be once a man reached his sixties, aware that old age had the power to force a man into accepting much worse.

When he fell into sleep here on the Tambopata he usually dreamed of Inez, seeing her as she'd been thirty years earlier, at the age of sixteen. On the night of Jacob's diagnosis of his son's case of River Sickness, in his dream the former couple was entwined in their usual lovemaking formation, lying side by side in the spoon position. The inside of Inez's knees squeezed his thighs as her pelvis rocked back and forth, her back in a great forward curve across the bed, her long black hair draped down around his face. She tipped her head back to listen to his whispered words interspersed within their duet of muffled moans. Jacob's hands gripped the bulge of bone protruding from her lower back, a feature that had always turned him on even more than her small, vibrant breasts. She'd been his river dolphin lover. Brown instead of pink, but equally mysterious, and similarly enchanting.

"My son has fallen in love with your river faster than I ever thought he would," Jacob whispered to her in his dream.

"This is a good thing, yes?" Inez cooed into his ear.

"I think so."

"It is what you wanted."

"It is. It's just that I'm feeling a little guilty all of a sudden, like I'm purposefully shaping him into what I want him to be."

She put a finger to his lips. "What you need him to be, Na-oosh-doh. He is your descendant. He needs to take over your work when you go to the other side. Do not forget this."

"Yes, I know. I just wish . . . I wish he came to it on his own."

"But he did. You only invited him to come here. He did not have to travel all this way. You did not force him to fall in love with my river."

She closed her eyes. Her back arched into his chest as she sank into the convulsions of an orgasm. Jacob held onto her tight while her whole body shuddered. Then he woke up.

During their nights on the porch Eddie frequently guided his father into reminiscing about his first time on the Amazon three decades before. Not only was it the area he was most intrigued by, but it also seemed to have a deep pull over the renowned aquatic biologist, a mysterious tug much different than the Mississippi's hold on him, as if he'd left something behind here in Peru all those years ago. Maybe not a wife and a child, but something.

"Mom calls the Amazon a whore," Eddie announced one night.

"She does? Well, that's a real shame. If this river was a woman, she certainly wouldn't be a harlot."

"What would she be then?"

Jacob tipped his head back, gazing up into the rafters, stroking the salt-and-pepper stubble of his chin.

"If the Amazon was a woman, she would be a virgin caught in a perpetual deflowering by the lust of man's endless greed." Jacob dropped his head back down, then turned to meet his son's eyes, which were wide open with astonishment. "What?"

"I don't know, Dad. I guess I didn't think you were capable of being so . . ."

"Eloquent?"

"Yeah, that."

Jacob chuckled. "I'm just a scientist who likes words more than formulas. And there's something about the Amazon that hits me down deep inside. Even though I wound up spending the majority of my time right here on the Tambopata, which is only a tributary."

"Why?"

"I got stuck, I guess. I was staying with these Ese' wa people. They liked me, called me Wa-noo-dah. The Water Man. A band of gold miners had been working their way up into the Ese' wa's territory, poisoning their river as they went, leaving dead bloated fish and sick Indians behind in their wake. I went toe-to-toe with those assholes. Abandoned my research for months so I could fight them."

Eddie's pride in his father, which had been slowly evolving every night, swelled out into the room, filling the air between them with a particular kind of warmth, a filial love so entirely foreign to Jacob that he initially failed to recognize it as such.

"So I take it you didn't pop their boat with a fishing hook this time," Eddie teased.

"No. These guys deserved much worse than that. What I ended up doing actually made me a fugitive in Peru for many years, until National Geographic was able to clear my name for good."

"What did you do?"

There was awe in Eddie's voice. Jacob rose up to meet it.

"I poisoned the bastards with their own mercury."

"Cool."

The Source

ON WHAT WAS TO BE their last night in the village before journeying upstream towards the source of the Amazon Jacob retired early, resisting his son's pleas for an extensive round of drinking, as Eddie had already acquired a fondness for the local brew. Jacob wondered how he'd feel about the beverage if he knew the truth about its fermentation process, how the village women chewed the cassava root over and over in their mouths, spitting into a vat contained in a hollowed out tree, the enzymes in their spit converting the sugars to alcohol. Better off for the kid not to know, Jacob decided. On this night he didn't really need any extra rest. He was simply eager for another dream world rendezvous with Inez, a regular nighttime occurrence during this second stint on the Tambopata. In his dreams that night he became a river dolphin, and found her swimming beside him. In the dream Inez told him, without using words, that he should bring Eddie to visit the village shaman before departing, something Jacob had been considering anyway. Meanwhile out on the porch Eddie was researching heart surgeons for his father on the satellite phone, trying to learn more about the highly regarded program at Dartmouth started by a woman named Dr. Stone. He'd already heard back from the president of the Medical College there, who praised Dr. Stone, and also mentioned her protégé Dr. Markus Greene, who might already have a heart for Jacob, ready for transplant. Before heading to bed in the hut Eddie scanned his Gmail inbox. He found multiple messages from Hannah. At first he expected to read she was pregnant. But the purpose of each message was simply to ask Eddie to come home, and give them one more chance.

In the morning Jacob announced a one-day delay in their departure, and the plan for Eddie to visit the village shaman.

"Have you ever done a hallucinogen, son?" Jacob asked him over their tea on the porch.

Eddie shook his head. "I've never even smoked pot."

"All right. Well, today you're in for the ride of your life. You up for it?"

"Sure. What the hell."

So after breakfast they walked down a narrow trail to the outskirts of the village. The shaman, a wiry, tattooed old man cloaked in eagle feathers, with a jaguar-tooth necklace and few teeth in his mouth, was waiting for the men on an elevated wooden platform. Walking up the steps Jacob knew the medicine man was drunk, just like his predecessor had been during his own ayahuasca experience three decades before. The chief back then had explained it was a common occurrence, how the alcohol helped ground the nature-priest, a man who'd transcended any need for drugs in order to access highly altered states of mind, who could slip into his spirit animal at any moment without the ayahuasca's assistance. While hugging the wobbly, bony man Jacob only hoped the shaman wouldn't fall off the platform while chanting his songs, like the priest leading Jacob had done, abandoning him in the midst of the most intense part of his trip, while he'd been fighting through the demons to reach his spirit animal.

After some limited chit-chat in the Ese' wa language, Jacob mustering up a few sentences, the three men settled in. There was a small fire going in a sunken stone circle in the middle of the platform. Eddie knelt by the fire as instructed, obviously nervous, his bare torso blazing white. Jacob paced behind his son, while the medicine man packed a clay pipe with the fine white powder. He had Eddie hold the end of the pipe to his nostril, close the other nostril with a finger, and snort in the powder. Eddie closed his eyes and dropped into the shaman's waiting arms, who lowered him to the floor before moving over to his drums. Eddie's body twitched with spasms. The muscles in his face contorted. His fists clenched and opened. The shaman sang his songs, played his drums. Soon Eddie was writhing, screaming out loud, locked in a fight for his destiny. Jacob lay down and closed his eyes, part of him hoping he might slip into his son's vision, the way two people can sometimes share a dream. He pictured himself as a river dolphin, and patrolled the murky water in search of his son. He came to a place of great chaos, splashing water and blood, screams, swarms of piranha, a few caimans. Jacob knew his son's spirit was in the middle of all this, trying to battle his way out. He knew because the ayahuasca had put him into a similar place. The shaman's singing penetrated the water, slowing the attacking fish, giving Jacob a window to his son. But as he moved towards Eddie, who was still in his human form, yet to transcend his body, two hands, a woman's white hands, reached down into the water, took hold of Eddie by his arms, and lifted him up and out of the river.

When he woke up hours later, both the shaman and Jacob were drunk on cassava beer, Eddie didn't want to talk about what had happened.

"Did you become your spirit animal?" Jacob asked eagerly.

Eddie shook his head.

"Did you see it, at least?"

Eddie nodded.

"And? What was it? This is important stuff Eddie."

"I don't want to talk about it Dad."

"Fair enough. Maybe someday down the road. So let's start packing for -"

"I did have a strong vision, though," Eddie stammered. "It showed me that I need Hannah, Dad. She saves me. Maybe we can try this again, on the Hudson, somewhere down the line. But I need that woman in my life to go forward. I have to go back to her and rescue what we had."

Jacob held his tongue, literally clamping down on it with his teeth, knowing both lives were not possible for Eddie, a choice he himself had made a long time ago. He must let his son go, allow him to be ensnared by the trap of marriage, the most deadly of all attachments. Jacob considered marriage to be worse than a drug or alcohol addiction, and was always aware that he'd barely escaped its vice grip all those years ago himself.

The biologist was so furious about his son's decision to retreat back to New York that he wanted to leave Eddie at the village with no way back to Puerto Maldonado and the flights home. The chief, however, under the burden of hospitality, felt the need to arrange Eddie's travel to the city downriver, guided by his right hand man Onda. So father and son shook hands in the doorway of the hut the next morning, after not speaking much the evening before.

"Sorry, Dad," Eddie said.

"I'm sorry too, son."

"I'll give it a second chance. I promise. We can try again on the Hudson."

"Maybe," Jacob muttered.

"I just have to fix things with Hannah first, Dad. She's such a huge part of who I am."

There were many things Jacob wanted to say in reply to this statement, namely some of his long held philosophies about the impermanence of romantic love, the trap of family, and the kind of wisdom that only years spent immersed in nature can provide. But he kept these words to himself, forced a half-smile, and turned to go meet the chief to begin their journey.

As Jacob and the chief made their way upriver the scientist considered how fortunate he was to have the career he did, work that always called him to move forward, the rivers pushing his physical body onward into the next challenge, helping him more easily transcend life's difficult moments, like the one he'd just had with his son. Many careers locked a man in a round trip commute by car, his work a circle around his house, the work weeks fencing him in. Here Jacob was, making progress up the river, its rushing current already washing away some of his paternal disappointment. Near the end of their first day the Tambopata became only a series of one rapid after another, forcing the men to stash the boat and continue on foot. After long days on the overgrown trail they slept in hammocks at night, wary of the deadly fer de lance snakes roaming the jungle floor after dark.

On the third day from the village their feet took them across an unofficial line separating one biosphere from another, as the Amazon gave way to a cloud forest environment, the trail heading steadily upwards through hanging green lichens cloaked in bands of cool mist, brilliant red bromeliads splashed against the white and green. Jacob drank in the cool air, happy to be out of the humidity. Although he'd spent most of his career in tropical environments, humidity always stifled his mind. He led the way along the little used trail, likely a route the Incas had taken in their trading journeys to the rainforest, using his cherished machete liberally. The chief's pace slowed dramatically during the day.

"My legs only know flat," he admitted in between deep breaths, ashamed to be falling behind a white man in his seventies.

"I know, Ama. You're a flatlander! It's okay. Honestly, I'm in no rush whatsoever. The world can wait a few extra days to know if the Amazon is truly the longest river in the world."

"Okay good."

After a few days of trekking through virgin cloud forest they reached an alpine, treeless environment, and a dirt road heading off in the distance. Too sore to continue onward by foot, the men waited until a truck hauling potatoes rumbled to a stop after passing their waving arms. Ten back-breaking hours later, after riding atop burlap sacks of Peru's agricultural gift to the world, the truck rumbled into Cusco. They woke up the next morning in their hostel room perched above the narrow streets of the artsy San Blas district. Jacob was immediately blown away by the ancient capital, a city the Incas had called *The Navel Of The World*. This made perfect sense to the scientist. If the one-thousand mile stretch of empire controlled by the Incas had been the entire world, then Cusco would surely have been its belly button. The perfect stone walls they built almost eight hundred years before still defined the city cradled by mountain ranges on all sides, interspersed with fertile valleys allowing sharp beams of sunlight to slip through the high clear air, striking the architecture from myriad angles, illuminating stone churches and park fountains. The gold fringed steeples and spouts of playful water caught this natural light, the first light that ever existed, reflecting it for everyone lucky enough to be in the enchanted city at that moment in time.

The men rested in Cusco for two days. Jacob indulged in dark strong coffee, imagining the rich brew repeatedly jump-starting his failing heart, keeping him going long enough to at least lay eyes on the source of his favorite river, challenging himself to hide the chest pains from the chief, and anyone else in their presence, even as they were growing in both frequency and intensity. The chief relished the fresh trout from local mountain streams served by mom and pop restaurants, giggling like a schoolboy during their strolls around the neighborhoods, the altitude combining with sights and smells he'd never encountered in his rainforest home environment. At night in their room Jacob would lurch up in bed, clutching the thick wool blankets to his chest, struggling not to scream out in pain. His jaw went numb for hours at a time. His shoulder ached, and froze up repeatedly. He was convinced these were miniature heart attacks that he was enduring. After the two full days of rest, the chief having finally adjusted himself to the altitude with the help of copious amounts of coca tea, the men were set to take a taxi to the bank of the Apurimac, the upper most branch of the Amazon, above where it became the Ucayali and spilled off into the embrace of the jungles below. Using a pair of laser beam measuring devices set on small tripods along the banks, a system similar to the one road surveyors use, they made their way along the rushing river, surrounded by high altitude plains that reminded Jacob of Alaskan tundra, populated by moss and rock and occasional herds of vicuna, a tiny Andean deer.

One afternoon a ten-foot wide shadow moved along the ground, covering the river from bank to bank. Jacob looked up to see a harpy eagle high above them, the largest bird of prey in the world, with talons big enough to carry off a small child. He shouted to the chief, who said a prayer to honor the great eagle, both men breathless for a moment, enraptured by the sight of the majestic bird.

"My spirit animal," the chief said, pointing up.

"Ahh," Jacob said, closing his eyes, seeing his river dolphin spirit self, reliving his hallucinatory journey all those years ago, the strangest aspect of which had been that he, as a dolphin, had wound up in a tiny pond high on the shoulder of a New England mountain. The fact that his future heart surgeon lived in Vermont added new depth to this vision, a detail that had bewildered him to this day.

Jacob snapped his eyes open, more eager than ever to reach the source. The chief was on his knees, praying out loud to the eagle, which was circling directly above them.

"Great harpy eagle, ta' koo, please help guide my friend Jacob in his next journey to find a new heart, which will be the hardest adventure of his life. Asho, ta' koo!"

Jacob walked over to the chief and placed a hand on his shoulder.

"How do you know about my heart, Ama?"

The chief shook his head. "The shaman told me," he said, standing up. "He saw the sickness in your heart when you came to him with your son. He said you'll find the right doctor. And now the eagle will help with this."

"Thank you, Ama."

"No. Thank you, na-oosh-doh. You are the heart of our people. Without you, the Ese' wa would be no more. Poisoned. Gone."

After a grueling week on the highest tributary of the Amazon, enduring frigid nights and constantly soaked feet, the two men finally reached the source, a tiny stream born from a spring on a cliff near the summit of Nevado Mismi. It was marked simply by a white wooden cross. Jacob was dismayed by this chosen marker, as he was hardly a fan of religious symbols. The cross made it look like someone had died there. But the setting soon easily overwhelmed such petty thoughts. The men were standing on the ceiling of the New World. The vast former kingdom of the Incas stretched out beneath them in all directions. They were merely brief guests in a land inhabited by spirits, mountain deities giving fleeting permission to their presence. Jacob cupped his hands under the dripping spring, brought the water to his lips, and tasted the origin of the world's greatest river. Pure, crystalline water, like no water he'd ever tasted before.

Jacob took some hours to sit beside the steady flowing spring, enraptured by the setting, filling up so entirely with a degree of peace he'd never known to exist, a contentment so all-consuming he could have died right then. He was ready for death, would have let death take him without a struggle. Thinking of all the hours in planes and airports awaiting him, followed by cars and highways leading him into days and maybe weeks in a hospital, compared to these last months on his favorite river that were culminating in this moment, he wasn't so sure the effort to get a new heart and go on with life was worth it. What if he never got out of the hospital? He couldn't think of a worse place to die than a hospital, especially when compared to where he was right then, a guest of Inca gods, communing with the ultimate source of the world's greatest river. Closing his eyes, tracing his life back to his very first stream, the one he'd followed out of his mother's backyard in Vermont without ever turning back, he thought he could have willed his dying heart to stop beating right then. He heard the mountain spirits calling out to him in their language of wooden flute songs carried by the winds, inviting him into their version of heaven. But the image of his son rose up to compete, Eddie's last words overriding the flutes, and tethering Jacob to his now thinning strands of life. Standing on the edge of one world and the next, he could only hope that enough doors had been cracked open inside his son by the prying efforts of this own words combined with the Tambopata and the ayahuasca. After getting a new heart, assuming he survived, Jacob would head straight for Westchester, and make one final effort to extricate Eddie from the bonds of his existence there and into that eternal flow the rivers offered, the priceless reward of deep inner peace that only a great river could provide a man with, something no woman or offspring would ever be able to give him. Rejuvenated by his decision to continue living, Jacob then followed through on an action he'd been planning for months. He reached into his pack and removed two glass vials. He filled each one up with the clear cold water spilling off the rock, sealed them tight, and tucked them deep into his pack.

"For good luck," he said to the chief, who was closely watching his every move.

The chief nodded in affirmation of this purpose. "For good luck," he spouted playfully.

Days later, leaving the Amazon's ultimate source high in the Andes after all it had taken to get there, required a huge expenditure of Jacob's will power. He'd never been so blown away, so awestruck and enchanted by a river's source. The Nile's origin came close, those mountainous, emerald green jungles in Rwanda, inhabited by gorillas and humankind's first gods. There the clouds collected in steep rifts, caught by the vegetation, their moisture transferred into hundreds of cool clear streams that would meet at Lake Victoria, the ancient body of water that was the origin of more than simply the great Nile River. From this one clear blue lake, deep in the heart of the Dark Continent, modern civilization had flowed forth. Water born into the world from clouds created by the primitive jungles, this vast, wild garden within the gates of the original Eden, became a portal from one world to the next, flowing north. Flowing forward into time, where this same water, carried into the future by the timeless Nile, would be drunk by the thirsty hanging gardens of Babylon. It would flow onward to provide a bath for hedonistic Romans. This original water would be blessed by a priest in a French cathedral, flow through the canals of Venice, power steam boats, and assist with nuclear fission. Some of this water returned to the African jungles, the world's first Eden. And some wound up here, giving birth to the Amazon. Jacob's favorite river had been alive then, too, giving birth to future civilizations of its own, cultures content with their jungle home that provided them with everything they needed, people with no desire to build dynasties in the sand.

As the only scientist he'd ever known to anthropomorphize water, Jacob was wondering if these original, African H2O molecules that were on his mind, having endured their role as a pawn in mankind's reckless quest for progress, having survived the industrial revolution, would be pleasantly shocked at arriving in these mountains around him, reborn in what was now one of the last oases of the primitive, indigenous world. One might even expect that this well-traveled water might refuse to descend beyond the spring on this cliff, breaking the circular cycle it was a part of, clinging to its new identity as the source of the world's largest and longest river, remaining high in these mountains. In his mind the water knew that the Apurimac was an aqueous gateway leading from a world almost lost into one that was losing itself. Yet, just like it was for him, the water had to continue onward. Jacob spent one last day alone on the river outside Cusco, saying a final farewell to the Amazon, vowing to the river's spirit that he would cherish his memory of it as he lived out the rest of his life. It was the same vow he made to every river before he left it for the next one. Except this time there might not be a next one.

Jacob had never undertaken a mission like this one, making his way from the Peruvian Andes to a farmhouse in northern Vermont. His trips had always been forward, embarked upon in the name of the next goal. The next goal was always the next river. And, inherently, the next woman. But there was neither a river nor a woman where he was headed. Only a big lake called Champlain, and a heart surgeon named Markus Greene. So it felt to Jacob like he was going back- wards. He tried to focus on the journey's ultimate purpose, one dramatic attempt to extend his life. There were other rivers to live for, other aqueous mysteries still waiting to be discovered, no matter what Eddie chose in the end. Next on his plate would be the looming mystery of the Mekong. He was studying Thai on the flight from Lima to New York City, dutifully making his way through a series of instructional CD's. Jacob told himself that this effort, something he did to prepare for every river, was proof that his spirit still wanted to continue moving forward. The heart transplant was a necessary event if his body was going to be able to keep carrying his mind any further down what had already been a very long path of continuous freshwater revelations. Beyond the underlying urge to make it to the furthest possible endpoint of his destiny, a motivation his mother had instilled within him long ago, there was also his legacy to consider, and with that came the foreboding problem of his son.

Jacob struggled to convince himself that he actually wasn't backtracking, telling himself over and over that to undergo a heart transplant procedure at his age would be the biggest challenge of his life. If he was able to recover, the operation would enable him to continue moving forward to the next river. Jacob had never let doubt or regret slip in to establish themselves in his psyche, as they were trying to do once again during the overnight flight, trading an ancient world for a modern one in the span of eight hours. He could have stayed on his first river, with the mother of his son, forever. But he chose to leave her and the Mississippi in exchange for the Amazon and Inez. This move had initiated a lifetime spent plumbing the depths of wisdom held by the murky flowing freshwater of the next river, and by the salty succulent fluids of the next woman who called its banks her home.

He could have stayed to be the Father and the Husband, a good family man with a government job, some stable fisheries and wildlife position in Missouri. But pushing papers in an office cubicle, the likely end destination of such a career path, was his personal nightmare, so he ran as far away from that fate as he could, bidding farewell to Twain's River and his newborn family with half a tear in his eye. Maybe the degraded nature of the all-American river's outlet, where it spilled into the oil-stained gulf beside steamy, gritty New Orleans, made leaving easier, turning the decision into a gut reaction to flee such a gratuitous example of mankind's potential for eco-destruction in exchange for the relative purity of the Amazon.

While flying through the night, heading back to the country he was always leaving, Jacob considered what was still the single most pressing reason for him to get a new heart, and hopefully keep on living for another twenty years. Eddie. He desperately wanted a second shot at him, even if it had to occur on the Hudson, a river barely worth his attention. This desire for his successor to be his own son, as if Jacob was the king of rivers with a scientific empire to pass down, grew even stronger as he made his way back to the United States. On the plane Jacob turned to his Blackberry for distraction. He wanted to learn more about this surgeon he would be trusting to replace the only heart he'd lived with for seventy-two years. He Googled the name Dr. Markus Greene. Overwhelmed by pages of relevant links, Jacob made forays down many of them during the course of the flight, learning more than he'd bargained for about this poet-turned-heart-surgeon currently charged with felony organ theft.

246   ⟶   I. ALEXANDER OLCHOWSKI

As a firm believer in the innocent-until-proven-guilty foundation of the American justice system, Jacob didn't let this detail color the impression of the surgeon before he even met the man. He followed the web of cyber-threads on his miniature screen, learning a variety of tidbits, from a company profile of Scoreboard Franks to a French baker named Lufont to the famous poet Robert Frost. The one tangent he wound up being captivated by was an obscure article he stumbled on in a recent issue of the Middlebury College newspaper. The piece was about an English professor at the college who had been doing in-depth research on Mr. Frost for a new book. Part of his efforts involved spending overnights at the poet's cabin in the mountains outside Middlebury, where so many of the man's poems had been written. This professor had recently come to realize that all the original wood from the cabin's walls had been removed, piece by piece over what must have been many years, replaced one at a time with virtually identical, newer versions of each board. No one had any theories as to a potential motive behind such a strange crime. Local police were in the midst of doing an investigation. Jacob finished up his informal research on this heart surgeon he would soon meet by reading some of Robert Frost's poetry. The soothing, sing-song verses and country settings eased his mind, ushering him into a long nap. When he woke up the plane was making its descent into JFK.

4

MASTERPIECES

Intravenous Faith

THE HEART SURGEON drove the aquatic biologist out of the city and up the Taconic Parkway towards Vermont. Once off the tight confines of the Saw Mill and onto more relaxing stretches of road the two men dove into conversation. Jacob asked Markus what it felt like to have a new heart.

"I've been reborn, Dr. Pearlman. Literally. And so too will you."

"I'm not looking to be reborn. I just want to be able to keep on living. I have a son to track down in Westchester."

"I see. But what about the rivers?"

"I hope there will be more of them, yes. That's where my son comes in. I want him to take over wherever I leave off."

"I see. From what I've read about you, you've had some career. It's not every day I have a National Geographic Hall Of Fame Adventurer sitting in my passenger seat."

"Ahh, yes. Well it's not every day I'm being driven by a heart surgeon poet, you know."

"I guess we're even then."

"I guess so."

After driving in silence for some time Markus spoke up again, attempting to swing the conversation back to what still remained his favorite subject. It was a shortened version of the usual screening evaluation he gave to all his heart disease patients.

"Speaking of getting a new heart, Dr. Pearlman, I feel like it's basically impossible not to consider the factor of love. Given the connection between the two, I mean. What are your thoughts on love? If you don't mind me asking."

The aquatic biologist took in a long breath.

"First of all, call me Jacob, and I'll call you Markus. Second, I'm not convinced there's a connection between those two things, but I'm also not a heart surgeon. Or a poet. And third, when it comes to love, the human world hasn't had much of a hold on mine. I have a son, but I only just recently started to get to know him. And I think that distance has been the best thing for both of us, at least when it comes to our survival as grown men, which is the most important thing, really. Self reliance. My heart has more in common with the heart of an Amazonian river dolphin. Or a Nile crocodile. I've been in love with many rivers, Markus. The world's greatest rivers, and the water that is their blood." Jacob sat forward, a sudden urgency tightening his body, squeezing out his next words. "But right now I'm more concerned with my own blood, with the outcome of my descendants. Once I straighten things out there, which will be the hardest thing I've ever done, I can return to my true love. The next river. The Mekong."

Markus nodded slowly. "Perhaps, following the procedure, you'll let go of this concern over your son's outcome."

"I highly doubt it."

"You never know. Kathryn and I believe in what we call our people. Those we can form even stronger connections with than we make with our own families. Like the president of Dartmouth Medical School. Karl Fredericks has been a son, a brother, and a father to me. Sometimes all three at once."

"Huh," Jacob said, making a sincere effort to ponder this concept. "Couldn't these people you speak of also just be called friends?"

"Sort of," Markus admitted. "But the concept is deeper than friendship. It's a spiritual kind of thing. Has something to do with evolution. Kathryn can explain it better."

"Do you have any children, Dr. Greene?" Jacob asked bluntly.

"No, I don't," Markus answered. "Maybe a certified bachelor like myself has no shot at knowing anything about love. So don't listen to me -"

"What do you love, Markus? Poetry? Surgery?"

"I like those things. But I love the mountain behind my house, a few old trees, and a surgeon named Kathryn Stone."

"Ah, I spoke to this Kathryn. She has a strong, clear voice."

"Kathryn taught me everything I know about heart surgery. And now she's teaching me everything I failed to learn about love. Or something like that."

"She must be quite a woman. Will I have the pleasure of meeting this Dr. Stone?"

"Oh, yes, you certainly will. She is going to assist me during your transplant procedure."

"Perfect."

Markus had planned to let Jacob settle in for a few days of rest, eat some good meals, maybe even take a hike up The Hump. But the aquatic biologist made it clear over coffee the next morning that he wasn't interested in any kind of delay.

"I'm seventy-two years old, Markus. No time to waste. How soon can we do this? I need to get down to Westchester as quickly as possible."

"We can do it tonight if you want. Kathryn only needs a few hours' notice. She cleared out her schedule for the whole week."

"Excellent. Tonight it is, then."

As the day progressed, leaving Jacob alone to prepare in whatever way he felt necessary, Markus was surprised by a slow buildup of nerves. He had more than a few transplant surgeries under his belt, and Kathryn, with her steady hands and depth of experience, would be there by his side the whole time. It didn't take him long to figure out the source of his nervousness. Dr. Jacob Pearlman was a world-famous scientist who made great contributions to humankind's understanding of freshwater ecosystems. He'd singlehandedly facilitated the preservation of many cultures, species, and landscapes dependent for their existence on the rivers he'd studied over the years. He was the kind of larger-than-life conservationist, a John

Muir type who would live on for generations through the books and movies chronicling his career, regardless of his current familial dilemma.

It would be up to Markus and Kathryn whether or not this career would continue any further. Markus felt the burden of his duty build through the course of the day, a concrete heaviness spreading across his shoulders, slumping his back under the weight of expectation. Jacob did nothing to instigate these feelings. The scientist seemed to be cultivating an air of detachment from the whole scenario, aware that success and failure were equally likely, that his death was perhaps moving in closer, surrounding the farmhouse on all sides, ready to pounce and carry him off if the new heart didn't take. Eager for distraction and peace of mind, Markus made repeated trips down into the basement to spend time with the one remaining heart. There was something strangely familiar about it, as if he knew this heart much better than he'd come to know any of the three he'd been cultivating before his arrest. He felt a kind of inherent intimacy with this particular heart that he couldn't exactly place. But there was no time to dwell on this phenomenon for long. Practical matters were dominating his thoughts, most especially his awareness that there wouldn't be time to use this last heart as raw material for cloning any new ones, so Markus would have to start over from scratch after the operation, something he'd accepted after Jacob had first called him from Peru in urgent need of a transplant. To find another heart like the little girl's he'd first started with would be an extremely difficult task, especially with all the eyes now watching his actions. Floating in the fish tank full of blood, the large, healthy heart had been beating since early that morning, after it responded immediately to the frequency of shocks Markus employed to jump start it, the same staccato rhythm of current which had inspired his original heart to come to life. The sight of the beating pulmonary organ suspended in blood calmed Markus a little, helped confirm that a large part of the procedure would be out of his hands. The surgeon could only do so much. Every transplant came down to a moment of truth between muscle and patient. Once Markus sewed it in his job would be done, but the heart would not resume beating on its own. Some combination of Eric's will, and the strength of his personal faith, would have to take over from there.

Kathryn arrived in the late afternoon. The three of them hung out in the living room for a while. It didn't take long for Jacob to feel comfortable in her presence. Each were masters of their respective fields, so certain threads of connection were immediately available. Markus sat back and let them chat, happily taking note of some weight lifting off his shoulders. Both he and Jacob were happy that Kathryn was present. Her calm confidence put both men at ease. Eventually it was time to move to the operating room downstairs. Markus dimmed down the lights, turned on the stereo, and loaded a Mozart Flute Concerto into the CD player. Kathryn painted a straight line of black paint down the center of Jacob's bare chest. His eyes kept glancing down at the circular saw resting on the shelf beneath the heart/lung machine.

"That's some tool down there," he said, trying to smile.

She chuckled. "It always does a perfect job."

"As long as you follow this line, right?" Jacob said, nodding down at his chest, his tan and weathered skin divided in two equal halves by a black line.

"Exactly."

Kathryn motioned for him to lie down on the operating table. She stuck the IV needle into his arm, administering the cocktail of drugs that would knock him out for the next six hours. Eric kept his eyes focused on the sealed glass vial of spring water he'd brought back from South America. He'd requested that one of the water samples be present during the operation, hoping the spirit of the Amazon's source might be able to bring them all some needed good luck.

Five hours later the two surgeons reached their pinnacle moment. Jacob's chest was splayed open beneath them. The cavity was a mass of blue-gray organs, empty of all blood. The heart/lung machine beeped in a perfect rhythm, pumping Jacob's blood back and forth, keeping his heartless body alive. His seventy-two year old heart lay slumped on a steel counter top beside the little red and white cooler holding the new heart. Kathryn did one last inspection of their prep work, then gave Markus the thumbs up to continue. He lifted the heart out of the cooler, admired it for a moment, and then lowered it into Jacob's open chest, setting it into the biodegradable scaffolding that would hold it in place until he was able to sew it in. Kathryn was his focused assistant, ready with every tool he needed, needles and plastic thread, scalpels and suction tubes. Markus' hands moved with intense precision as he worked to attach the new heart in place, peering in close with his magnifying goggles. He worked for over two hours at this task, until the same take-your-breath-away, life-versus-death moment that arrived during every transplant proce-dure was fast approaching. Kathryn had been doing most of the grunt work up to that point. She'd been the one who sawed through the chest plate. Now she strained with the effort of closing Jacob's split chest back up with the steel cables, something her nurses usu-ally did for her. Markus kept his attention glued on the heart/lung machine, its performance now more crucial than ever. Once Jacob's chest was closed back up it was time to cut him off from the ma-chine. They switched places. Kathryn manned the controls while Markus positioned the defibrillator pads on Jacob's chest. As the lead surgeon, he had the climactic role of shocking their patient back into life. Mentor and apprentice connected eyes, their patient in between them.

"Kiss me," Markus said, leaning forward over Jacob.

Kathryn shook her head. "Bring him back, Markus. Then ask me that question."

Markus shocked Jacob with the pads. The biologist's body

lurched up off the table. He shocked him again. Kathryn monitored the machine, which kept telling her the transplanted heart had yet to beat on its own. Markus increased the frequency of his shocking. Minutes went by. A faint smell of smoke filled the air. The two surgeons exchanged nervous glances. There was only so much electric current their patient could endure. Markus was reaching the limit, but his handmade heart had yet to beat for the first time inside a body. Kathryn grabbed a hold of his wrist to stop him.

"Markus, please. That's enough. I think we're going to lose this one."

"We can't lose him!" Markus shouted.

He glanced up at the IV bag half filled with anesthesia. His eyes found the sealed glass vial of clear water on the steel counter beside the operating table. Markus moved to grab it. He poured its contents into an empty bag and attached the bag to the IV stand, replacing the one holding drugs designed to help wake a patient up out of the artificial coma they'd induced.

"What are you doing?" Kathryn asked.

Markus watched the Andean spring water course down the thin plastic tube, entering Jacob's bloodstream through a needle stuck into the underside of his arm. He let the clear cool water course into Jacob's blood for some time, ignoring his assistant's pleas for an explanation. When half the bag's contents had been transferred into their patient he picked up the shock pads once again, placed them on Jacob's chest, and jolted him one last time. He stepped back, holding his breath.

"Turn it off," he told Kathryn, nodding at the heart/lung machine.

"But Markus -"

"Just do it."

She turned off the machine. The EKG screen continued to show a flat green line, maintaining its constant monotone that announced their patient was dead. Kathryn circled the operating table. She offered Markus a hug. He caught her shoulder firmly with his hands.

He kissed her, his tongue working hard to convince her lips to part, which they finally did. It was a long, deep kiss that left them each staggering. Kathryn shook her head.

"Why did you do that? There's nothing to celebrate. We've lost him -"

"That kiss wasn't a celebration."

"What was it, then?"

"A prayer."

The EKG's steady tone of death then fragmented into a series of pulsing tones. Kathryn sucked in a breath and held it. Markus dashed towards the screen. The flat green line was now spiking up and down in regular intervals, indicating a beating heart. Markus let out a yelp of joy as he returned the anesthesia bag to the IV stand. The water had been fully deposited into their patient, who was now breathing on his own. Kathryn removed the oxygen tubes from Jacob's mouth. She moved up close behind Markus.

"Kiss me again, Dr. Greene," she whispered into his ear.

Upstairs in his living room Markus dragged the mattress off the futon and onto the floor beneath his wide window. The cool night air spilled in through the open screen. Kathryn pulled him down on top of the worn mattress. She stripped off his blood-stained scrubs. Markus let himself get lost in her touches, reveling in large expanses of skin against skin. He was captivated by her glistening golden pubic hair, caught himself comparing it to corn silk garnished by light drops of dew catching the half-moonlight. Her cat-like movements kept him constantly guessing. They played at foreplay like teenagers for so long Markus started wondering if that was all they needed, the myriad of playful things that fingers and lips can do. Then he slipped inside her, almost by accident. He stayed in there without moving, their bodies intertwined, holding on to the moment with a kind of desperate intensity. The futon mattress became a raft being tossed by the stormy seas they were making. Crashing back on firm ground for a moment they shuddered together in the earthquake of a shared climax. During the aftershocks they let the ground of their friendship be split open by the force of pent up passion, falling as one into the crack. For Markus it was a thunderous, surreal session of lovemaking. When he took a moment to catch his breath, rising up above the hot sultry atmosphere surrounding the mattress, he gazed out the window and imagined Camel's Hump as Mt. Olympus, where Zeus was busy conjuring up lightning bolts to honor their passion.

After it was all over, listening to the floor for any sound coming from downstairs, Markus hesitated to say what was on his mind. He thought any words spoken might only lessen the heightened quality of this extended moment they were still in the midst of sharing.

"We need to have a party, to celebrate this union. To celebrate us," he said firmly.

"Why?"

"Because the president painted it on the wall of his cabin. So it's going to happen anyway."

Kathryn's forehead twisted with confusion.

"I'll explain later, when there's more time," Markus added.

"I don't know, Markus. What kind of union are you talking about? Marriage is so good at ruining something like what we have. Whatever it is we have."

"I'm not proposing a wedding. Just a party, to celebrate us. We're too complicated to get married. We're friends, co-workers, and, I hope, lovers. Maybe we'll even have a kid someday. Who knows!"

"It is an intriguing idea. And a good excuse for a party I guess."

"Hell yeah it is! Not to mention we just performed a successful heart transplant on the oldest patient ever."

"That sure is something to celebrate. We should go down and check on him."

"Did I tell you how sexy you were during any of that?" Markus asked her while they stood up to collect themselves. "It was all a kind of blur."

"No. You didn't say a thing, actually."

"Good. I'll write you a poem about it then."

"Okay."

Markus grew suddenly serious. "I've been meaning to ask you something, Kathryn."

"What?"

"When you went to my house to check on my hearts, after I got busted, how many were down there?"

"Just the one. Why?"

"That's strange. There were three hearts left when the cops took me away. I have no idea what could have happened to the other two. The police never got a search warrant, I know that much."

Kathryn shrugged her shoulders. "At least there was one left by the time I got there."

"I guess."

A Union

AND SO THERE WAS A PARTY. It had the spirit of a wedding, without the ritual of I do, without any tuxedos or a white gown. Markus and Kathryn wore special sets of surgical scrubs hand-embroidered by Bethany. Markus knew the celebration had to be held up on the shoulder of Camel's Hump, in a meadow beside the alpine pond, because the president had painted it there. Since neither of them had grandparents still living, the three-mile hike up to the spot was only a challenge to the catering company. Burdened by their own supplies, and also by the many loaves of bread and rolls Bethany baked for the occasion, the caterers made a last-minute decision to contract out a few llamas from a local farm to carry everything. The guests only had a couple weeks' notice, as winter came fast to northern Vermont, and Markus wanted Jacob to be able to attend. Already back on his feet, the aquatic biologist appeared eager to get on with the next phase of his life. Whether that meant a mission to Westchester in order to extract his son from suburbia, or a trip to Thailand and the mouth of the Mekong, Jacob wasn't saying. And Markus hadn't asked him.

The weather lined up perfectly. A high pressure cleared the air with crisp breezes. The sky was a deep, piercing blue, with fluffy clouds billowing across at various altitudes. The canopy above the trail held rainbows of color splashed across the leaves. The day unfolded gracefully, which hardly surprised Markus, given that it was already painted into the president's mural of his life. The eclectic group of guests created lively combinations of personalities. Conversations danced through the cool clear air, buoyed by the easy riffs of a bluegrass band. Rupert bonded instantly with Jacob. The hot dog baron was fascinated by the scientist's firsthand accounting of the Amazon. After hearing about the famous clay lick along the Tambopata River, where hundreds of macaws gathered every dawn to get their daily fix of salt, Rupert knew he had to take a trip down there. Jacob promised to use his extensive contacts to set up a personalized itinerary for the newly retired CEO.

"Just make sure you come back," Jacob warned. "I've known more than a few men so seduced by the Amazon they never returned to their lives. Hell, she seduced me for almost two years. I had to force myself to leave. And then I had to go back again three decades later to get another fix!"

Bethany and Kathryn also found an immediate kinship as they further explored the connection they'd felt on their first meeting, what had been a fleeting encounter at Markus' graduation from med school. The two women discussed their respective passions, motherhood and surgery, baking and rock-climbing. Both craved an insider's perspective on the sides of Markus they couldn't know. Kathryn wanted to hear stories of Markus as a child, while Bethany yearned for some details about the adult version of her only child. The women strove to help each other fill in some blank spots of the man they each loved from opposite ends of love's spectrum.

The president found himself enraptured by White Dancing Coyote, eager to hear the medicine man's perspective on the surreal ability of his painting to influence reality. Finally Karl had met someone who could understand that the cabin mural had directly influenced Markus' path through life.

"You are a shaman, Dr. Fredericks. Your paint brush has the same power as my prayer pipe. And it seems that Great Spirit has chosen wisely. You've done good with the gift He gave to you."

"I used it to create Markus, something I only realized twenty years after I started painting, when he stepped into my life. He's become the son I never had."

The Lakota elder nodded slowly. "The true shamans often don't have children of their own. Too much of an energy drain. We need to conserve our life force for other outlets. Your painting. My praying."

"I have four daughters," the president pointed out. "And I love them all."

White Dancing Coyote smiled wide. "Congratulations! Rules are meant to be broken, Doctor. Especially in the spirit world."

"It's funny. I feel like I created Markus as much as I created my four daughters. Without consciously trying. And by using a different method, of course."

"You did," the medicine man confirmed. "You painted him to life."

"And then I painted new details, once I became aware of this power," Karl continued. "Like the dog I thought he needed. But I think I might have gone overboard. Crossed some kind of boundary. I knew the paintbrush wasn't going to be enough to complete the circle of Markus' life, that I had to act with my own hands as well. Can I tell you what I did?"

The medicine man shook his head slowly. "I don't take confessions like the priests do. Whatever went down is between you and the Creator. Great Spirit will bring judgment in time, on the backs of the Four Winds. This judgment I can't influence, because it has already taken place. But if you happen to cross paths with a hawk, you might explain to the bird why you did what you did."

The president had a look of bewilderment. The shaman continued.

"Hawks have a direct line to Great Spirit. They're the intermediaries between us humans and the Creator. And if you see an eagle, you won't need a hawk at all. An eagle is the Creator taking on a physical form. To listen to us humans. If you see one, tell the eagle everything."

The day's best revelers proved to be some of Markus' friends from Hanover, the regular townspeople he'd bonded with during med school. Jim the carpenter plied his amateur card tricks on anyone he could. Rick the cop convinced the caterers to let him roast a rack of ribs in an open fire. And then there was Chip the electrician, who filled his bong with pond water and blew the smoke from his hits into the llamas' faces, until he got hit with a giant glob of putrid spit. The Boys, as Markus referred to them, congregated around the keg, and were the first to start dancing to the bluegrass music. Some of Markus' friends from the distant past were also in attendance, including Jake Boletti, the class clown who'd broken down his shyness, and Ishmael, from the monastery, who was now a wilderness guide in Alaska. Also present were the parents of the little girl whose heart now beat inside him, along with their son Markus Jr. Ken Gabriel was there, flanked by his fiance Wu Kwan, one of his former tutoring students. Kathryn invited some of the girls she'd grown up with at the orphanage, a few of her current heart surgery residents, and her best friend from UCLA. The only moment of chaos came when the stoned llamas broke free of their tethers to storm the table that held a towering pile of Bethany's bread. They devoured a few loaves before the caterers were able to restrain them. Since most of the guests were earthy types, the remaining loaves, moistened with llama drool, still got eaten without much hesitation.

After dinner Markus and Kathryn each made a speech honoring their relationship from their dual perspectives, trying to explain to the guests what kind of a union they were all there to witness and celebrate, a friendship that could oscillate back and forth between platonic and romantic, colleagues connected by the intensity of their work, two childless adults entering middle age still debating the possibility of reproduction. The speeches inspired tears and laughter in equal proportion. After it was over champagne corks flew as Kathryn and Markus held each other on the dance floor, moving slowly to Clapton's romantic ballad Wonderful Tonight. The party extended deep into the wonderful night. Fireworks were launched above the pond, their colorful displays momentarily overriding the sharp sparkling stars. When it was finally time to descend the mountain Markus convinced the caterers to let him strap tiki torches to the llamas. The quirky pack animals were spread out among the group as they all walked down the winding trail bathed in the flashes of torchlight, the band strumming tunes on the way down.

Markus lingered behind at the tiny pond after the group had left. He needed a few minutes alone with his mountain. The starlight was enough to illuminate the great mound of boulders rising in the sky above, outlining the bold summit he knew so well. He sat there reveling in the scene, making sure the details of the best day of his life would be sufficiently stored into his memory. After replaying the entire day in his mind, he was left with only two words.

"Thank you," he said out loud to his mountain and the stars, to his parents and Kathryn, to everyone and everything he loved. Instead of taking the trail down, Markus followed the small creek born out of the alpine pond. The stream led him all the way out of the forest, where it skirted the edge of his backyard to join the Winooski, then into Lake Champlain, then the St. Lawrence before finally merging with the sea. He could have followed the creek forever. Being a land-loving heart surgeon content with the embrace of mountains and trees, it felt like he was channeling the spirit of his recent patient. But at the bottom he reluctantly let the little river flow onward without him, trying to be satisfied with that fleeting taste of what Jacob Pearlman's whole life had been like.

Markus only stopped inside his house long enough to grab his walking stick, a journal, a pen, and a pack of matches. By the middle of the next day, after ten hours of some hitchhiking and a lot of walking, he reached the president's cabin on the trail-less flank of a nameless peak. Markus stepped inside. He sat down in the worn chair. He grabbed the smooth wooden board resting on the shelf in front of him, a tablet lightly grooved with the marks of a feather pen. He set the old thin board on his lap, and placed his journal on top of it. Markus laid the pack of matches on the floor beside him, and wrote a poem. When he headed out to walk back into town, he left the matches and the poem placed on the table inside.

ENDLESS BEGINNINGS

Suddenly, she seemed to me, cat-like in my bed
be-
between shiv-
shivering between kisses
making love
Made Pure
in Vermont.

The moonlight watching,
a witness to it all,
the sweet seduction
of two souls two each other
each to the other
one for the lover
in both.

I'm taken away
by the soothing sway
of this rocking we have found,
in the here of the now
and the now of the hear,
of this singing inside
and the ring in my ear.

Memory recorded as melody,
harmonies of the future,
a lifetime of listening
to endless beginnings.

When Markus finally made it back to his house the next day
he found a note on his kitchen counter. Beside it was a glass

vial filled with clear water. Beside that was a bottle of white pills.

Dear Markus,

So I'm off to try and rescue my son from the living death he's chosen. But time is short. The Mekong is waiting for me. I must answer its call. As for you, Markus, take a honeymoon with your beautiful wife, if that's what you call her. Laugh, skinny dip, make lots of love, and smoke a cigar in my name. I brought TWO samples of the Amazon source water to Vermont. Kathryn told me one likely saved my life. Maybe this second one will help you whenever you need it. Hopefully you won't have to go so far as using an IV to inject it! Drinking it should work just fine. But then you're going to need these anti-diarhea pills. Trust me from experience. Anyway, take the Amazon's original water, the first water of the New World, as a thank you gift, whatever you do with it. I owe you so much more for this rebirth you've given me. I owe you the rest of my life. Literally. You are a true healer, Markus Greene. And more than a healer. A resurrector. Is that a word? It should be. Oh, you're also a damn good poet too. I couldn't help flipping through some of your journals while you were gone. Sorry!

Anyway, cheers to rivers, and hearts, and poetry, and women. And yes, cheers to love, something I still have a shot at finally understanding one day. I look forward to finding more of my people along the way. One of whom is you, Markus.

Thanks again.

Jacob (The Water Man)

Markus folded up the letter and stuck it in a back pocket. He reached for his phone, and dialed Kathryn's number. He wanted to take her out for dinner, a long overdue first date. But before he could finish typing her number a call came in. It was the president.

"Markus. Hi."

"Hi Karl."

"I have something to tell you. A weight to get off my chest that I thought I could just keep to myself forever. But I can't. I need to make a confession to you."

"Oh boy. What's up?"

The president paused a long time before speaking. "You never had a diseased heart, Markus."

"What?"

"Your heart was perfectly healthy. The ultrasound image you and Kathryn saw in her office a few days later was planted there by me. I bribed that French Canadian technician. She was in on it. That image was the heart of one of your sickest patients."

Markus closed his eyes. Goosebumps spread across his skin. He had trouble holding the phone to his head, trying to stop his hand from shaking.

"So I never needed a transplant?! Karl, what the hell -"

"I know. I don't expect you to forgive me anytime soon. Just know I was only acting in my best interest for you. I wanted to help you cure yourself from the imaginary illness you created in your head. All that bullshit about losing your love."

"Was Kathryn in on this? Tell me the truth Karl."

"No. She had no idea that image wasn't your heart."

"But when she took it out she must have noticed it wasn't diseased?"

"Nope. She probably didn't look all that closely at it, Markus. Why would she? But she did save it. Kathryn gave your heart to me."

Markus was having trouble breathing. "I have to hang up now."

"Sure. But don't you want to know what I did with your heart?"

"Christ. Fine, let's get it all over with."

"It was Kathryn's idea to go feed the hearts in your basement. But I was the first one down there after you were arrested. That night I took away the three cloned ones you had, and left one heart in their place. Your heart. Then Kathryn fed it while you were away, thinking it was one of your original specimens."

"And then I fucking sewed it into Jacob Pearlman."

"Yes. You did."

A Return

A BLUE FORD FOCUS was traveling south on I-87, heading towards Westchester. At some point near New Paltz the car slowed down in the left bound lane, then made an illegal u-turn across the median strip. Inside the car Jacob typed the name that was reverberating inside his head into the GPS. *SARANAC LAKE.* His phone rang at the same time. It was Markus' number.

"This is strange, Markus."

"What's strange?"

"I turned around. It was some kind of an impulse. I'm heading to Saranac Lake right now. Something told me to go visit your mother, and forget about Eddie, at least for now. I have no idea why. I only heard her mention the name of that town she lives in once. At your wedding. Or whatever that party was called."

"I know why you turned around. It's a long story that could be made short over the phone. But I'd rather tell you the long version. In person. What are you going to do after Saranac Lake? Still going down to Westchester?"

"I don't think so, Markus. Something is telling me to leave Eddie alone. I'm going to look for a permanent assistant instead, someone at least half my age with a healthy heart, a person I can teach everything I know about the world's greatest rivers, so he or she can carry on my work. Someone other than my son. I'm letting him go all over again. And I want to thank you for helping me do this. It feels right."

"Don't thank me, thank my -" Markus stopped himself just short of spilling all the beans over the phone, a tempting notion.

"I understand. Good luck with that, Jacob. I'm sure you'll find the right person."

"I think I already have. He just doesn't know it yet."

"Okay."

After hanging up the phone Markus pondered these last words of the scientist, intrigued by who this person might be, even a little jealous for some reason. He didn't linger on these mysteries long, knowing he and Jacob would meet up sooner than later, when Markus would be able to fill him in on the origin of his new heart.

As the weeks became months Markus found himself living in the prime of a life he'd never expected to have, even after becoming a heart surgeon. He was married to a caring and brilliant woman, whose beauty in his eyes was deepening by the day, a woman who was also his best friend. As part of their vow to not let marriage change too many parts of their lives, Kathryn kept her place in town, where she slept after longer operations. Markus extended his sabbatical from surgery by engrossing himself in another home renovation project, this one shared with the company of Jim the carpenter instead of bourbon and eighties rock. And the work took place upstairs, where the two men converted an entire half of his farmhouse into a master bedroom suite. The bathroom was the most decadent aspect, a sprawling space with skylights and tropical plants and a heated wave pool. The large bedroom had all the drawers and closets built into the walls, so the only furniture was a great bed in the middle, sunken into the floor, two steps leading down into its oasis of large pillows and billowing down comforters. The porch was almost as big as the bedroom, half screened, and directly facing Camel's Hump.

When the construction was complete Markus made a gradual return to heart surgery. The charges against him had been dropped, thanks to the insistence of the little girl's parents that he not be punished. New Hampshire then promptly reinstated his license. He didn't need to take chances anymore. So he left his basement locked and dark. At the hospital, his original patients having been forced to gravitate back to Kathryn or another colleague during his absence, Markus decided to learn new skills, and leave the transplants to other colleagues. He soon came to love the laparoscopic bypass surgeries, how neatly efficient they could be, and settled into a four-day work week, earning more money in those four days than most people did in three months, indulging in his home and his wife during the great expanses of free time even as his father's words, spoken through the macaw all those years before, began haunting him. Had his father been right all along? Was a man's happiness so predictable, even for a man like Markus, one not fashioned in the regular mold? Markus had to admit that the combination of his challenging career, significant cash flow, and loving wife were bringing him to a previously unattained state of satisfaction. His situation had marked differences from what had defined his father's working life. Markus had no child to support, and his wife made even more money than he did. Kathryn had already told him he could call it quits any day if he wanted, and she would continue bringing home all the bacon they would ever need.

After a vigorous yoga session together on the deck one spring Sunday morning, followed by an equally energetic round of love-making on the bed, Markus endured the now familiar paternal tug that bare sex with his wife produced. The end destination of this biological pull was usually his vivid memories of his dog Niko, the closest he'd come to having a son. Kathryn was still on birth control even now, six months after their wedding. And she was at an age where her reproductive window was steadily closing. They lay on their backs, gazing up at the slowly spinning ceiling fan high above.

"It might be time for another talk," Markus said, fighting back the tears that remembering his dog always inspired.

"A kid talk, you mean?"

Markus nodded his head up and down against the side of hers.

"Yeah, I guess we are getting to a now or never kind of place on that one," Kathryn said, a marked resignation in her voice.

"In a way, I guess I always considered myself beyond the reach of predict-able human urges like reproduction."

"You've never gotten beyond the reach of sex though!"

"Yeah. Who has, right?"

"No one. Not even monks and nuns, I bet."

"But I have gone away from it for long periods of time. During my travels. For most of med school, and all of residency. I've was like a sexual camel, really. No pun intended," she joked, acknowl-edging the mountain looming above the house. Kathryn leaned in to kiss his neck. "Until now."

"I was too."

"Yeah right!"

"It's true. Compared to the average guy, at least."

"I guess I'll give you that."

His hand found hers under the sheets. He squeezed it tight.

"It has to be your decision in the end, Kathryn. You'll be the one with a bowling ball in your belly for nine months."

"True."

She released a long sigh, exhaust fumes such a life-altering deci-sion produced.

"You don't care one way or the other?" she asked him.

Markus closed his eyes, and let go of her hand. He knew that a few words on the subject, uttered right now, would be able to sway her one way or the other. There was no time for a hike up his mountain for clarity, no chance for a call to the president for advice. Since their marriage Kathryn had dropped only a few subtle hints about the subject, most of them indicating her wariness of the idea. Markus knew how much childbirth would set back her career. She was at the top of her game, a world-renowned transplant surgeon. It would be selfish of Markus to ask her for a child if she didn't fully want one herself. His parents would get over the Greene line ending at him. There were way too many people on the planet as it was. Then he saw Niko again, bounding through the woods, smiling. He snapped his eyes open. He rolled up on top of her, smiling himself.

"What?"

"I don't need a kid. Not if you don't. But I think we should get a dog."

Kathryn kissed him. "Okay, Markus. We can always adopt a child someday down the road if we want."

"True."

He rolled back off her, excited by his new plan. "So where can we find a dog?" she asked.

"There's a certain sheep farm I want to visit. Today."

Markus hadn't told anyone about how he'd gone about letting go of Niko, not even Kathryn. He filled her in as they drove down the dirt road towards the farm, which was located only about thirty miles from his farmhouse, a fact he'd always been aware of, barely able to contain himself from making a visit earlier. He pulled off the road at the same spot he'd last seen his beloved dog, Niko sprinting off thinking his master was following, that curved, fluffy tail bounding through the tall grasses. The two surgeons stepped out of the car and walked over to the edge of the field. Markus pulled a silver whistle from his pocket. He blew three quick, sharp notes, his old signal for Niko to come.

"Do you really think that will work?" Kathryn whispered.

Markus shook his head. "I don't even know that he's here. Maybe the owners gave him away. Maybe he ran the other way," Markus said, spinning in a circle, suddenly assaulted by waves of guilt more potent than any he'd felt since that moment five years before, while releasing his dog into a second life. And then, in the rare way reality can slip into the realm of Hollywood cliché, a fairy tale moment Walt Disney would have struggled to pull off, a black and white dog came streaming down the lime green hillside, dodging bewildered sheep, leaping boulders, heading straight towards them. Kathryn pointed at the tree line, where another dog, a gray, wolf-like animal, sprinted out of the forest and down the hill trailing Niko. Seconds later Markus was on his back. He didn't wait for Niko to re-enact their first encounter, He flopped down on his back, breathless, waiting for that eager border collie tongue. Then his dog that was no longer his dog was upon him, kissing his chin, grinning, peering into his soul with that piercing blue eye, melting away his guilt, while the brown eye looked into Markus' heart, and forgave.

A short time later Markus and Kathryn sat with Skip and Maggie, the owners of the farm. The couple told him how Niko had literally tamed their female husky Yala, who had been disappearing for days at a time. Markus could see his former pet's fierce loyalty being torn in half. While he and Kathryn indulged in fresh camembert at the kitchen table, Niko sprinted back and forth between his two masters. Skip smiled slowly.

"Yeah, for close to a year I'd watch him standing on the road, looking off into the distance. But the sheep and Yala always drew him back to the farm. He was looking for you, Markus."

Both men knew the dog would have gone with Markus if Skip had told him to, or stayed at the house if Markus commanded him to. Luckily for both of them there were puppies, a whole litter of border collie and husky blends, the second batch Niko had fathered with Yala.

"You go, man," Markus said upon hearing this news from Skip, slapping Niko on the ass. "That's my boy!"

Markus and Kathryn had the pick of the litter. They wound up choosing a female, one Kathryn had immediately gravitated to, a black and white puppy with two brown eyes.

Last Beginnings

ONE DAY ON THE MISSISSIPPI, while training to be Jacob's assistant, Markus shared the story of getting a dog instead of having a kid. He had to fill in a blank space of shock, the wake of silence that had lasted for days following his tidal wave revelation that Jacob had inherited his heart.

"Well, that turned out to be a good decision, seeing as how you're going to be away for half of every year," Jacob said, observing Markus try to start their outboard motor, distracted by a group of half-naked black women washing their clothes in the mud-infused water.

"Not having a kid?"

"Well yeah, that too. But I meant the dog. Getting the one your wife really liked, since she'll be spending all this time alone with it."

"True. You're right. I must have known that this future awaited me."

"Of course you did. You knew it all along."

"Yeah, because the president painted it, I'm sure. And Siddhartha, my favorite book, ends at a river."

Jacob was shaking his head. "Those are just coincidences. You're here on the Mississippi because I have your heart. That's what I think."

Markus looked upstream, the direction they were heading, trying to envision the Rockies, a range of mountains he hadn't seen since his days as a poet. Something about the scene, his new mentor, Twain's River, the women singing now on the shore, allowed Markus to see this was his last beginning and his first ending, both happening at once.

Later in the day Markus asked Jacob if it was hard being back on the Mississippi, what had been the natural choice for Markus' initiation, without foreign languages to learn or bribes to hand out, malaria to catch or roving bands of militants to avoid.

"I mean, given your family history with this river," he added.

Jacob shook his head firmly. "There is family, and there is our people, like you taught me. I lost my mother shortly after my transplant, but I have your mother. I lost my son to the prison of the city, but I have you."

"What about your women?" Markus asked.

Jacob smiled a knowing grin, Buddha-like, imbued with happy wisdom. "I only lost one of them, the one I married. But I've never stopped loving any of my women. There will always be another woman to love, just like there is always another river to fall for."

"I'm already falling for the Mississippi."

"I thought you might be. I call it the River Sickness. Like herpes, it's highly contagious, and stays with you for life."

Markus was going to be a different kind of Water Man than his predecessor. The River Man would become his name when he ventured to the Mekong the following year. The plan was that he would dedicate six months of each year to the rivers, returning to Vermont for the other half of the year to take aquatic biology courses at UVM and work with Jacob on the non-profit they were forming, while basking in the glow of his loves: his mountain, his wife, and their dog.

Endings

JACOB PEARLMAN'S FUNERAL, even though it took place outside Cusco, where his ashes were scattered into the Apurimac, was attended by thousands of people. His son Eddie gave the eulogy. Eddie's speech, heartfelt and eloquent, culminated with a description of his ayahuasca trip, the first time he'd mentioned its details out loud to anyone.

"I was underwater, in a river," Eddie told the captivated audience. "Hundreds of piranha tore at my skin. Their teeth were like thousands of razor blades. Caimans were closing in to finish me off, everything was a swirl of blood and splashing water. Then I saw a pink dolphin through all the chaos. It was tossing the caimans out of the way with its tail, clearing an opening in the swarm of piranha with its nose. Then a giant catfish appeared in the open space the dolphin had created. An arapaima they call it. I heard the shaman's song shift into words I could finally understand. He was telling me to become the catfish, my spirit animal, and swim away to freedom with the dolphin. But at the same time a pair of human hands broke the surface of the river and reached down to me. They were a woman's hands, the hands of Hannah, my wife. She lifted me out of the river and into safety."

There was great applause. Hannah beamed in the front row of chairs. High above, too high for anyone to see it, a harpy eagle soared in circles. Eddie didn't hear the cheers, couldn't look his wife in the eyes. Only he and one other person there, the chief of the Ese' wa, knew the deeper meaning of the vision he'd just shared. The first thing Eddie Pearlman did after returning from his father's

funeral was donate his entire life fortune, valued at over two bil-
lion dollars, to the non-profit group River Keepers, which Markus
and Jacob had founded in Vermont. Eddie's only statement to the
unsatisfied press calling him repeatedly for interviews was that his
father had been right all along, and that he vowed to live out the rest
of his life in poverty as an example of the evils of over-consumption,
as a living plea to save the rivers. Because, he tried to tell everyone
he could, the rivers could save us from ourselves. Without healthy
rivers, Eddie Pearlman preached, we have nothing.

Rupert Greene, inspired by Eddie's unlikely philanthropy, sold
off all his stock in Scoreboard Franks, and gave most of the money
to River Keepers. The rest he stashed in a special account to be
drawn from twice a year, in order to fund his biannual pilgrimages
to visit the macaws of the Tambopata Clay Lick. After making this
drastic move he informed his wife that it was now her turn to bring
home their bacon. That wouldn't be a problem, Bethany told him,
as they watched another sunset garnish the lake with pinks and reds.
And she wouldn't even have to leave Saranac Lake to do so. Her
bread was being sold across all of northern New England by that
point. She informed him how even Pierre Lufont admitted being
jealous of her baking empire, a fact that brought Rupert so much
joy that after hearing it he stayed out on their dock well into the
night, trying his best to harmonize with the screaming loons.

While Rupert was howling crazy loon calls into the Adirondack
night, the president was in his cabin beside a small stream on the
trail-less flank of a nameless peak. He was admiring his mural lit
up by the lantern chandelier. Karl hadn't worked on it recently, not
since painting the Mississippi from outlet to source, with a boat
occupied by two men, one much older than the other, heading
north through Missouri. He'd decided it was time to set both himself and Markus free, in one fell swoop, by taking matters into his

own hands. Karl sat down in a chair. He placed the wooden tablet, grooved with the marks of Robert Frost's feather pen, on his lap. He reached out to pick up the journal page resting on the table with one hand, and the pack of matches that lay beside it with the other. As he read the poem out loud a slow smile spread across his face. Karl hadn't smiled in a long time. His wife was dead. His daughters were all begging him to come live with their families in various locations around the country. They were worried about him, as daughters should be. He'd been in the cabin for days, not eating, waiting for this moment. But lighting the match was proving more difficult than he thought it was going to be. What finally gave him the surge of strength to strike it, and hold it up to the piece of paper, was the thought of that young French Canadian brunette, the ultrasound tech he'd bribed to trick Markus. Karl dropped the burning poem on the floor, watched the flames spread out across the dry wood, then shoot up his canvas lining the walls. He leaned back in the chair, closed his eyes, and waited for the fire to consume his sin first, the only time he'd cheated on his beloved wife. The flames would forgive him, before devouring his body and his painting together, setting himself, Markus Greene, and the ghost of Robert Frost free, all at once.